THE INN AT VERDE SPRINGS TRILOGY
BOOK ONE

THE RENAISSANCE SISTERS

Wendy Cohan

LUCID
HOUSE
PUBLISHING

LU(C I D
HOUSE
PUBLISHING

Published in the United States of America by Lucid House Publishing, LLC
Marietta, Georgia, www.LucidHousePublishing.com
©Copyright 2023 by Wendy Cohan
This title is available in print and as an e-book via Lucid House Publishing, LLC.
Cover and interior design: Jan Sharrow
Author photo: Sarah McIntyre Photography, Albuquerque, NM
All rights reserved. First edition of *The Inn at Verde Springs Trilogy* Book 1.

The Renaissance Sisters is a work of fiction and the events described are not biographical in nature. All characters and events in the book are wholly derived from the author's imagination and life experience, and any resemblance to real people or events is coincidental. Some geographical and business locations are mentioned by name to orient the reader. However, the setting of the novel, Verde Springs, is purely fictional and intended to evoke small-town life in the American Southwest.

Library of Congress Cataloguing-in-Publication Data
Name: Cohan, Wendy 1960-
The Renaissance Sisters/Wendy Cohan
Description: First Edition. Book 1, The Inn at Verde Springs Trilogy/Marietta, Georgia:
Lucid House Publishing, 2023
Identifiers: Library of Congress Control Number: TK
ISBN: 978-1950495375 (paperback)
ISBN: 9978-1950495405 (e-book)
Subjects: 1) Contemporary Romance 2) Sisters Fiction 3) Divorce Fiction
4) Women's Fiction 5) New Mexico 6) Landscape designer
7) Unexpected inheritance 8) Narcissistic ex 9) Child abandonment 10) Bed and breakfast
11) Eating disorder 12) Renaissance Fairs
FIC027020
FIC044000
FIC027100

To my sister, Kim Anne Kenley,

who always has my back.

"You must not, ever, give anyone else the responsibility for your life."

— Mary Oliver

Crawley: Gaelic name of Irish origin, Ua Cruadhlaoich, meaning

"Descendant of the hardy warrior."

PROLOGUE

February 2, Groundhog Day, Tacoma, Washington

*H*arper Crawley sat across from her husband of eight years, trying not to glare. It wasn't good for the already-developing frown lines on her forehead, the gift of a life spent outdoors. At thirty-two, her marriage was over, due to Kevin's unfortunate habit of sleeping with his harem of young architectural interns. Once was an aberration, she supposed, and a non-negotiable request for marriage counseling. But twice meant reaching out to the best divorce attorney she knew. Now, watching her lawyer in action, Harper thanked her lucky stars that Heather Diamond had asked her to design a northwest native-plant garden last year, and they'd gotten to know each other.

"We're asking for spousal support for four years, since Ms. Crawley's income potential is less than her spouse's, even though my client works full time and runs her own business. As does Mr. Geddes," Heather acknowledged.

Looking irritated, Kevin looked at his counsel and nodded.

His attorney, Fred Kohn, said, "Based on his wife's current financial circumstances, we're in agreement with the settlement your client is requesting, and *my* client wishes to proceed with the divorce."

"After Ms. Crawley signs the settlement agreement, I'll messenger it to your office, Mr. Kohn. Thank you for taking the time to meet with us," Heather stood and reached out to shake the attorney's hand.

It was done.

Feeling the life-force drain out of her and into the pavement beneath her feet, Harper hoped the feeling was temporary. It's not like she wanted Kevin back—she could say good riddance now and avoid a lifetime of heartache. It was just the shock of being completely alone for the first time in a decade, with her sister 2,800 miles away.

She only had to hop in Ricky, her VW Super Beetle, and drive across the Narrows Bridge to Gig Harbor. Then she'd be on her own with a bar of Belgian chocolate and a good bottle of Malbec to keep the early February gloom at bay, all alone in her half-empty house. A few short months ago, she'd have called it a home.

As she drove over the choppy gray water, she tried hard to look at the bright side: early January's revelations had been the absolute low point, and somehow, she'd made it through. Barring a scary health diagnosis, she had nowhere to go but up for the rest of the calendar year. In the love and marriage department, she deserved a hell of a lot more—even if it had taken eight long years for her to get the message.

Harper poured a glass of wine and clicked on the big-screen TV to watch reruns of *Flip or Flop*. That firecracker of a husband sure wasn't hard on the eyes. Harper liked a gym body well enough, but she preferred a body honed by physical labor, preferably outdoors, like the guys on her landscaping crew. Since finishing grad school and spending most of his time in the office, Kevin's body had grown to be less than chiseled. *But she wasn't going to think about him.* It was just a nasty habit—much worse for her than the junk food she was currently eating—but habits could be broken.

Restless, she switched to *Fixer-Upper*. Chip needed a haircut and she needed Joanna's cheekbones. Much to Harper's surprise, she teared up at a scene of the couple's children playing with the Gaines family's baby goats. Since she'd turned thirty a few years ago, she'd started to *want* certain things. Damn Kevin—who she wasn't supposed to be thinking about. He'd wanted to delay having a family, telling her that "the timing wasn't right"— when he'd actually meant that children didn't fit conveniently into the lifestyle of a married man pretending to be single.

Her phone rang. *Paige.* She'd better take the call or her big sister would worry. "I'm here."

"How did it go? Are you still standing?" Paige asked.

"No, I'm in bed with the heat cranked up, eating chocolate and thinking about getting a pygmy goat herd," she said, not mentioning the kid part. She didn't need to—her sister already knew everything there was to know. "It went about as expected," she said. "Heather did a great job. Kevin isn't happy that he has to pay spousal support, but he's agreed to the settlement."

"The hell with him and the Mercedes convertible he rode in on. I hope the roof springs a leak during one of your torrential rains," said Paige. "What did he expect? You run a damn good business, but landscape design isn't as lucrative as commercial architecture. Doesn't he remember who worked her ass off putting him through grad school for two-and-a-half years?"

"I know, I *know*. And deep down, he knows, too," Harper jumped in, before her sister could work up a full head of steam. She took another swallow of wine, holding the glass's long, delicate stem with chocolate-stained fingers. Her hands were small but strong, from years of physical work making the Pacific Northwest an even greener, more beautiful place.

"So, for how long?" Paige asked, in the shorthand of sisters.

"Four years. I could have asked for more, but I've got decades left to build up my business. I'll make it work," she said, running her hands through her short brown pixie cut. Full level brows and high cheekbones completed the picture. Deep-blue eyes, so different from her sister's green, were her best feature—although at the moment, she looked like she'd recently attended a funeral. *Well, in a way, she had. Marriages die, too—sometimes, slowly and painfully.*

"Well, that's something. But I hope you at least asked for money to upgrade your car. You drive that ancient VW you bought in college, while he drives that little toy car designed for men with tiny dicks."

"Paige! Kevin doesn't have a tiny dick. The problem was his habit of sharing it with other women—and that wasn't something we agreed to in our wedding vows. Plus, he's a lying, narcissistic jerk," she added.

"No argument from me. I still would have insisted on being equally compensated in the personal vehicle department," Paige said, sounding like the MBA she was.

"I have Lucy."

"Your work truck? She's not going to last forever—you work her too hard."

"What are you talking about? I *love* Lucy," Harper said.

"Hmm," Paige said, sounding skeptical. "Well, you *seem* alright. *Are* you alright?".

"Probably not, but I will be."

"I guess you'll live. I'm won't give you any of that "what doesn't kill you makes you stronger" bullshit—but I'm calling you tomorrow, and if you don't answer, I'm getting on a plane."

"You don't have to, Paige. In fact, save your money and we'll go somewhere warm and sunny together—someplace with a pink sand beach and margaritas on the rocks. I just need to let the dust settle for a few weeks, or maybe months. But I promise not to jump off the Narrows bridge—he's not worth it. And, I promise to answer my phone."

"I love you, Harper."

"I love you more."

Harper lay her phone face down on the bed and sighed. Maybe she should get a dog—just in case Gig Harbor's residential zoning laws didn't allow backyard livestock.

CHAPTER ONE

March 17, Santa Fe, New Mexico

"*P*aige, you have to come with me, tomorrow. You're much more likely to understand lawyer-speak. Besides, you're the big sister," Harper said, finger drying her short hair into an acceptable tousled look, while inexpertly using La Quinta's hand-held hair dryer.

Paige sighed, still suffering from east-coast jet lag. "Alright. But that means I'll have to change my airline ticket. I hope there's enough cash in Aunt Sabina's bank account to cover the fee." She arched her elegant brows meaningfully above eyes the color of a cat's.

Harper sighed. Her older sister looked annoyingly put together in a charcoal-gray wool jacket over a white blouse that was somehow still crisp—even after the long flight from her home in Virginia. And Paige's shoulder-length caramel-highlighted brown hair was practically perfect. She, on the other hand, wore basic black as if she were a New Yorker: black skinny jeans, black rock-concert t-shirt, and a slim-fitting black bomber jacket. As least she didn't have mud on her ankle boots, which was a shockingly rare occurrence in her line of work.

"Thanks, I appreciate your sacrifice. Now, let's go out and get some comfort food. Last time I was here, we ate at this traditional New Mexican place—Maria's, I think. I want to drink a toast to Aunt Sabina and send her off properly. She was a cool lady, and she deserves it. It's a shame the funeral turned out to be a bust. It must be sad to lose most of your friends along the way."

"At least the few people who *were* there had nice things to say. That Ruth person seemed nice. I didn't know Aunt Sabina as well as you did, and now I wish I'd taken the time to get to know her better. Are you going to miss her?" Paige asked.

"Of course, I'll miss her, but I know she was at peace. We talked about it, once, and she said she'd done everything in life that she'd set out to do. How many people can say that? I know she was lonely and missing family—I couldn't get here as often as I'd have liked—and like you said, she'd outlived so many of her friends. But I really think she's okay, wherever she is. At least I hope so.

The day had gone by quickly. They'd retrieved their aunt's ashes from the mortuary, then held a brief get-together with Sabina's few remaining friends, including Ruth Watkins, her longtime housekeeper. Paige had planned to head home first thing in the morning, leaving Harper, as executor of Sabina's will, to handle the legal paperwork. But that didn't sit well with Harper.

She closed her eyes and yawned, thinking back over the many trips she'd made to visit her aunt. Sabina had lived in a small house on the outskirts of Santa Fe for the last few decades of her life. In contrast, while living in a town with forty-six inches of rain annually, Harper had enjoyed her winter sunbreaks in the southwest, and over time, she and Sabina had grown close.

As a child, Harper had only been remotely aware of her estranged father's older sister, and she'd had no familiar face to associate with her aunt's name. But after their mother died, while she was a junior in high school and Paige was finishing her final semester of college, Sabina had reached out. Tomorrow, she'd learn her aunt's last wishes, and what it would mean for her own life, and her sister's. *Rest in peace, Aunt Sabina.*

Harper was feeling uncharacteristically anxious the next morning, and Paige was taking entirely too long to get ready. Finally, they were in the rental car, heading down Saint Francis toward the downtown law office where her aunt's will would be read.

"Stop!" Paige commanded. "Swing into the drive-through so I can get an espresso. I was up all night with heartburn. You can take your favorite Mexican food and—"

"Not my fault. I said it was *good*—I didn't say I'd tried everything on the menu. I don't know why you had to be so adventurous, Paige. You should stick to enchiladas, like I do, and go light on the green chile." Harper crept along the steadily moving line until they reached the intercom. "One grande espresso, one tall cappuccino, please," she called out to the attendant.

Ten minutes later, they entered a southwestern-themed office building and walked straight into the open elevator. Harper pressed the button for the sixth floor and attempted to slow the hammering of her pulse, which the jolt of caffeine wasn't helping one bit. She wanted to get the reading of the will over with as quickly and efficiently as possible, and then they could both go home.

"Do you think it'll be straightforward?" Paige asked.

"I don't see why not, but guess we'll know when we know."

They entered the small office at the end of the hall and took adjoining seats in soft leather chairs. The place had a woman's touch, decorated in soft desert tones, with arched *nichos* filled with local pottery. Harper recognized the black-and-white designs of the Acoma Pueblo, so intricate and precise. Her aunt had collected it, too.

"Sorry to keep you waiting. Ms. Gonzalez will see you now," the receptionist said. "If you'll follow me?" She turned and led the way to an outside office with a view of the snowcapped Sangre de Cristos.

"Welcome, Harper! I'm sorry we didn't have a chance to talk, earlier. It's been a busy week," Cherie Gonzalez said as she stood to greet them.

Harper had met her aunt's attorney once before, when she'd signed a document giving her Sabina's power-of-attorney for healthcare, but she didn't know the woman well. "No worries. I'm glad you had time to meet with both of us today. This is my sister, Paige. She'll be here for another couple of days," she said, ignoring Paige's raised eyebrow, "but I can stay longer, if necessary."

"Of course. There's a fair amount to go over, so let's get started," the attorney said, resuming her seat behind the desk. "Generally, your aunt kept her legal affairs in order, and I'll go over everything in detail. First of all, Sabina has left you, Harper, her SUV. It's a newer model, and per her instructions, it's currently at the local dealership getting required maintenance. But you can pick it up at the dealership, on Cerrillos, as soon as that's done. My secretary will give you the details."

"Wow, that was so thoughtful of Sabina!" Harper immediately had visions of trips to the coast, the Olympic rainforest, and weekend visits to old college friends in Bellingham. And if her landscape design business ever went belly up, she could even sleep in it. She shuddered and made an attempt to focus. *She needed to have more confidence that she could stand on her own two feet—she'd done it before, and she could do it, again.*

"Okay, moving on, there's the house on Arroyo Seco. There's no mortgage to pay off, but Sabina has left it to her long-time housekeeper, Ruth Watkins." Cherie paused, glancing at them briefly. "I know it might seem strange, but she and your aunt were close, and Ruth was getting on in age as well. And it's a Godsend for Ruth, since she's not able to work full-time anymore. Your aunt was one of her last remaining clients, and Ruth was committed to helping Sabina maintain her home for as long as she could. Now, if there are any personal items either of you would like from the house, I can speak to Ruth, and I'm sure something can be arranged. She's a lovely person."

Harper nodded. *The house wasn't theirs.* And, of course, she'd like some personal items from the house: some cherished ceramics and artwork, her aunt's basket collection. Old photographs. She and Paige didn't have much in the way of family anymore, but history was still important, wasn't it?

A frown creased her sister's forehead. "We're Sabina's only living relatives. Isn't this kind of a surprise to you, Harper?"

"A little, I guess, but Sabina never promised me anything. The car will come in handy, you know, considering." She smiled at Cherie and shrugged her shoulders. "My husband and I recently finalized our divorce, in February. At least, now, if one of my vehicles breaks down, I'll have a reliable backup."

"Oh, I'm sorry. Divorce can be so difficult! I began my career as a divorce attorney but I've since branched out. I know it can be rough. Shall we continue?" She dropped her eyes to the stack of documents in front of her. "Moving on, there is the situation of back taxes, which will be deducted from Sabina's estate and paid directly to the San Miguel County Treasurer's Office, before the remainder is disbursed to you and your sister—and that should only take a couple of weeks."

"I'm sorry—hold on a minute. I *know* my aunt paid those taxes. I drove Sabina to the county treasurer's office myself, last November. I stayed for a full two weeks, and we spent Thanksgiving together." She remembered that very clearly—the same way she remembered that her ex-spouse had been cozied up with an intern at Snoqualmie Lodge, an interesting fact she'd learned a month later from December's joint credit card bill. *Gosh, men could be dumb.*

"Do you know if she paid the taxes in full?" Cherie asked. "The county is usually good about keeping accurate records. Also, the property has been in arrears for the past *several* years. If Sabina had let me know about the situation, I could have helped her with those transactions, or at least given her a reminder," Cherie said. "I'm so sorry this has come up, now. I know your aunt had hoped to keep everything simple for you and your sister."

Harper frowned. "I just don't understand how this could have happened. May I see the tax document?"

Cherie nodded and turned the document to face her, and there it was in black and white, from the San Miguel County Treasurer's Office, in a letter addressed to Sabina Crawley (O'Neil):

- 1614 Arroyo Seco – $4,365.00 – Paid in Full
- 21750 Verde Springs Drive – $15,483.00 – Taxes Past Due

Harper slid the paper wordlessly over to her sister.

"You mean, she's *paid* her taxes on the Arroyo Seco house, but… there's *another* property? And she's behind on the taxes by over fifteen grand?" Paige asked to clarify.

"Oh! I'm so sorry. I assumed you both knew about the ranch. Sabina and her ex-husband, Hugh O'Neil, ran the property for a decade or so. They raised laying hens, and when they were done laying, poultry. After they divorced, Sabina leased the ranch out for quite a while, and she'd kept up with the property taxes, apparently, until recently. I'm afraid it's fallen into some disrepair. I did encourage your aunt to sell the property—it's quite valuable as development land if you wanted to subdivide, as long as there's reliable water. It would be good to check that out, first thing."

"I'm…*speechless*," Harper said. "This is…mind-boggling."

"I can see that. It's very odd that she didn't mention it to either of you. Well, while your sister is here, why don't the two of you drive out to the ranch and have a look? Besides the car, which Sabina wanted you to have, Harper, the remainder of the estate is equally divided between the two of you—so you'll need to reach an agreement, together, on what you decide to do with the ranch."

"Holy shit! We own a ranch! In New Mexico! An actual piece of property that's worth something," Harper whooped, in the privacy of the stainless-steel elevator.

"Let's not count our chickens before they're hatched," Paige said. "You didn't tell me Aunt Sabina and Uncle Hugh were in the poultry business."

"Very punny. I think it was one of Uncle Hugh's many business adventures that went bust. Sabina had mentioned it a few times, but I didn't even know where the ranch was. She'd just say things like, 'when your Uncle Hugh and I ran the chicken ranch.' I had *no* idea she'd held on to it for all these years—but now I'm dying to see it. Aren't you?"

"Maybe don't use the word 'dying.' We only held Aunt Sabina's memorial service yesterday, and we haven't even decided what to do with her ashes," Paige said. "The urn's still sitting in our room at the La Quinta, until we figure out what to do with them. But, *yeah*, I'm curious—who wouldn't be?"

After a quick lunch, they headed out of Santa Fe, turned south-southeast, and followed the directions from Google Maps.

"If we decide to keep the place in the family, there's no way we can call it the chicken ranch—because I know for a fact that 'The Chicken Ranch' is *actually* a legally licensed brothel sixty miles west of Las Vegas."

"I had no idea you'd had such a comprehensive education," Harper said, as she admired the northern New Mexico scenery.

"I learned about it in one of my business law classes. We reviewed a case study—The Chicken Ranch won. What else did it say on the deed?" Paige asked.

"Cherie wrote some notes for us. It's just outside of a dot on the map called Verde Springs."

CHAPTER TWO

*F*our lanes narrowed to three, and then to two. Piñon pines and junipers dotted rolling, red hills, and the landscape along the roadside changed from sparse grassland to sagebrush. Along the washes, Harper recognized the furrowed bark of Fremont cottonwoods and the russet glow of scrub willows.

There wasn't much wildlife to be seen in the warmth of the afternoon, although once, Harper ran over an already-dead snake. She shuddered—living with scaled and venomous reptiles in the neighborhood would take some getting used to. Finally, she turned right into a dusty gravel driveway overgrown with vegetation, and knee-high weeds scratched at the car's under-carriage.

On the left, a row of low-roofed buildings, their sides bleached silver, stood forlornly in the desert sun. Harper wondered what color they'd once been, but trying to envision them in their once-new incarnation brought up nothing. Further on, she glimpsed a sizeable grove of bare-branched trees she didn't recognize, and beyond them, what had to be the main house.

Much larger than she'd imagined, it sat on a slight rise with a distant backdrop of blue-shadowed mountains. Its arched front matched the old pueblo style, and its hand-carved wooden doors came with a *nicho* above, currently empty of its patron saint. They'd have to do something about that—it didn't seem right to leave the house unprotected. To one side was a shaded patio covered by a terra cotta roof, its absent tiles as noticeable as missing teeth. Adorned by hand-hewn spiral columns and ornate corbels, the space called to her. This had been someone's home: she could imagine Sabina and Hugh sitting here on a warm evening, relaxing after a hard day's work, before things between them had gone south. Now, it was a house in need of love, and money.

There was plenty of space around the house for water-wise plantings. Harper's designer's eye envisioned the massive doorway framed by two matching desert willows, in the deeper rose variety that Sabina had planted, years ago, at her house in Santa Fe. Harper couldn't see operating this lovely property as a chicken ranch. *That just wasn't going to happen.* Nor would she and her sister sell to a developer who would create another water-hogging golf course, surrounded by second homes, within driving distance of Santa Fe. Not in her lifetime, and not if she had anything to say about it. *Did love-at-first-sight apply to rural agricultural land?*

Harper glanced at Paige, sitting quietly beside her. "Well, shall we?" She held up the enormous, medieval-looking, cast-iron key Cherie Gonzalez had handed them.

"After you," Paige said, unfastening her seatbelt and stretching. "I don't see any chickens, but there *is* something about this place. I can understand why Sabina held onto it as long as she did. It's got character."

Harper smiled in agreement. Then, she turned the key in the lock and stepped inside. The home's many windows had been shuttered for protection against vandals and would have to be pried open—but there was enough light coming down through an old central skylight to see the basic layout, once her eyes adjusted.

"A skylight? I hadn't expected that," said her sister, pointing up.

"They're not all that rare in homes built before electricity became common. It made sense to make use of the natural light during the day, and they probably used candles or lanterns at night. Check out these floors! I think they might be original to the house," Harper said.

The central hallway was laid with brick in a herringbone pattern, and the living area, or salon, to the right, had wide plank flooring that likely hadn't seen a coat of wax in thirty years. The windows were grimy with years of accumulated dirt, but at least the house wasn't filled with trash. They could start fresh. She'd never been afraid of hard work, and her sister was the most productive person she knew. *They could do this.*

"Let's keep going. I want to check out the kitchen," Paige said, interrupting Harper's thoughts.

Located at the back of the house and adjacent to the tile-roofed patio, the kitchen was large, airy, and bright, no doubt built to feed all of the people who'd helped run the place in its heyday. It had an ancient timeless feel with hand-carved wooden cupboards, vintage blue-and-white Mexican tile, and a faded, or dirty, painted border where the adobe walls met the room's high, beamed ceiling. A *viga* ceiling, found only in the American southwest, as far as she knew, and especially common in New Mexico.

"I don't see any water damage and it doesn't smell like mold. But the house sure smells like *something*," Paige said, wrinkling her nose.

"Age. Dust. Mice droppings?" Harper guessed.

"Stop! You're freaking me out. I'll wait for you outside," Paige said, turning to exit.

"Oh no you don't—this is *your* inheritance as much as it is mine. Let's head upstairs. We haven't even seen the bedrooms yet," Harper said.

"You first," Paige said, following close behind her.

The wide stairway was enclosed by a hand-carved banister, and there were a few warped treads that would have to be replaced. But as much as the large house looked weary and abandoned from the outside, it was far from a teardown. *No way.* Even without a good look at the bedrooms, she could see that it had massive potential.

The second floor's wide hallway was flanked by seven large bedrooms, four of them with a view of the Pecos Mountains in the distance. A long time ago, someone had thought carefully about the placement and layout of the house, and it had likely stood here, largely unaltered, for more than a hundred years. With a little luck, it might stand for a hundred more. *With a little love, it could be a home, again.*

"What do you think?" asked Harper. She might as well get the conversation started. Unlike her sister Paige, whom she couldn't read at the moment, Harper had the opposite of a poker face.

"Well, I can already see the wheels turning in your optimistic little head. I mean, it's *not* as bad as I thought it might be, from looking at the outside. Still, it's going to need some work unless we sell it 'as is.' Tell me what you're thinking."

Harper winced at the word 'sell.' "I know it's early to be saying this, and we'd need to hire a professional contractor to tell us what we're dealing with, but…"

"You're already a little bit in love, aren't you?" Paige asked.

"Am I that easy to read? I know it's not fair to you, because we're equal partners. But can't you imagine running our own B&B, here? We'd have to think of a really elegant name for the place—this house deserves it. She's like a dignified lady that everyone forgot. I think she deserves to be dusted off, dressed in finery, and given a great big reveal. And the gardens! Oh, my God, Paige! I could design the most *spectacular* gardens here."

"The town—Verde Springs—already has a nice ring to it, and it probably stands out on a map," Paige said, wearing her thinking face.

"Does that mean you can see my vision?" Harper reached over and squeezed her sister's hand. "You know how long I've wanted to do this, but Kevin's always been adamantly against anything like a B&B. He actually bought me a novel, once, that took place in a B&B. And he wrote inside the cover, 'I hope reading this book satisfies your curiosity, so we'll never have to own one in real life.'"

"Kevin, Kevin, Kevin," Paige said, shaking her head. "Bursting your balloon like that."

"Well, he's had a chance to have *his* dream career, and I supported that. Now that I'm on my own, I deserve a chance to go for mine."

"I'm not saying *yes*. But if you, or *we*, decided to do this, would you give up your landscape design work?" her sister asked. "I thought you loved that?"

"Not necessarily. I'd have to brush up on my low-water techniques and learn the plants native to the high desert. But I could use my skills to make this place a paradise. Maybe I could even do a little freelance design work for some of the local resorts or a couple of the gated communities in Santa Fe. So…are you at least willing to think about it?" Harper asked.

"Well…," Paige hedged. "I'm willing to not tell you, to your face, that you're out of your ever-loving mind. And we *do* have a little bit left in Aunt Sabina's savings account, after the amount that was applied to the back taxes. It's not much, but I'm willing to fork over a little cash to pay for a professional inspection, not only of the house, but of the whole property. How many acres do we have, again?" Paige asked.

"Fifty-six. It looks like a lot of it was farmland, once, and I don't think it's unmanageable. The driveway is in relatively good shape. One pass with a brush-hog should do it—and it wouldn't take much to get those trees and scrub pruned back."

"At least you've got the skills for this kind of thing. You and Kevin did a beautiful job rehabbing your house in Gig Harbor."

Harper nodded. "And *you've* got the financial-planning skills and your business background. That'll come in handy with any paperwork we'd need to get a business up and running."

"True. I guess we make a good team," Paige said, smiling for the first time since they'd made their way up the overgrown ranch drive. "But, no promises, okay? At least not yet. My life is in Virginia, and I'm working on getting tenure at the university. You know I'd have to be a *silent* partner, more or less."

"Yeah, I know. But you could spend summers here if you're not teaching a class." Harper said. "Maybe Christmases, too. Christmas in New Mexico is magical! Maybe you could think of this place as your home away from home."

"It's kind of isolated, and it's too far from the ocean," said Paige. "Not that I'm complaining. It was very nice of Aunt Sabina to leave us the ranch. Nice *and* unexpected. I'm just not sure I'd ever want to live here."

Harper nodded in agreement. Her sister embodied "city chick" from her weekly pedicures to her upscale-casual wardrobe, heavy in cashmere and chunky jewelry. "Well, I think we're done here unless you want to check out the chicken coops, up close and personal."

"Hard pass," Paige said. "But I *am* getting hungry. Let's grab a bite to eat somewhere not too far from here. Maybe check out the towns nearby?"

"I could demolish a burger and a beer," Harper said, although that might not be what her sister had in mind. "Let me think. Aunt Sabina used to love to drive out here to a small country steakhouse. I don't remember the name…"

"Do we have cell reception? I can Google it. Okay…it seems like there's only one. *Los Olivos.* And it's on the way back to Santa Fe," Paige replied.

Fortunately, *Los Olivos* stayed open in the afternoons, so they could have an early dinner, *and* it was open on a Monday, which was definitely *not* a New Mexico thing. Towns usually followed their own rules in rural areas, something Harper would have to remember, *if* she decided to relocate. *Who was she kidding? When…*

CHAPTER THREE

"*D*o you really have to go?" Harper asked, as she watched her sister pack her Louis Vuitton suitcase.

"I've already been gone longer than I planned to be. I've taken too much personal time and I don't want to jeopardize my job."

"I know. I'm sorry. It's just that I could really use your help figuring out what to do."

"I'm only a phone call away, and I can trust you to do due diligence and not make any crazy decisions without talking to me. Right?"

Harper nodded, crystal clear on the terms of their agreement. She'd stick around for as long as it would take to get a thorough property inspection, work out a plan, and present it to her sister. Then they'd talk about whether they wanted to move forward together—or, if they could come up with a long-term plan for Harper to buy out her sister's share of the ranch.

She couldn't think of one good reason to stay in Gig Harbor permanently. Although she had plenty of ongoing clients for her landscaping business, her work was strictly seasonal. And she'd had more than her share of hundred-day stretches of rain and gloom in the winter months. Ever since things had gone south in her personal life, she'd been craving blue skies and endless sunshine. Discovering Kevin's infidelity and filing for divorce were two gigantic dark shadows she'd prefer to leave behind her.

Although it had only been a few months since they'd separated, she'd already grown tired of running into well-intentioned people who would ask about Kevin, or casually remark that they hadn't seen the two of them together for a while, and Harper was completely over the need to explain. She needed a fresh start, and the surprise gift of inheriting her Aunt Sabina's property in Verde Springs couldn't have come at a better time. Young and vital, she still had plenty of energy to start her life over in a new place. *She was lucky, wasn't she?* For now, she'd focus on that sense of gratitude. It seemed like a good place to start.

When they reached Albuquerque International Sunport, Harper shifted the car into park and embraced her sister. "Safe travels, Sis. See you soon, I hope."

"No promises, remember?" Paige reminded her. "I know you already have your heart set on this project and I understand the reasons for that. But it's a lot for *anyone* to take on, and you're barely past signing your divorce papers. Please think about this, Harper. Maybe it's too much to take on right now."

"I will, I promise. I just…can't stay there anymore. It wouldn't be good for me." She swallowed hard. "What if I saw them together, somewhere? Or, God, what if she gets pregnant?" *Although it wasn't the only factor, Harper and Kevin's disagreement on whether and when to start trying for a baby had created distance between them.* "Maybe it wasn't that Kevin didn't want a child—maybe he just didn't want one with *me*."

"Stop it! Don't even go there. You'll become a mother when the time is right, and with the right man. A *better* man. I'm sure of it. And you'll be a great mom. Now, I've gotta run." Paige kissed her sister's cheek and opened the car door. "Love you too much!" she called in farewell.

"Love you more!" Harper sang out in return, but Paige had already closed the door and her words were lost in the ambient sounds of the busy airport.

Caleb Johansson picked up the phone vibrating at his hip with one hand and turned off the compound miter saw with the other.

"Johansson."

"Um, is this Caleb Johansson, General Contractor?" Harper asked.

"Yep."

"Do you also do general inspections of properties? Including farms and ranches?" she asked.

"Sure."

"I was wondering if you had any openings in your schedule. I've, well, *we've*, just inherited a small ranch outside of Verde Springs. It's been more or less derelict. That's not right—that sounds terrible—it's really a *beautiful* place. Let's call it "unoccupied" for several years. We need to see how much work it would take to get it up to a livable, or saleable, standard."

"When?"

She didn't understand why he couldn't put two whole words together—she'd been doing it since she was a toddler. "Well, I guess, as soon as you can come and take a look. I don't live here—I'm just in the area to handle everything. My aunt recently passed away, and I'm her executor."

A short pause, then, "Oh. I'm very sorry for your loss." Another pause. "It must be tough to make big decisions when you're dealing with a loss like that. How can I help?"

Ah, the four most useful words in the English language.

Wow! He *was* capable of complex speech that made communication so much easier. "Can you let me know your availability? Preferably sometime this week. I'm staying in a hotel in Santa Fe."

Caleb whistled. "That'll cost you. Is the property in such rough shape that you can't stay on-site even for a few nights?" he asked.

"Well, I'm not overly fond of bats," Harper said, alluding to her recent discovery on the second floor. And he laughed, a pleasant sound she wouldn't mind hearing again.

"Me either. I'd probably squeal like a girl. Sorry, that sounds sexist. I'm *not* sexist. I mean, anybody would squeal in a dark room with bats flying around. Too many scary movies have been made involving bats. They're probably harmless," he said, back-pedaling fast.

Harper swallowed her impatience. "Look. I just want to know if you're available to inspect the property—or not. And...you *were* highly recommended."

"Can I ask who recommended me?" Caleb asked.

"My attorney," Harper said. She could be succinct too. "Now, can you do the inspection or not?"

"Let me think," he said, pausing. "Yeah, I'll find a way to make it work. Does tomorrow afternoon work for you?"

"What time were you thinking?"

"It depends," he said.

Was he hedging? The landscaping contractors and subs Harper worked with tried this every time, and there was no way she'd fall for it, now. "I'd like a *window* of time, she said firmly. "Noon-to-two? Two-to-four? You tell me."

"I'll call you tomorrow late morning and let you know," he said. "That's the best I can do."

Harper thought of asking why, but nothing good could come of it, and she'd already grown tired of this conversation.

"Well, you have my number. I hope to hear from you. Goodbye, Mr. Johansson."

"It's Caleb."

"Fine. I'll see you tomorrow, Caleb." Harper disconnected the call and let out a whoosh of breath. Despite the challenging phone conversation, she'd liked the sound of the contractor's voice, especially his moment of laughter. She needed more laughter in her life, as it had been notably absent for the past few years. She had a brief but pleasant feeling that her life might be about to change—a moment of buoyancy, or simply a longing to make it a reality.

CHAPTER FOUR

Caleb Johannsson loaded the toolbox on his pickup with the necessary tools of the trade, including, on a whim, his old surveying equipment. Initially a land surveyor right out of college, he'd studied to become a home and property inspector, and a few years later had started his own construction company. In a small town, it made sense to have a lot of "tools" in his toolbox. He preferred projects he could complete on his own, but he had a pretty good skeleton crew he could call on for larger projects.

A stickler for details, he worked at his own speed. If a client didn't like it, they were free to look elsewhere. Caleb had spent too many years under the domineering thumb of his contractor father, learning the trade. But he'd also vowed to never be *that* kind of boss—or to ever work under one. So, self-employment had seemed like his best option.

He always enjoyed the drive from Verde Springs along the county road, with pretty little washes filled with native scrub, and in the higher elevations, willows still in their rich winter colors. Having run out of time to shave this morning, he rubbed the stubble on his chin and considered what property his new client might be referring to. If he wasn't mistaken, it had to be the old chicken ranch. No one had lived there in quite a few years, and by now it had probably been taken over by rodents and other undesirable critters that would creep out a city girl.

Had she sounded like a city girl? Just because she didn't want to sleep in an abandoned building with bats flying around didn't mean she was a city girl. *He shouldn't judge.* Caleb took another sip of coffee from the mug in its holder. *Focus.* He had a job to do, which, by definition involved not pissing off a potential client, at least more than he already had. Anyway, she'd sounded cute on the phone and he kind of hoped she would be. *Stop it*, he told himself. It's just that it had been a while—for one very good reason.

He rolled to a stop a respectable distance from the old adobe building. Then he stayed in his truck sipping coffee and taking it all in. The ranch house in question wasn't little and quaint like some of the older structures he'd worked on. It stood on a slight rise with a backdrop of mountains, still majestic, and definitely in need of some TLC. He loved bringing an old building back to life—respecting the original design by not modernizing it too much—one of his strengths as a builder. But he was here to give his client a general inspection of the property, not sell a perfect stranger on *his* vision of what the place could be, starting with a new name: 'the chicken ranch' didn't suit her at all.

A car approached on the gravel drive and he glanced briefly in the rearview mirror. A substantial SUV with a fresh wax job pulled up beside his truck. It didn't look like a rental, so clearly, his potential new client didn't seem to be hurting for money, a good thing to keep in the back of his mind moving forward.

He sighed and got out of the truck. Time to make nice, not always one of his strengths, especially in recent years. "Hey. I'm Caleb Johansson. Here's my business card," he said, extending an arm toward her. His intuition had been right—standing in front of him was a knockout brunette with killer blue eyes.

"Thank you. Harper Crawley. My sister Paige and I inherited this property together. She's returned home to Virginia, and I'm staying here until we can see what we're dealing with before we make any big decisions."

Caleb nodded. "I'm happy to provide whatever services I can."

"Would you like to start with a tour of the house?" she asked.

"After you," Caleb said, gesturing for her to lead the way.

First off, he noticed, you rarely ran across a hand-carved door of this size and presence, and this one came with ornate brass handles on its double panels. It opened into a spacious central hallway with doors on either side leading to good-sized reception rooms. In the center of the wide hallway, a large skylight illuminated the dust moats that floated downward in shafts of muted light. Beautiful and moody, the interior of the house beckoned him forward.

"Kitchen?" he asked, taking a couple of hopeful steps.

"At the back. It opens onto a covered patio with a tile roof, minus a few tiles that need to be replaced. The rest of the house has a metal roof, though."

Caleb nodded. "That's why the interior is pretty well intact. I don't see much water damage. Boy, they sure don't build things like they used to. This is one grand lady," he said, his voice echoing in the cavernous space.

The kitchen was large and square with windows on two sides. He preferred it when kitchens were located, like this one, in a sunny corner of a house. It made sense and helped you to greet the day in a good mood. Caleb noted another set of wide double doors, also hand-carved, that opened onto the covered patio. The attractive outdoor space was large enough to accommodate dining, and maybe even an outdoor kitchen or bar, as long as it fit the general ambience of rustic elegance, New Mexico style.

"All it needs is a trellis of mature trumpet vines," Harper said, nodding her head with satisfaction. "That'll be my first project."

"Nice space. *Very* nice," he agreed, smiling "Have you been upstairs yet?"

"Yes, but only briefly. Here, you can check it out." Harper led the way up the grand staircase to the hallway, gesturing to show him that it opened onto seven generous bedrooms.

Mighty nice view on the way up. Focus. "Plenty of room up here. Bathroom?" he asked.

Harper shook her head. "No. The house must have been built before indoor plumbing, and they never got around to retrofitting the upstairs. There's a full bath on the first floor, though, off the central hallway. I skipped over that, but we can check it out when we're done here."

Caleb had a good head for measurements and could tell with fair accuracy the size of the rooms as well as which would make the best master. When he opened the closet in the largest room, out flew a bat or two, and damned if he didn't let out a squeal.

"I'm sorry, what was that?" Harper asked, calmly, with a glint in her eye. "I thought I heard someone squeal like a girl."

"You got me. But, hey, you were prepared. *You* found them yesterday." He cleared his throat and took a deep breath. "Now that I know what to expect, I'm just gonna poke my head in there and assess what we're dealing with," he said, bravely. *Time to pull up his big-boy pants and behave like a professional.*

"Go right ahead. I'll wait here," Harper said, crossing her arms and leaning against the wall farthest from the closet.

Caleb poked his flashlight into the space, slowly moving the beam up the wall until he reached the *viga* ceiling. When the light caught a couple-of-dozen beady little eyes glaring down at him, he fumbled his way backwards and slammed the door, then leaned firmly against it.

"Yep. You've got some bats in there," he said, unnecessarily.

"You don't say," the woman grinned. "The question is, what're *you* going to do about them?"

"Oh, no. Not me. I have someone for that. I'll give you a name. Bats are a protected species in New Mexico, you know. Now, about that bathroom downstairs—we should probably check that out. Yes, we definitely should," he said, moving quickly out of the room and down the hallway. He didn't exactly *run* down the stairs, but he took them two at a time while she trailed along behind him like she had all the time in the world. If she was admiring the view, it would only be fair. *Did his toolbelt make his butt look big? Get a hold of yourself, man!*

Geez, Harper thought, moving her eyes downward so far that she nearly missed a step. Objectifying her potential contractor didn't seem like a great way to begin her new life, at least the life she hoped to build. And it was *definitely* not worth breaking her neck. She caught up to him. "So, what would you like to see next?"

"Well, I'm thinking of climbing up on your roof," he said.

Why did that sound so interesting? It must be his voice—he probably couldn't help it.

"Roofs are expensive to fix. If it doesn't need replacing, you'll save a lot of money," he explained.

"Do you need to borrow a ladder for that?" Harper asked. *Did the ranch even have a ladder?*

"Don't worry, I came prepared. I do this for a living," he said, patiently. Are you coming up, too?" In his experience, most women he knew weren't that big on heights.

"Happy to—if you think it's necessary," she said with a note of resolve in her voice.

"It never hurts to see for yourself what you're dealing with," he said.

She swallowed hard and nodded her agreement, noting that her palms were instantly sweaty and her heart began to beat at hummingbird speed.

In less than a minute, he'd removed the extension ladder from his truck, raised it to a few feet above the roofline, and quickly ascended. Once he'd stepped onto the roof, he squatted comfortably and turned to glance down at her.

Oh, God. Oh, God. Not my thing. But I want to see for myself. It's the responsible thing to do. Besides, she didn't want to back down, now. Perhaps her 'I thought I heard someone squeal like a girl' comment had been unwise. Taking a deep breath, she slowly ascended the ladder, repeating a spontaneous mantra of "don't look down." When she'd reached the top, she had a clear view of the roof's general construction and her hunky contractor's muscular thighs—but she felt no need to release her death grip on the ladder and step onto the roof itself. *She just couldn't manage that last act of faith.*

"Here, I'll give you a hand," he said, standing up and reaching out.

"No!" Harper shouted, too quickly. "I mean, I'm *fine* right here. I can see everything I need to see. So, what are we dealing with? Talk to me."

He turned away from her, *thank God*, and walked toward the center of the roof. "Well, it looks like you'll need to redo the flashing around the skylight. And if *that's* true," he said, moving toward the chimney on his left, "yeah, looks like you'll need to redo the flashing around the chimney as well. Probably the second chimney, too, he said, moving easily across the roof to confirm it. "Yep. They're both toast. I'll check out the back of the roof and the juncture where the metal roof overhangs the tile one," he said. "Likely, it's overhung enough to prevent damage. It's a good design. We'll need to replace the missing clay tiles, maybe eighteen or twenty. Probably should order two dozen, though. Sometimes they break during installation." He turned back to face her. "Oh, hey, you okay there?" he asked, glancing at her with concern.

"Why wouldn't I be?" she asked.

"Well, some wom—*people* don't like heights. No sweat. You can go on down and I'll join you in a minute. I need to take a few measurements," he said, removing a tape measure from his toolbelt.

"I'm fine," she said, and her voice squeaked. *Like a girl's—God!*

"Okay. Hang tight. I won't be a minute."

True to his word, he measured one of the chimneys and appeared to ballpark the other with a practiced eye. He measured the two adjoining sides of the skylight and then met her at the roofline.

"Are you sure you're okay?" he asked again.

This time she nodded. "But can you wait right there while I go down? Okay, I admit it. I'm not that good with heights."

"I'm right here. I'll hold the ladder," he said, helpfully. "It's not going anywhere. Take it step-by-step, and it takes as long as it takes. Safety first. No one's running a stopwatch," he said in a gentle voice.

She took a couple of deep breaths and stepped down. He held the ladder steady and she took two more steps. As each foot approached the ground, her confidence grew and her momentary light-headedness faded. Finally, she reached the packed dirt of the courtyard and stepped away from the ladder. Only then did he begin his own easy descent.

Quietly, he packed up the ladder and secured it to the truck, giving her a minute to steady herself. Intended for her benefit, or not, it was a nice thing to do.

"Where to next?" he asked, turning to face her.

"Um, the chicken coops, I guess? I can't imagine what we'd do with them. Tear them down, probably. But I guess we should know what kind of shape they're in before we decide," she said.

"It depends on what you'd like to do with the property. Have you thought about that? Any ideas?" He sounded genuinely curious.

Harper debated how much she should tell a perfect stranger, and forthrightness won. "Well, *I'm* not the only one who gets to decide— my sister is an equal partner—but I kind of fell in love with the ranch at first sight. I know that probably sounds ridiculous, but it's true. So, in my wildest dreams, I'd turn the main house into a B&B, plant some beautiful gardens, and try to breathe some life back into this place."

"I don't think falling in love with a house, or a patch of land, sounds ridiculous at all," he said. "It's happened to me more than once.

That's part of what makes me so committed to my work. Restoring old homes is what I live for, other than Ellie."

"Your wife?" she asked, politely.

He shook his head. "No, my daughter. I have full custody."

Harper swallowed this bit of information, which caused her to revise her initial opinion of him. "So…is that why you couldn't give me a firm time yesterday?" she asked, using her remarkably perceptive intuition.

"Yeah. My housekeeper had some family obligations and she wasn't sure she could watch Ellie. I have a couple of backup people, but I hadn't had time to arrange anything, yet."

"But you found someone?" she asked.

"Yeah, I did," he said, not elaborating. "And then I called you, and here I am."

"Do you ever bring your daughter to work with you?" She was genuinely curious about how he managed single fatherhood—it couldn't be easy.

"Almost never—not since Ellie became mobile. She's only four-and-a-half, and there are too many ways for her to hurt herself. Not to mention snakes, spiders, and scorpions. You gotta love New Mexico."

"And bats," Harper couldn't help adding, with a grin.

"How about those chicken coops?" Caleb said, by way of deflection.

Did she detect a blush? It was hard to tell—he looked like he spent a lot of time in the sun.

They walked down the drive a hundred yards and moved toward the row of seven largish coops. A few strips of peeling tarpaper clung to the exterior walls, but up close, the wood appeared to be in better shape than she'd initially thought. Like the house, the coops had metal roofs, which hopefully had limited the amount of interior water damage.

Caleb pushed open a door, which creaked eerily on its hinges, but a little WD-40 could fix that. Light entered the space from a small square window, opposite, enough to see the bits of faded straw and chicken droppings that littered the floor. Roosting boxes sat a few feet off the ground with perches suspended above. On the far wall, the slanted roof was a little low for Caleb, but Harper still had some headroom above her. While not exactly struck with inspiration, she didn't think the coops were total teardowns, but she'd happily listen to a competent professional's opinion.

"What do you think?" she asked him.

He rubbed a hand over his attractively stubbled chin.

"Well, they're not in bad shape, but there are a *lot* of them. A couple of decades ago, this was no small operation. Unless you're going to start raising chickens again, you probably don't need to keep all of them." He ran his hand lightly over the silvery wood on the walls. "Old barnwood like this is worth good money." Wagging his head back and forth, he appeared to consider the situation. "If it were me, I'd decide how many of them you're willing to keep, then offer the rest for sale on Craigslist under building materials. You could use some of that money to do something with the remaining buildings. They could be some sort of craft workshops, art studios…"

"Maybe, live/work spaces for short-term rental?" she said.

"Yeah. You got it—whatever floats your boat."

In her mind's eye, she could picture a few colorful, leggy hens prancing around the place, entertaining the guests. Probably entertaining the local coyotes, too.

"Are you free for lunch?" Harper asked, spontaneously. "My treat. I don't know much about the area in general, and I could use an insider's point of view. We can discuss plans for the property later on, after you've had time to go over your notes and price things out."

"Sorry, I can't today. I'm all booked up," he said, glancing at the time on his cell phone. "But, tell you what, I could drop by later this evening after I'm finished with another job. Oh, I also wanted to ask you if you'd like an official survey," he said. "I could even mark your boundaries for you—that is, if you want me to."

There he went with that voice, again.

Of course, I want you to. "Um, yes. I could meet you back here, late afternoon? Can you text me when you're on your way? Meanwhile, I'll check out the town, grab some lunch, and find a park or something to chill in. So, does grass even grow around here?" she asked. "It looks like it's all scrub and sagebrush, except where there's water."

Caleb smiled. "It does when it rains—but right now we're in a drought. Well, for the last decade or two, we've been in a drought. Okay, so that's a plan. When you're in town, check out Maggie's. You won't be sorry."

"Will this Maggie person feed me?" Harper asked, very interested in the answer to that question.

Caleb smiled and nodded. "Tell her I sent you."

CHAPTER FIVE

*W*hile staying at a hotel on the outskirts of Santa Fe and commuting to the ranch, she hadn't yet taken time to check out Verde Springs, which was eight or nine miles further down the county road. She had a few hours to kill, and there was no time like the present…

Now, as she stood on the main street, the quaint little town looked like something out of an old western, or its newer incarnation, the *Longmire* TV series. Roughly five blocks by ten blocks wide, it featured a small central square surrounded by a sheriff's office, a grocery store, and several boarded-up buildings that included a hotel straight out of the Old West. A rustic, southwestern version of a diner anchored one corner of the square, judging from the glorious scents reaching Harper's nose. *Maggie's Diner*, the sign read. It was hand-painted, without any neon in sight.

She practically sprinted across the winter-brown grass, aiming for the yellow stucco building with tall green-trimmed windows. Double doors with gold lettering welcomed her to enter, and it was a good thing no one got in her way. Stepping inside, she saw the "Seat Yourself" sign and grabbed a booth by the window overlooking the sidewalk, so she could people-watch and get a feel for the town's vibe. It appeared to be relaxed: if it weren't for a young man with dreadlocks whizzing by on a skateboard, she'd swear someone had turned back the clock a couple of decades. She'd bet her bottom dollar that her Aunt Sabina had eaten at this little cafe, and that it hadn't changed all that much in thirty-odd years. It was exactly the kind of place that had great pie, something to keep in mind if she planned to stick around...

"Have you had a chance to look at the menu? What can I get started for you?" a friendly voice asked.

Harper looked up to see an older woman with a turquoise stud in her left nostril. She was wearing a Maggie's t-shirt, and her nametag read "Skye."

"Hi. Sorry, I was distracted. No, I haven't had a chance to look at the menu—but I'm kind of starving and not that picky. Tell me what's good, or what Maggie's is famous for."

"Green chili cheeseburgers, sweet potato fries, and agave wine margaritas. I know it's early, but—"

"Sold! I haven't eaten all day," Harper said.

"Alrighty, then. I'll ask Maggie to throw some extra fries on there."

"Thanks. Oh, and I'm supposed to tell Maggie that Caleb sent me."

"Caleb Johansson? Yeah, he comes in all the time. He and Maggie are good friends. Don't worry, we'll treat you right. Give me ten minutes and I'll be back with a plate that'll make you happy," Skye said.

What a helpful and generous person, Harper thought, smiling and leaning back against the booth. About a quarter of the booths were occupied, and only a few of the tables. To her right, a double door led to a charming patio with tables and chairs were stacked on one end. In late March, the garden looked dry and lifeless. It all looked very sad—and daffodil bulbs were the obvious answer. Hyacinth, too. If she got to know this Maggie person, she would definitely recommend some bulbs.

Her phone buzzed. It was Paige, keeping tabs on her little sister—and, to be fair, checking on the "rustic" former chicken ranch they now owned together.

"What's up? Make it snappy. I haven't eaten all day, and you know how I can get," Harper said by way of greeting.

"Well, hello to you, too. How are things going?" Paige asked.

"Okay, so far. The contractor showed up, I accidentally made him squeal like a girl, then he coached me down off a ladder, and now I think we're friends."

Paige laughed. "I'd have given a lot to see any of the above. So, do you have news to share?"

"No, we're meeting again later this afternoon after he finishes work. He offered to survey the place, and I said it sounded like a good idea."

"It does sound like a good idea. Who knows what we might find on fifty-six acres that have been sitting vacant for a good long time? Maybe he can tell us where the bodies are buried."

"I think he's more interested in finding out where the boundaries are. By the way, the old coops aren't in terrible shape, and Caleb thinks we could do something with them. I'm still considering our options."

"Oh, so, it's *Caleb*, now? What's he like?" Paige asked.

"Well, the man definitely knows how to wear a toolbelt," Harper said, keeping her voice low. *Small towns were known for their healthy grapevines.*

"Down, girl," said her sister. "Keep it professional."

"Yeah, yeah. He's a busy guy and a single dad, but it doesn't hurt to look. And he turned me on to this amazing diner in Verde Springs, where I'm about to eat something called a green chili cheeseburger, loaded, with as many sweet potato fries as they can fit on the plate. So, I kind of owe him."

"Oh, my God! Stop. You're making *me* hungry, and my body doesn't even like spicy food. Okay, now I'm hanging up, for real. Call me *mañana*."

Harper's green chili cheeseburger delighted every single one of her tastebuds: hand ground and perfectly seasoned organic beef, locally grown green chilis, a big slab of New Mexico goat-milk cheddar, and the best sweet potato fries she'd ever eaten. Harper sat back in utter bliss, thinking. Maybe she should check out the area's cafes and see if they used locally grown produce or herbs. There had to be a surplus of aged chicken manure somewhere on the ranch, and it made *great* fertilizer. As long as she was busting her butt to beautify the high desert, she might as well plant something that would add to their potential income stream. Diversification was important.

She paid her bill and waved to the dark-haired woman standing over the grill making magic happen. "That was delicious! My name's Harper, and I'm new in town. Caleb sent me. Thanks for the wonderful food—it was just what I needed." She gave a little wave, and the woman smiled in return.

"Nice to meet you, Harper. I'm Maggie. Say 'hi' to Caleb for me. And thanks for coming in." She flashed a quick smile in Harper's direction, then turned her attention to her work.

※

Harper headed out of town and back to the ranch. She arrived before Caleb and decided to explore a little. First off, she used her tape measure to gauge the width of the driveway, then drove the total distance trying to come up with a ballpark number. The road badly needed another layer of gravel laid down before monsoon season, if they were lucky enough to *have* a monsoon season this year. Next, she took photos of all seven of the individual chicken coops and texted them to her sister. She added a note explaining that Caleb had suggested keeping some, and tearing down the rest, saving the weathered siding to sell to folks looking for reclaimed wood. It could bring in a little cash to help with their rehab project.

Harper worked her way around the back of the house, using her tape measure to determine the size of the patio. She'd do some sketching tonight, drawing out lush gardens full of native plantings. She'd throw in some fantasy southwestern furniture, maybe she'd snoop a little on Pinterest, although that was way more up her sister's alley.

She heard the sound of tires on gravel and made her way to the front of the house to greet Caleb. This time, he wasn't alone.

"Hi, I'm Ellie," said the little girl after climbing carefully down out of the tall cab.

Caleb nodded at his daughter. "New skillset. She's proud of herself."

"And rightly so," Harper said, smiling. "Hi Ellie, it's nice to meet you. I'm Harper. I'm glad you could come out to the ranch with your daddy."

"Her sitter had to go home early. There's a flu bug going around and her husband needed some help. I hope it's okay," Caleb said, raising one shoulder in a little shrug.

"Sure. I'll help you keep an eye on her. By the way, thanks for the tip about Maggie's. That place was the bomb!"

"I'm glad you liked it. Maggie's a good friend. Well, should we get to it? I took the liberty of grabbing some survey maps for the property while I was in town. I didn't know if you had anything like that laying around."

Impressive. It showed initiative and thoughtfulness. Being new here, she had no idea where the county land offices were even located— Santa Fe, most likely.

"Thanks, Caleb. That'll be a big help. Lead on, and I'll follow you. Ellie? Is it okay if I tag along with you?"

"Sure. Do you have any chickens? Daddy said we were going to look at a chicken ranch."

"No, not at the moment. Do you know where I could find some? This used to be a commercial chicken ranch that produced both eggs, and well, chickens. But it hasn't been for a long time. Now, what *I'm* looking for is chicken *poo*: It's like gold for your garden, and I want to plant a very *big* garden here. Maybe a *couple* of very big gardens—with lots of pretty flowers."

"I like flowers. I like sunflowers the most because they're the biggest. And the best," the little girl said, accurately and with discernment.

"Me too. When I plant my gardens, maybe you can come and help me plant the sunflowers," Harper offered. "Hollyhocks, too. They seem to be everywhere in New Mexico."

"Daddy, can I?" Ellie asked.

"May I?"

"Daddy, may I?

"I don't see why not."

"Good." Ellie skipped ahead of them down the dirt track, not quite a road, but wider than a trail. Harper was curious where it led. Owning a big chunk of land was a distinctly new experience.

Caleb seemed to think the rough track led to a boundary marker. He handed Harper a role of neon orange flagging tape to carry, while he balanced the surveying tripod on his excellent shoulder.

On a property of fifty-six acres, it had taken them almost twenty minutes of brisk walking to reach the first corner. Old lichen-covered fence posts held sagging barbed wire, but the boundary corner had been secured by one of those square wooden boxes filled with rocks. *Big* rocks, no doubt cleared from the surrounding fields. It seemed miraculously intact.

Caleb held out the map. "According to the official survey, the corner pin should be pretty close, maybe a few more feet to the east."

When all three of them bent to look, Harper sensed that Ellie had done this before. She seemed to know exactly what to look for, as did Harper, from her years of working in landscape design and installation.

"Sometimes it's easier to feel it with your foot than to spot it with your eyes." In his sturdy Redwings, Caleb tapped the soil to the south of the rock-filled-box marking the corner of the property, while she and Ellie walked the fence line carefully to the east.

"Maybe it's behind this box of rocks, and that's why we can't see it. Could they have built the fence corner just inside the boundary?" Harper asked him.

"If we don't find it after a good look here, that's worth a try," Caleb said.

Before Harper could stop her, Ellie slipped through the barbed-wire fence and immediately called out. "I found it, Daddy. Come look."

"Yes, you sure did, baby. But you could have scratched yourself on the fence-wire. Next time, wait for me, okay?" he said, in a firm but gentle voice.

"But you were taking too long," she said, matter-of-factly.

"Sometimes we need to be patient, remember? I would have been there in a minute or so. Baby girl, I'd hate for you to get scratched on rusty metal. Promise me you'll be more careful?"

She nodded, still standing on the other side of the fence. So, Caleb straddled the barbed wire with his long legs and lifted her over, while Harper reached out and helped Ellie to the ground. *Teamwork. She didn't have any idea how on earth he did this parenting thing alone.*

"Should I flag this, then?" Harper asked.

"I would. Mark it in a couple of places, so you'll be able to find it again. And, it never hurts to let people, especially neighbors, know someone's occupying the property, again.

"Speaking of, I'm not actually occupying the property yet. I know you've only just seen the house, but how long do you think it would take to make it habitable?"

"Habitable like camping, or actually livable?" he asked.

"Well, no bats, for starters. Seal up any cracks that would let critters in. Utilities hooked up. It's still pretty cold at this elevation, so heat of some sort. A wood stove would do—we can add a real furnace later on if the one the house came with isn't functional." The dollar-signs were adding up—and they didn't need to spend money they didn't have.

"Two or three weeks, tops. Maybe sooner if no other urgent jobs come in. March and April are the windiest months in New Mexico. When I get calls for emergency roof repairs, they take priority. So, it could be more like a month, if I'm busy."

Harper calculated in her head. "I could probably make three or four weeks work. I have to head back to Washington State to pack up my house and wrap up a few other things."

"So, you're going to go for it? I'd love to see someone do something with this old place. It's got so much more character than a new build," he said.

Harper backtracked. "Well, it all depends on how much money you think it would take to get it up and running. My sister, Paige, is an equal partner in this. Although the property is probably valuable, it'll only bring in quick cash if we sell some of it. But that wouldn't be our preference—we'd like to keep it intact if I can."

Paige was pretty settled in Virginia, with a secure teaching job and a comfortable condo. But Harper would have some moving expenses, and then a substantial period with no income. She sighed. Was this idea of turning the ranch into a B&B just a ridiculous fantasy? She turned her attention back to the corner post and took a good look at the property—*their* property—which sloped gently up to a small rise where the house stood, regally, like a queen surveying her kingdom, or, queendom? She shook her head. *No, it wasn't fantasy—it was possibility.* For the first time in months, she was moving forward. And, at the moment, moving forward alone felt just fine.

CHAPTER SIX

"So, any news?" Paige asked. "Have you been able to keep your hands off the sexy contractor?"

"Yes, I've been very appropriate. Besides, I've fallen in love with someone else," Harper said, as she sampled her last meal of Mexican food for a while.

"Well, don't leave me hanging."

"Her name is Ellie, she's four-and-a-half, and she wants to come over and help me plant sunflowers, because they're the best. I'm considering getting her a puppy," Harper said.

"That sounds like a Hallmark channel moment—but aren't you forgetting something? If you're serious about this, you have a nearly two-thousand-mile move to make in the next few weeks. Not to mention, a giant black hole of a cash flow problem," Paige reminded her.

"You're such a buzz-kill," Harper grumbled.

"*Someone* has to keep it real. So, let's talk money. How are we going to bring this old chicken ranch back to life and get it to pay for itself before it becomes San Miguel County's next 18-hole golf course?"

"Good question. I have no income at the moment—and in our divorce settlement Kevin and I agreed to use our savings to pay off the Gig Harbor mortgage so we could split things equally when we sell the house. Right now, I only have enough left in what remained in my landscape-business account to pay for the move to New Mexico. But I can cash in my 401(k), if I have to," Harper said.

"That's not the best move—you'd take a big hit. We could try applying for a small-business loan to help with repairs," said Paige. "But probably no lender will touch us until we can come up with a viable business plan for the ranch."

"Well, there's *one* option we should consider. I'll keep Lucy, of course, because I need a work truck. But it would help if I could sell Ricky before I leave Gig Harbor. And when I get back to New Mexico, I could sell Sabina's SUV. I haven't had time to get attached to her, yet." Harper believed cars came with genders and personalities, and no one could talk her out of it.

"But that SUV is perfect for the terrain around there, and Aunt Sabina obviously wanted you to have it," Paige argued.

"I know she did. But if we can make the ranch pay for itself and keep it in the family, I think that would matter to Aunt Sabina a whole lot more. I looked up the blue book on the SUV—it's in decent shape, and it's less than two years old. It'll give me money for groceries, gas, and materials, so Caleb can at least get started on repairs. Besides, I don't have the luxury of owning multiple vehicles or paying car insurance on all of them."

"Okay, then, keep me posted. And don't fall too hard for the kiddo, or her daddy. There might be another woman in the picture—estranged wife, girlfriend, fiancé, take your pick—kids don't grow on trees."

"I'm aware of that fact—you did an excellent job coaching me on the birds and bees. But I already have an 'in.' When the three of us were walking back from checking the corner pins, I heard Ellie say, 'Daddy, that lady is *nice*.'"

"Well, you *are* nice, mostly, except when you're stomping around yelling at people and speaking sailor in three languages."

"Thank you, I think? What can I say? It comes with the territory. I've been running landscaping crews for almost ten years," Harper said, by way of justification. "Guys tend to talk trash—and some of the women I hired, too. I guess playing in the dirt makes us a little 'earthier' than other people."

"Well, clean it up, missy, especially if you're going to be hanging around small children. And if you're going to get a puppy, wait until you finish moving and settle in."

"That sounds like you're giving me the green light."

"I am, *cautiously*, giving you a yellow light. Maybe even chartreuse. If you're willing to sell both of your cars and pay for the initial repairs yourself, it's proof that you're willing to invest in the property. Therefore, as your big sister and co-heir, I'm willing to invest in *you*. I'll chip in for the big-ticket items, and we'll make sure it all comes out even in the end. However, I'm imposing a strict time limit."

"How is *that* going to work?" Harper asked.

"You've got a year to do your thing, try to make a go of it, and see if it's even a viable proposition. After that, we're going to sit down and look at the books, together, and have a serious discussion. Agreed?"

"I don't have a better idea, and I guess it's fair. I know I'm not the boss of the world, and half of the property belongs to you. Let's go for it."

"I know you want to do this, Harper, and I hope it works out for you. More than that, I hope it's the best thing for you. I just…don't know if it's the best thing for *me*," Paige said.

"Do you want me to buy you out, Paige? Because I probably wouldn't be able to do that for a *long* time—we're talking card-carrying senior citizen," Harper said.

"Like I said. You've got one year, and then we'll talk. Not only that, but I'll try to come out and spend the summer and help you as much as I can. Anything we do to improve the property will just make it more valuable, if we *do* eventually decide to sell."

Harper felt a sudden surge of tears. *Her sister had faith in her and wanted to help her. More than that, Paige would be here for her as she rebuilt her life from scratch in an entirely new place.* She cleared her throat. "That means a lot to me, Paige. You have no idea."

"Of course, I do! When Dan and I split up you offered to share your house in Gig Harbor with me—and then you flew all the way from Washington state to help me pack up and move to my condo. And, you said *very* mean things about Dan's equipment. By the way, that wasn't *our* problem, either."

Harper smiled, remembering. "If I'd only known then, what Kevin was up to while I was away, you and I could have run away together and joined the circus."

"I guess you can only work with what you know at any given time—and I think you've handled things really well. But, you know, it's two hours later in Richmond," she yawned, "I'm off to bed. Call me when you know more, about anything. It must be hard with so many things up in the air."

"No worries. I'm taking things one day at a time. The green chili cheeseburgers at Maggie's are helping a lot," Harper said. "'Night, Paige."

CHAPTER SEVEN

*E*arly the next morning, Harper made a quick trip to the ranch before her flight back to Sea-Tac. She wanted to thoroughly explore the vicinity of the chicken coops, reasoning that no one in their right mind would want to haul the constant supply of manure any farther than necessary. She dug her shiny new shovel into several suspicious mounds covered with unnaturally lush vegetation, and voila, she found green gold: decades-old, aged, chicken manure. By now, the once-pungent piles had composted into the finest organic matter, ready to mix with the sandy soil and fine gravel to create the perfect substrate for her gardens.

Using non-toxic paint, she painstakingly outlined the planting beds closest to the house, and instructed Caleb where to deposit a good foot of chicken manure using his front-end loader. The stones she'd use to surround the beds could come later—there was no shortage of them around the ranch. Finally, she ordered two, fifteen-foot desert willows with gracefully contorted branches to be installed upon her return. She'd done what she could in the few hours she had—but it was the start of something she hoped would one day be beautiful.

※

After two busy weeks in New Mexico, she was headed home to the land of chanterelle mushrooms and licorice ferns—and to the life she'd once shared with a man who had sorely disappointed her. *But she wasn't going to think about him right now—or maybe ever.*

During the long flight to Sea-Tac, she listened to the Dixie Chicks' "Wide Open Spaces" album on her wireless headphones. She smiled as she revisited her pleasant memories of Caleb and Ellie, the flocks of white-winged doves that roosted in the trees near the coops, and the friendly staff who kept her well-fed at Maggie's. She was leaving Verde Springs filled with visions of puppies and sunflowers and fifty-six acres of reasons to be happy. She only had to 'believe in herself, work hard, and be nice to people,' Aunt Sabina's three-part motto. *She could do that.* The cherry on the sundae was having a big sister who believed in her, and who'd be joining her in a few short, busy months.

Her life was changing in a big way, but every life involved evolution: even the Dixie Chicks had dropped the 'Dixie' and were now just The Chicks.'

A little over two weeks flew by as she wrapped up one life and prepared to begin another. And after a ridiculous amount of hard work and multiple trips to Home Depot, she was finally done. Standing in her now-empty house felt like an out-of-body experience. Steady rain drizzled down the tall windows as she looked out on the white-capped waters of Puget Sound. The Pacific storms helped green plants grow, and as a landscape designer, she'd benefitted from nature's generous bounty for nearly a decade. Shove a stick in the ground in the Pacific Northwest, and in a few years, you'd have a tree. She would miss the abundance of water—just not the kind that seemed to fall continuously from November to June, if you were lucky.

Something she *wouldn't* miss? The possibility of running into Kevin or his new partner. Once she got to New Mexico and built a brand-new life for herself, she could ditch that internal alarm for good. *Chill and relaxed would be her future motto...*

The few close friends she had in Gig Harbor, Tacoma, and Bellingham would no doubt be calling her next February in desperate need of a sun break. She'd love to be able to offer her future B&B services, gratis, but she wasn't there yet—she'd have to come up with a "Friends-and-Family" rate and hope her friends weren't offended. Meanwhile, her spousal support, though modest, would help keep the lights turned on until the ranch was able to make it, or break it, and she had her end-of-year sit-down with her sister.

The movers had come and gone. She had a full tank of gas in Lucy, a fresh oil change, and four new, heavy-duty tires. Sadly, she'd had to let Ricky go. But the sweet, young college student who'd bought her old VW bug was ecstatic, and Harper knew she'd treat him right.

"Goodbye, house," she said, softly. "I hope the next people who live here are happier. You were a good house—it wasn't your fault." And with that, she closed the door on her old life, hopped into Lucy, and began the slow return trip to sunnier skies and infinite possibilities. With one last look at the blanket of gray hanging two hundred feet above her head, Harper smiled. *Three hundred days of sunshine a year sounded just about right.*

Driving to New Mexico alone gave Harper the opportunity to shop for cool things that would add ambience to their future B&B. Thankfully, she and Paige shared a vision for the ranch house's renovation and decor: rustic, southwestern elegance; hand-crafted, classy, and never garish. The interior would blend seamlessly with the exterior, which Harper had plans to transform with glorious gardens dominated by native plants and Xeriscape specimens.

High on caffeine and non-nutritious road snacks, she drove like a long-haul trucker for the first two days, singing along to all of her favorite tunes: Brandi Carlisle, Band of Horses, and Lord Huron made for excellent company. There was something so totally freeing about a solo road trip, that she didn't even mind the incredible distance.

When she reached Durango, instead of heading directly toward Santa Fe, she detoured due south through the Four Corners area, hoping to stop at some rug galleries. In Farmington, a massive flea market caught her eye. *Good Golly, the entire town must have organized a spring cleaning!* Needing to stretch her road-weary legs, anyway, she pulled Lucy over and retrieved a diet Coke from her cooler. When she finally got to the ranch, she'd need to do a seven-day cleanse of nothing but celery juice and kale. *Bye-bye, nachos with pourable cheese topping and pickled jalapeños.*

The flea market booths contained mostly kids' clothes and toys, the larger ones, tools and farm machinery. There were some diamonds in the rough, including a bargain pair of pink cowboy boots that looked like they'd fit Ellie, and, of course, she had to buy them. Alas, there were no red cowboy boots in a size eight.

Then she came to "the basket lady," whose booth featured dozens of baskets of all types, utilitarian, made-in-China, and even a few intended for collecting eggs. Mixed in among them, Harper spotted a few gems. Her Aunt Sabina had collected Native crafts, including basketry. She'd gifted several nice baskets to Harper over the years, and they were already traveling in carefully packed boxes on their way to the ranch. But Harper had two large reception rooms to furnish, a huge country kitchen, and seven bedrooms. Baskets could serve so many purposes: art, craft, and as storage containers to organize small items. They were also lightweight and easy to transport, and she had plenty of extra space in Lucy's big truck bed. *Time to shop.*

"These are really beautiful! You must have been collecting for quite a while," Harper said, admiringly.

"Yes, going on forty years. I'm moving in with my daughter in Denver. She doesn't have room for all this," she said, waving a hand. "I'm ready to let my baskets go to a good home."

Harper picked up a beautifully made basket in alternating light and dark fibers. "I'm moving, myself, to the Southwest. I'm furnishing an old ranch house that I hope to turn into a B&B. Do you know much about the history of these baskets?"

"Some. I picked up a lot of these when we lived in Gallup. My husband worked at Red Rock State Park near there for a few years. Here, let me show you." She sorted through her baskets, slowly and lovingly, then pushed several well-crafted pieces toward the front of the table. "These are from the Four-Corners area. I'm sorry, I don't know which pueblo or maker."

"They're lovely," said Harper, picking up each piece to examine it more closely. "I like all three of these." They agreed on a price and the woman took Harper's credit card to run through the square on her cell phone. *The wonders of modern technology.*

"Miss, if you need quilts, you should go see my friend, Marguerite." The woman gestured down the row of tables to one stacked with folded quilts.

"Thanks very much, I'll check them out." At a glance, they appeared to be worth a look. Turning back, she said, "I promise I'll give all of your baskets a good home."

"These are lovely," Harper told the quiltmaker, whose name was Marguerite. "I'm furnishing a B&B in the Southwest. Your colors are so vibrant! I might get a quilt or two, now. But if I asked you to make several more in certain color combinations, would you be willing to do that? And do you make pillow cases? I'd want those as well."

"I can do that. Go ahead and show me what you have in mind," Marguerite said.

"I like the two full-size quilts with the large geometric shapes in these desert colors—but on the vibrant side rather than the softer end of the spectrum. I'd love to buy this queen-size quilt, now," Harper said, picking it up in her hands, "and the two matching twin quilts."

After paying for the reasonably priced items, Harper added Marguerite's business card to her wallet. "Thanks! I'll be in touch, soon. The house I'm furnishing is amazing, but it needs a lot of love. These bright fabrics will look wonderful against the adobe walls. I'll be back to pick them up in a few minutes."

She gathered her baskets and made her way to Lucy. She transferred them to the bench seat, passenger side. Then she drove the short distance to Marguerite's stall and loaded up her quilts, inside, where they wouldn't get wet in a sudden spring storm. Road-weary, even after taking the short break, she knew she wouldn't make it to the ranch before she grew too tired to drive. *Safety first.*

She locked the truck and returned to ask Marguerite one more question: "Is there a nice place to stay around here? I could keep driving, but I won't be able to get where I'm going tonight."

"Oh, sure. There's lots of nice, clean motels around here. If you head back out on the highway, you can take your pick. It's getting near dinner-time—do you need to eat first?"

"I can *always* eat," Harper said, smiling. "Do you have a recommendation?"

"Yeah, Red River BBQ, the best barbecue in New Mexico. My grandkids told me it's even on Yelp—just look for the five-star review. It's in a strange location, like, in a neighborhood, you know? Your GPS should get you there. Tell 'em I sent you," she said, with a warm smile.

Marguerite wasn't exaggerating. Full of excellent barbecue and colorful dreams, Harper got a solid eight hours of sleep.

She hit the road early, determined to make it to the ranch by mid-afternoon. The Decemberists' "June Hymn" played from Lucy's stereo as she gazed out the window at "O'Keefe Country," tanked up on caffeine and a couple of two-dollar breakfast tacos she'd found in a truck stop. Three road-weary hours later, she pulled up in front of Maggie's to grab dinner to go: chicken enchiladas '*enmolada*,' with deliciously dark, creamy sauce. How lovely to be welcomed back, to be recognized, and to be far, far away from the Pacific Northwest's chill. The people here in New Mexico were warm, and she was *craving* warmth: it would keep her going until she found her feet again, or until her big sister joined her. For as long as Harper could remember, Paige had always had a way of making her feel like everything would be alright.

As the April sunlight began to fade, Harper chugged up the ranch drive. Two freshly dug holes immediately caught her eye, one on each side of the ranch house's massive front door, in precisely the spots Harper had reserved for her desert willows. The holes hadn't been on Caleb's punch list: it was thoughtful that he'd done it, or asked his crew to take care of it. When the trees were delivered in a few weeks, they'd have a comfy place to settle in. Harper planned to amend the soil like crazy so the beautiful, drought-tolerant trees would thrive. "Buy a five-dollar plant, dig a ten-dollar hole," was her general rule when planting anything worth having, and these two specimen desert willows had cost her a bundle, as most big trees do.

She opened the heavy front doors and entered, noting the clear light shining down to illuminate the grand space. Caleb had cleaned years of accumulated dirt and debris from the old glass skylight, and what a difference it made!

The tile floors had been cleaned and waxed, and the entire interior had been freshly painted the warm, eggshell white she and Paige had agreed on, a shade called "Spanish Villa." Now, the untouched natural wood contrasted beautifully with the clean backdrop. Art, textiles, and even the baskets and quilts she'd brought with her from Farmington would bring the space to life. Harper choked up a little, thinking of how badly she'd wanted to create a welcoming refuge for her sister, for her friends, for visitors, and for herself. In a few short weeks, the house had been stunningly transformed. Caleb and his crew of subs had done a truly outstanding job—she'd have to find a way to thank him.

Harper brought in the rest of her things from the truck: the baskets, the quilts and pillowcases, and her take-out from Maggie's. Dropping her new purchases on the wide staircase, she wandered into the kitchen and noticed that it, too, had been spotlessly cleaned. And Caleb had cleverly built her four custom barstools, staining them cobalt blue to match the blue-and-white patterned Mexican tiles. They weren't makeshift, either: he'd used old, reclaimed wood and had designed them with subtle New Mexican craftsmanship. Pulling up a Damien Jurado playlist on her phone, she settled on the nearest stool and stuck a plastic fork into her still-warm enchiladas. For the first time in months, she felt like she was *home*.

CHAPTER EIGHT

*K*evin Geddes sat at his computer in the spacious downtown loft that he shared with his intern, Erica. More than likely, their relationship wouldn't last forever. Young and ambitious, Erica would move on. *C'est la vie.* There were plenty of fish in his sea of young professionals.

Opening his online banking account, he slid on his designer reading glasses to take a look. Scanning the entries, a series of charges from unfamiliar states immediately jumped out at him: Nevada, Utah, New Mexico? *What was Harper up to?* The debit card was attached to a joint account that they could both use until the Gig Harbor house had been sold. Harper had agreed to do most of the hands-on work, and he knew there would be expenses for repairs and cleaning, so he'd given her permission to use it. But that's *all.* Now he'd have to have a conversation with his ex-wife, and Harper had been anything but cordial throughout the entire divorce process.

He dialed her number and left a message. "Hey, it's Kevin. I found some charges on the bank statement that aren't mine, and they don't appear to be associated with selling the Gig Harbor House. You should not be using the debit card without my permission—that's not what we agreed on. Call me as soon as you get this."

Harper stared angrily at her phone. Had eight years of fidelity and reluctant ego-stroking done nothing to earn Kevin's trust? She'd been in a 'situation' and she'd handled it. As often happened when traveling, her Washington bank had mistaken her trip to New Mexico as fraud from a stolen bank card and had temporarily blocked access—and in some of the places she'd traveled through, she hadn't even had cell service. She'd needed to use their joint debit card twice at the gas pump, and once at the motel in Farmington, and thank God, it had worked. She'd fully intended to make up the money in one way or another. Kevin had no right to get righteous with her, after she'd spent a measly few hundred bucks, at a time when she'd had no good alternative. *She'd nip this in the bud, right now.*

"Uh, yeah, Kevin," she said, leaving a voice mail. "The bank temporarily blocked my personal debit card because I was traveling out of state. I was in the middle of a transaction and I couldn't drive my truck with an empty gas tank. As I'd planned to, I'll transfer the money back into the joint house account. Today, okay?"

That's done, she said, handling the situation efficiently and promptly. Then, she took the joint debit card out of her wallet. Using her handy multi-purpose tool, she cut it up into little pieces and threw them in the trash.

Almost immediately, her phone rang. "Harper, what's going on? Why are you traveling all over the place? I thought you were taking care of the house and getting everything done like we agreed—not taking a spontaneous vacation in the Southwest."

Why did he always think the worst of her without a shred of evidence? Who *was* this person she'd spent a decade of her life with? Including dating him and supporting him for two years before he asked her to marry him. She was embarrassed by the fool she'd once been. *But no more.*

"Are you concerned about my well-being, or just my where-abouts? And for the record, I'm *not* on vacation," she said.

"I'm not in the mood to play games, Harper. Don't use the card attached to the house account without my permission. We agreed on that, as I'm sure you're aware," Kevin reminded her.

"No worries, then, it's on its way to the landfill. And I'm sure you're not aware that my Aunt Sabina died recently—*that's* why I'm in New Mexico." He didn't have any right, or need, to know that she planned to stay here, more or less, permanently.

No "I'm sorry." No "I know you two were close." No "are you okay?" After an awkward moment of silence, Kevin continued, "You should have told me."

"Why? You're not part of my life anymore. *You* decided that," she said.

"But this *changes* everything, Harper. Assuming your aunt left you her house, that revises your financial picture," Kevin said. "Santa Fe real estate doesn't come cheap. What's it worth?"

He was so pathetically predictable. "Well, she *didn't* leave me her house—so, you're out of luck. Sabina left her house in Santa Fe to her housekeeper."

"Still, if your financial circumstances change, you're supposed to let me know, or the court know, or *somebody* know. I don't need to pay spousal support when you're perfectly capable of earning your own living," Kevin mansplained in a voice that implied she was dumber than a box of rocks—and that he had been infinitely patient with her for a decade. *Not.*

She wasn't even sure that what he'd said was true. Letting the screen door slam behind her, Harper stomped outside and focused on the dark blue ridges of the Pecos Mountains. She needed to climb a hill—something steep and gravelly—to burn off the adrenalin. "Kevin, I'm not earning a *dime* at the moment. First, it's winter; second, I'm not in Gig Harbor; and third, I spent two full weeks working my ass off getting *our* house ready to sell. And until it does and the money is in the bank, I can barely keep myself afloat. I had to let Ricky go to cover my expenses and give me some quick cash for the road trip down here. And let's not even talk about *your* income potential!" she growled.

"What about all the money I'm giving you?" he asked.

"Dude, it's court ordered, as an *equal* division of our *joint* assets, remember? It's all coming out of the same pot. I've made some changes in my life, Kevin—changes that don't concern you. I'm leaving Gig Harbor and I have no immediate plans to return. I've had some moving expenses, and I needed to set up a new living situation, here," she explained, with award-winning patience.

"Where?"

She supposed that was a reasonable question, so she answered it. "In New Mexico."

"I don't understand. Why are you moving to New Mexico, if Sabina didn't leave you her house in Santa Fe?"

She could sense Kevin's formidable wheels turning, which made her even more defensive, if that were possible.

She counted to five, then took a breath: "Because...it feels like home? Because I like enchiladas? Because I don't want to be within a thousand miles of *you* for the foreseeable future? Take your pick."

His moment of silence was only a temporary reprieve. Then, "Did she leave you *anything?* You have to tell me, Harper."

She didn't think Kevin had a legal leg to stand on, but she threw him a bone—anything to get him off the phone. "She left me her car."

"Well, that's something. What's it worth? We should figure that into the spreadsheet."

Well, that backfired. "Damn it, Kevin! Our settlement was finalized nearly two months ago! We agreed on the spreadsheet and we divided our assets, equally. Just like we'll divide the funds from the Gig Harbor house, when it sells, equally. You don't need half of my Aunt Sabina's car, and you don't have a legal right to it! Besides, I've already arranged to sell it."

"Why do you need to sell it? What are you driving, then? That old truck? And you said you sold Ricky, too? Why?"

Giving up, she shouted into her cell phone, "BECAUSE I NEEDED THE MONEY!" And then she disconnected the call. *But she knew that wouldn't be the end of it...*

No one could trigger her like Kevin could—Harper couldn't stay still another moment. Grabbing her keys, she jumped into Lucy's cab and roared down the driveway, spraying the newly laid gravel, but she stopped before the ranch drive met the county road. Taking a deep breath, she turned onto the blacktop and made her way into town, to Maggie's—her current source of carbs, protein, and solace.

Harper ordered a wine margarita, chips and salsa, and a green-chili cheeseburger a la cart. After that, she was having a big piece of pie with ice cream, damn the calories. She pressed her sister's number and Paige picked up.

"Hi, what's up?" Paige answered.

"My blood pressure. Kevin saw a few charges from my trip down here on our joint debit card. I *had* to use that card because my personal debit card had a fraud alert and the bank temporarily blocked access. I always forget to call and let them know I'm traveling out of state, and this time it came back to bite me. So, I used our joint debit card to buy gas, twice, and to pay for my hotel in Farmington."

"Well, that's not exactly earth-shattering. What was it, a couple of hundred bucks? Why does Kevin even care?" Paige asked.

"The problem is, it led to a much larger conversation: he knows about Aunt Sabina dying, the car, and then my having to turn around and sell it—and now he's asking why I needed the money. Should I be worried?"

"No, I don't think he has any legal standing regarding your inheritance. And your immediate financial circumstances haven't changed in the short term—you're *not* earning any money, yet. But in the long term? I guess that *could* be a pretty big change, but it's after the fact. Sabina died almost six weeks after you and Kevin agreed to your divorce settlement. So, it shouldn't matter. Right?"

"I agree with you, but I'm worried enough to want to talk to someone, discreetly. Nobody who knows Kevin, and nobody in the state of Washington. Not even Heather—because she might feel a responsibility to disclose the details to someone."

"Who then?" Paige asked.

"I'll start with Cherie Gonzalez. I like her and I trust her—and she used to practice divorce law. Plus, she's familiar with Sabina's estate and probably has a pretty good idea of what it's worth. I'll call her tomorrow and make an appointment."

"That sounds like a good plan. Keep me in the loop, and don't stress too much. And try to get some rest. Aren't you completely bushed from all the work you're doing?" Paige asked.

"Yeah, I am. But I'm also jazzed because the sexy contractor did such an excellent job on the house. Paige, it's so beautiful! It turned out even better than I'd expected, and I can't wait for you to see it."

"Send me some more pictures!" Paige said. "Seriously, the more the better."

"I will." Harper took a breath and thought of other, relevant news to share. "Oh…I bought the four-year-old a pair of hot pink cowgirl boots."

"You did not! Oh, my God! What's next? If you buy her a puppy, I want one, too." Paige loved dogs, but they were against the lease in her condo complex.

"Puppies aren't currently on my radar," Harper said. "Keeping Kevin's mitts off my bank account is my priority."

Harper end her call and continued her intake of exceptional comfort food. *God bless Maggie.*

Early the next morning, laying in her makeshift bed on the hardwood floor, she heard the grinding gears of the moving van moving ponderously up the ranch drive. How odd to know that it was filled to the brim with furniture and belongings from another life. At least she'd have plenty to occupy her over the next week, unpacking boxes, setting up her office space and toolshed, and creating a few unique, cozy areas to call her own. Then would come the big shopping spree, outfitting the rest of the ranch house, so much larger than her small home in Gig Harbor. She'd save the inner workings of the kitchen for Paige. Still, no home was truly a home without a kitchen table and chairs—and that much, she could handle.

CHAPTER NINE

$\mathcal{S}$ince she only needed to get some advice, not file formal paperwork, Harper met Cherie Gonzalez for lunch at the Santa Fe café the attorney recommended. As a courtesy, Harper bought lunch and drinks, and offered Cherie a free stay at their still unnamed B&B. That was the best she could do at the moment: she'd almost run out of funds, and she wouldn't see any green in her checking account until the house in Gig Harbor, for which they'd accepted an offer, just yesterday, closed escrow.

"What can I do for you, Harper?" Cherie asked, between bites of her southwestern Cobb salad.

"I've run into…a situation. As I might have mentioned, I'm recently divorced. We signed the final documents on February second. Then, out of the blue, my Aunt Sabina died on March fourteenth." She took a bite of her pecan-chicken salad and waited for the attorney to do the math in her head.

"And the will was probated on the twenty-third, I believe." Setting down her fork, Cherie continued. "First of all, it's widely agreed that property settlements aren't subject to change based on future events," she explained. "I understand why the timing might make you nervous, but legally, your ex-husband has no claim on your inheritance, since you acquired it *after* your divorce settlement was finalized. Yes, it ultimately has the potential to change your financial picture, long term. But at most, he could ask for a modification of spousal support based on your overall change in financial circumstances—and there's no guarantee at all that he'd get it."

"That's the thing," Harper said. "I'm actually bringing in *less* than my forecasted income, due to the circumstances brought on by my aunt's death. And my expenses have increased dramatically, with travel and the ranch rehab Until I get the B&B up and running, I'll have no real income. We've recently accepted an offer on our former home in Gig Harbor, and my share is already factored into our joint settlement." Harper sighed. "Kevin knows about the car my Aunt Sabina left me, and he asked me why I needed to sell it pretty much straight away. And, he knows that I sold my older personal auto in Washington State, too. He's wondering why I needed the money now, when he's already started paying monthly spousal support. So, here's the real question: Do I have an obligation to tell him about the ranch, or not? I *really* don't want to if I can help it. Not only does Kevin make substantially more money that I ever have, but he's closely tied to some pretty big property developers, and not just in Seattle. He's worked on projects in California, Oregon, and even Park City." *And that was uncomfortably close to New Mexico.*

"I understand—you've already formed an attachment to the ranch and you're feeling protective." Cherie took a sip of white wine and said thoughtfully, "There's really nothing to worry about—he can't get his hands on the ranch. But, if you like, I can read over the details of your divorce judgement."

Harper nodded, feeling slightly more at ease. Still, she had to ask, "Is there any other way he can find out that Paige and I inherited the ranch? I don't even want him sniffing around."

"Technically, property ownership is a matter of public record. And once it's gone through probate, the will is a public document. If he knows what to search for, he won't have much trouble finding it. Is he an attorney, or…?"

"No, he's an architect and a developer," Harper explained. "That's what worries me. I know how his brain works—it pretty much only sees dollar signs."

"Okay, let's not invest too much thought into it, just yet. Let me do some research, but try not to worry. And this will be pro bono." Cherie smiled. "I'm well aware of your present financial circumstances, and your Aunt Sabina was one of my favorite clients. Plus, I've *been* where you are, and not that long ago."

"I'm sorry, Cherie. It's not been much fun, so far."

"Truly, it never is. But we've both moved on. My ex has since moved on to San Diego—*with* his boyfriend," Cherie said, lifting an eyebrow.

"Oh, dear." Harper didn't know what to say.

"As my mother used to say, 'that's the way the *bizcochito* crumbles.' I got over it with a lovely man who since passed away in an accident. Now, I don't date much at all. Maybe every now and then, if I have a social or professional occasion to attend and I don't want to go alone. I'm pretty focused on my career, and I spend a lot of time with my family. I have lots of nieces and nephews to spoil," she said, smiling. "So, I have plenty of love in my life."

Harper returned Cherie's smile, then took care of the check. On the drive home, she contemplated the reality of her *own* future. She *really* had to look into getting a dog. If things didn't work out, here, in a year or so, she and the dog could look for a new home and another fresh start, and at least she wouldn't be alone.

"Any news?" Paige asked, when they talked later that night.

"Not to worry, Cherie's on it. And it might take Kevin a while to find out unless he knows what he's looking for."

"That's good news, I guess. But, damn it, it would be just like that jerk to try to swoop in after we've done all the hard work; well, *you*, mostly. But I'm coming out, sooner than I thought I would. I have my flight booked for the weekend before Memorial Day."

"How'd you manage that?" Harper asked. Paige taught business law at the State University in Virginia. After going away to college, she'd come back to Richmond, the city where they'd both grown up. Of course, Harper knew the reason for that—Harper *was* the reason for that.

"I'm having my TA proctor the final exam, and I'm out of there the day after regular classes end."

"Well, hot damn! That makes my day, Paige. I have a lot of work to do, but the vision is coming together in my head. We've even had some rain, so the plants I've managed to put in are hanging in there until monsoon season. I think you'll like it here. It's already starting to feel like home to me."

"That's great, Harper! You really needed a win. So, how's Mr. Toolbelt?"

"Lately, he's been 'Heavy Equipment Man.' He's helping me landscape the entry garden near the house, just the big stuff I can't handle on my own. And Ellie *loved* the cowgirl boots—hot pink is her favorite color."

"Aw, that's adorable, and I'd love to see her wearing them. Well, I've got to get these midterms graded and then get some shuteye. Good work, Harper. I'm proud of you. You are so far from wallowing in your post-divorce misery, it's not funny! Seriously, you're a bad ass."

"Thanks, that means a lot. I'll feel better when we get this place up and running and bring in some paying guests—at least as long as Kevin stays in a different time zone."

As Harper drifted off to sleep, the phone rang, and she answered a call from Mr. Toolbelt/Heavy-Equipment Man.

"Hey, Harper. How's it goin'?" Caleb asked.

"Fine. Just getting ready to turn in. Will I see you in the morning?"

"Bright and early, but I need to be done before lunch. I have another job that can't wait—it involves leaking plumbing. So, the reason I'm calling is, I would like to invite you—*we* would like to invite you, to dinner—as a thank you for Ellie's cowgirl boots. She loves them so much that I can hardly get her to take them off when I put her to bed! Um, tomorrow night, if that's not too short notice? Ellie's kind of excited, and excited Ellie is a non-stop-nagging Ellie. I don't think I can take it anymore. *Please* say you'll come."

"Of course, I will. Thanks for the invitation. Is there anything I can bring?" she asked.

"No, thanks. Just you. Ellie and I have the menu all planned out."

"Alright, then. I'm looking forward to it." She'd bring something, anyway, probably a plant. She never liked to arrive as a guest, empty-handed. In fact, she knew *precisely* what plant she would bring. *And didn't everybody love chocolate?*

Harper drove into Pecos, the closest larger town, and only a twenty-minute drive from Verde Springs. She'd found a small plant nursery that seemed to have a little bit of everything, and the prices were even lower than the big box stores in Santa Fe.

"Hey, I'm doing some spring planting. Do you have any sunflowers in stock?"

"I think so. They're early starts—no flower buds yet."

"That'll do. The person I'm buying them for will be too impatient to wait for seeds to sprout." Harper picked up a couple of flats, since she had visions of planting sunflowers all around the ranch. *Then she'd let the birds do the rest—that's the way annuals worked.*

Working on the shady patio, she chose five of the strongest, healthiest young stems to plant in a hot-pink, plastic pot that looked unbreakable. With Caleb's help, Ellie could transplant the sunflowers outdoors when the nighttime temperatures were safely above freezing.

Harper dressed in her nicest stone-washed jeans, a plum-colored v-neck top in a soft, drapey fabric, and a pair of dark-brown leather cowboy boots she hadn't worn in years. Kevin hadn't liked her to be taller than him, but with Caleb—not that they were an item—that would hardly be a problem. She was only about five-seven, and Caleb was at least an inch over six feet, she'd guess.

She added a pair of dangly earrings Paige had bought her for her birthday one year, and a swipe of "peony" lip shimmer from her favorite natural products company. Then she drove Lucy away from the ranch, and toward her first real outing since she'd arrived in Verde Springs. A healthy-looking coyote crossed the drive ahead of her, just before she reached the county road. It looked very well-fed, or possibly, it was expecting a litter of little coyotes in a few weeks. The willows had begun to show little green buds. Spotted towhees trilled from the tops of the tallest junipers, and a curve-billed thrasher called loudly from its nest in a clump of cholla near the chicken coops. New life burst forth all around her, and she felt the thrill of being part of it all. Whoever said 'no one likes change' had gotten it wrong. *Change was good.*

CHAPTER TEN

*H*arper parked in front of a small, bungalow-style home with a tidy front yard. She walked up the nicely laid flagstone path and was about to knock on the door when it opened.

"Hi Harper! I'm glad you're coming to our house for dinner. Come in!" Ellie practically shouted. Caleb's daughter seemed a little excited, but Harper knew a lot of adults who could use a healthy dose of Ellie's social skills.

"Thank you, Ellie! I'm glad to be here. And I brought you something." Harper carried the pink plastic planter in one hand and a brown-paper bag with three of Maggie's chocolate-pecan brownies in the other.

"Hey, Harper! Glad you could make it. Come on in. Can I help you with anything?" Caleb had come out of the kitchen, irresistibly handsome in a deep blue, brushed cotton shirt and jeans that, for a change, weren't covered in paint splatters.

He cleaned up beyond a girl's wildest dreams.

She handed him the brownies. "Dessert, courtesy of Maggie, and you can show me where to put these. They're sunflowers for you and Ellie to transplant outdoors when the weather warms up."

"Ellie will love that! And thanks for the brownies. I might even have some ice cream to go on top."

"Now, you're speaking my language." Harper followed Caleb to the tastefully remodeled kitchen, then through a door to a utility room with a laundry, sink, benches, and hooks for hanging outdoor gear. A wide bank of multi-pane windows looked out on the small deck and backyard. Below the windows was a bench covered with living plants of various sorts. This was a good sign, as she didn't date plant killers. But this wasn't a *date*—merely a 'thank you' from a sweet little girl and her incredibly hot dad.

"Find a place anywhere in the jungle. I'll keep an eye on them for a few weeks, and then Ellie and I'll plant them, together. Are you hungry?" he said, turning his full attention to her. Caleb's full attention was pretty satisfying in itself—but, yes, she could always eat, and the smell of whatever he was cooking came close to making her drool.

"Absolutely. I've been looking forward to this all day." *Okay, don't go overboard.*

"You're in luck. I made my mom's lasagna recipe, along with a green salad. And I had to make cheesy garlic bread for Ellie. It's her favorite."

"Please marry me," said Harper, not really kidding. *So much for not going overboard.*

Caleb laughed. "Can I get to know you a little better, first?" He put a nice, warm hand on the small of her back and gently steered her to the living room, where Ellie was watching a New Mexico PBS kids' program. "Can I get you a glass of wine?"

"That would be lovely. I should have thought to bring some," she said.

"You brought plenty. Have a seat and I'll be right back."

When Harper chose the sofa, Ellie quietly moved from the floor to join her, eyes still focused on the colorful characters on the TV screen. Ellie leaned in for a snuggle and Harper instinctively put an arm around the girl's shoulders. Ellie's thumb went in her mouth, before she remembered and popped it back out. Heading toward five, she was determined not to be a thumb-sucker by the time she started kindergarten, an intention she'd shared, during one of their rambles on the ranch.

Caleb came back into the room, stopping for a moment to glance her way. He had an interesting look on his face, one she couldn't read, because she didn't know him well enough, yet.

Quite a few things about Caleb had appealed to her right off the bat, after their first, stilted phone conversation. But at the time, he'd been distracted and scrambling to find last-minute childcare. It's true that Mr. Toolbelt wasn't chatty, but he *was* more than capable of putting multiple words together. Which she appreciated.

"Here you go," he said, handing her a glass of red. "Ellie, five-minute warning. When this show is over, you go wash your hands, and then we'll eat. Are you listening?"

A head nod indicated the affirmative.

"How was your re-entry after the trip back to Washington? And the trip itself? Any problems?" Caleb asked.

"No problems on the trip, either way. I let the professionals do the work, packing and loading the truck. Then I met with several realtors, and my ex-husband and I agreed to list the house with a local company. We accepted an offer after only a few days and we're already in escrow. The market in the Seattle area is kind of ridiculous." She left out the part where Kevin had started poking his nose into her life, which had triggered a spate of anxiety that still hadn't quite abated.

"That all sounds good. And the ranch?" he asked.

"Caleb. Seriously! You can't imagine how thrilled I was to walk in and see it looking like that! It's perfect, and heartbreakingly lovely. I want to thank you for going above and beyond. And it was very thoughtful of you to have someone dig the holes for the desert willows. They're are arriving on Saturday."

"You're welcome. You're just lucky that no one's roof blew off while you were gone—early spring weather can be tricky. Otherwise, this isn't usually the busiest time of the year for me. Another month and I'll be swamped, though. I'm sorry I couldn't get all the bathrooms finished, but Gary will do a good job for you. Shouldn't take him more than a few weeks, since all of the framing's in."

"Thanks for that. And Gary seems to be on the ball. I can make do with the bathroom downstairs, for now. Well, as a 'thank you' for all your hard work, and the quick turnaround, I'd like to return the favor and have you and Ellie over for dinner. Maybe this weekend, if you're free."

"*I'm* free. But it's Ellie's weekend with her grandparents, in Santa Fe. Once a month, I drop her off there Friday after work and pick her up Sunday afternoon. But…if it's okay with you, I'd still like to get together. Or we could go out. Do you like to dance?"

Oh, God. Now, he was just showing off.

"I used to *love* to dance in my college years in Bellingham, a couple of hours north of Seattle. But I haven't danced much since then other than in my own kitchen, so I might be rusty. I might even step on your feet." She winced a little, making him laugh.

"My feet can take it." He gently removed the wine glass from her fingers. Then, he took her hand and led her to the kitchen while simultaneously calling over his shoulder, "TV off, Ell. Wash up, now." He pulled out a chair for Harper, took the foil off the cooling lasagna, and snagged the salad from the refrigerator in one smooth motion. *The man could multi-task like nobody's business.*

Since she'd walked in the door, she'd sensed some chemistry percolating nicely between them, and if it turned out to be combustible, she wanted to know her precise parameters. "Caleb," she began, not sure how direct she should be, but wanting and needing answers. "Um, what's the situation with Ellie's mother? Is she still in the picture?"

He shook his head, nodding subtly toward the bathroom, where they could hear the water running in the sink. "I can tell you more when we get together this weekend—let's text each other to make a plan. But, no, she's not in the picture. Ellie misses having a mother, and maybe she still remembers a motherly *presence*, but not much in the way of details. And that's probably a good thing."

It seemed a curious thing to say, and she sensed a story behind the words. "How long has she...*not* been in the picture?" Harper asked.

"Since Ellie was a little over two," he said, as Ellie breezed into the room and climbed up into her booster seat.

"Good job, baby girl! What do you want to drink?" he asked, changing tacks, smoothly.

"Just water, Daddy."

Caleb dished out a small square of lasagna for Ellie, then carefully picked out a pile of carrots and cucumbers from the green salad, adding them to her plate. "Ellie isn't a big fan of lettuce," he informed Harper, with a serious expression. "I hope someday that will change, but for now, we're just going with the veggies."

"And ranch," Ellie added, dipping a carrot round and popping it into her mouth with a crunch.

Harper nodded. "I totally get that, Ellie. I wasn't a fan of lettuce when I was your age, either, until I grew my own garden. My mother told me that lettuce was one of the easiest garden plants to grow from seed, so I tried planting it. And after I grew it, I had to try eating it."

"But did you *like* it?" Ellie asked, a doubtful expression on her face.

"Well, I didn't *not* like it. But let's be honest, there are lots of better things than lettuce: ice cream, and brownies, and Maggie's enchiladas. But greens are healthy for you, and now I eat a *lot* of salads."

"But I still might not like lettuce," Ellie said, apologetically.

Two pairs of adult eyes met in amusement.

"Okay, Ellie. Eat up. Harper, you're next," he said, adding a larger portion of perfectly cooked, gooey, cheesy lasagna to her plate. She helped herself to a large amount of salad to set a good example for the kid.

Soon, the only sound at the table was forks clinking on ironstone plates. Harper tasted rich tomato sauce with a hint of basil and fennel, quality ground beef, ricotta, and the rich taste of oozy mozzarella, baked to crusty perfection on the top, but melt-in-your-mouth in the middle. *Seriously?* It was the best lasagna she'd ever tasted.

"Oh, my God. Caleb! I want details," Harper said, before taking another bite.

"Secret family recipe," he said, winking at Harper. "You might have to earn it."

"I can keep secrets. In fact, if you teach me how to make your lasagna, I'll *only* make it for you and Ellie. Sooner or later, you're going to be swamped with work, or come down with a horrible cold and you'll need a good friend to take care of you, right? And I could make you lasagna and bring it over and feed you in your time of need," Harper said, making a strong argument. Her kitchen repertoire was pitifully small, and this recipe would be solid gold.

"I'm not saying yes, but I'm not saying no," he said.

Funny, that's the same thing her sister had said about the two of them keeping the ranch—but she really hoped she didn't need to wait a whole year to get the all-clear for Caleb's lasagna recipe.

Harper insisted on cleaning up, while Caleb helped his daughter get ready for bed. Ellie had wanted to save her brownie for her pre-school lunch, which Caleb thought was a good idea. Sugar, chocolate, and bedtime did not make a great combination—something he knew from past experience.

Mission accomplished, Caleb came back to the kitchen, poured each of them more red wine, and placed the brownies in the micro-wave to heat. The gooier the better. He placed a scoop of rocky road on each, then carried everything into the living room, while Harper carefully cleared all of the Ellie-debris off the coffee table.

He used the remote to click on the natural gas fireplace, sat back with a sigh, and closed his eyes. The fire put out a steady glow, the wine was delicious, and Maggie's brownies were out of this world. Since their mouths were full and conversation minimal, eye contact and body language communicated with growing clarity. It was if someone had lit a healthy spark in a pile of New-Mexico-dry kindling. They moved closer together, their shoulders and thighs touching comfortably and generating a pleasant warmth. Then Caleb set his wineglass on the table, turned his body to face hers, and leaned in for a kiss. She met him halfway, eagerly seeking his lips. She'd been wanting to taste them for weeks. He palmed her cheek gently in one big hand, his other resting lightly on her shoulder. Then he leaned in slowly and met her lips.

Harper experienced a lovely zinging vibration of energy—not an uncomfortable jolt, not a raging bonfire, but a warmth that felt like coming home and hinted at more. *It was the perfect first kiss.* When Caleb went in for a second kiss, Harper touched the back of his neck, gently threaded her fingers in his hair, and leaned in, answering any lingering doubts he might have had. She wanted a physical connection with him; and she was pretty sure, now, that he wanted her in the same way.

Suddenly a toilet flushed, a door creaked open, and another door shut. *Had Ellie seen them? What if she had?* Maybe this wasn't a good idea. On second thought, this was a *really* good idea—it just wasn't the right time or place.

"Caleb, I've had such a nice time, and I'd like to see you again. But I think I'd better go," Harper said, softly.

He nodded. "Yeah, the single dad thing is tricky. Ellie is so young still—that's why I haven't dated much since her mom left."

"Will I see you this weekend?" she asked.

"You'd have a hard time keeping me away." Caleb smiled. "I'll text you on my way back from dropping Ellie off at her grandparents, and we'll make a plan."

Harper stood up and Caleb walked her out to her truck. She opened Lucy's door, but then, with his hand on her arm, he turned her slowly around to face him. "One more for the road?" he asked.

She answered with her lips and he pulled her firmly against him. Everything perked up in the cool night air, and she felt that delicious warmth down low. How long since she'd been hit with such an intense rush of desire? His own response let her know that things could accelerate quickly. *Time to go.*

"I can't wait to see you this weekend," he said, huskily.

"Yeah, me too, Caleb. Safe travels with Ellie on Friday. Then, come and see me out at the ranch." Harper drove away smiling. *God, she loved New Mexico—it seemed to have the magical power to make all her dreams come true.*

CHAPTER ELEVEN

*F*riday afternoon and evening came and went with no word from Caleb. *Harper was pissed*—and equally pissed that she was worried about him, when they weren't even a couple. He'd seemed so certain of what he wanted. *And he'd wanted her*. Finally, she'd sent a text asking him to let her know he was alright and to call her when he could. She should have expected something like this to happen, when things truly seemed too good to be true. *But men blew off women regularly, didn't they?* At least that's what her single and divorced friends complained about, often. Why should Caleb be any different? *But he was different— she was sure of it.*

Saturday was a big day for her, even without Caleb going silent. The nursery had called to say they were dropping off the desert willows at one-thirty, and they'd sent two workers along to help set them in the ground. She'd spent all morning shoveling decomposed chicken manure and a balanced fertilizer into the holes, then meticulously mixing in the sandy soil to form a firm planting bed. She'd bought hundreds of feet of temporary garden hose, and she soaked the holes thoroughly in readiness for the trees' new homes. Wiping the dirt from her forehead with a bandana, she shoved it back in her pocket and picked up a shovel. She heard the sound of tires on the gravel drive and looked up to see Caleb's truck coming toward her. *At least he was alive—but could he have picked a worse time to show up?* She was wet, filthy, and smelled like decades-old chicken shit. *Absolutely perfect...*

He got down out of the cab, slowly, clearly not excited to be here. His body language was almost as easy to read as her opposite of a poker face. Dropping the shovel, she faced him with her arms crossed and her shit-covered gloves tucked firmly in her armpits. "Why didn't you call me last night?" Harper asked, getting right to the point. She didn't put up with bad behavior from men—not anymore. As soon as the ink had dried on her divorce settlement, she'd fully committed to her zero-tolerance policy, and set it in granite.

"I'm so sorry. I know I said I would, and I should have." Seeing as she wasn't throwing anything at him and she'd put down the shovel, Caleb took another step closer.

"If you aren't interested, we can still be friends. You do really good work, and I need to get a lot of work done around here," she said.

"It's not about what *I* want—not anymore. And I think...it might have to be *just* friends. God, I hate this, Harper."

"Look, I'm not really much of a mind reader, Caleb. We got pretty close, Thursday night—I don't think I'm making that up. Tell me what changed in the span of twenty-four hours? Go ahead, humor me."

"It's not *like* that. I mean, it's not personal. This...requires a longer conversation, maybe when we're not standing in the hot sun at high noon. Can we go inside, maybe have a drink? Sit and talk? I'll tell you everything."

A man who wanted to talk? Now there was an idea she could get behind. "Well, the trees are supposed to be here soon, and I have a lot of work to do before then. I can't take a break right now, and I want an answer. I *deserve* an answer. Can't you just give me the three-minute elevator speech?"

"If that's what you want. I'm happy to have a longer conversation, but things are tricky, right now. So, at dinner the other night, you asked about Ellie's mom."

"Yeah, and *you* said she was out of the picture," Harper pointed out.

"She *was*, I swear. But when I took Ellie to her grandparents on Friday night—her mom's parents—Mariah was there. I didn't have any warning: she was just there, all smiles, with gifts for Ellie, and wanting to be back in her life."

"And?"

"And, she wants to try again—for Ellie." Caleb took off his ball cap, ran a hand through his dark hair, and put it back on. "And, I have to *let* her—for Ellie."

Harper was gobsmacked. *This was the last thing she'd expected.* Of course, he'd want to do the right thing, the best thing, for his daughter. He'd told her almost nothing about his ex-wife, their marriage, or about why she'd left him to raise their daughter alone. To be fair, he hadn't had the chance. Still, she had to ask, "After two years?"

Caleb nodded. "I know. It's been a long time, and we haven't stayed in close touch. Most of our communication about Ellie has been through Mariah's parents, Bill and Kate. They're good people." Looking seriously sleep-deprived, he rubbed the stubble on his face and paused, swallowing. "You and I didn't get to chance to talk, like I wanted to. But after Ellie was born, Mariah developed severe postpartum depression. She really *tried* to be a good mother, but she constantly doubted and criticized herself, and no amount of support from me or from her parents seemed to help. And then, one day, when I came home, I heard Ellie crying in her crib. Mariah was sitting on the couch, hysterical, and she said she wanted to leave. I knew she was in crisis. And clearly, at that moment, she *wasn't* capable of taking care of a toddler while I was at work all day. So, I agreed that Mariah needed a break. Things were tense, but I still loved her. I got Ellie calmed down while Mariah packed a bag, and then I drove her to her parents' house. At the time, I thought it would only be for a few weeks." Caleb smiled grimly. "I couldn't have been more wrong."

"So, what happened? Did she get help? Counseling? Did she try medication?" Harper asked.

"Yes, of course, she tried—and who am I to judge whether she tried hard enough? I've never walked in Mariah's shoes. But at some point, it seemed like she wasn't willing to try anymore—she even stopped asking me to bring Ellie down to Santa Fe to see her. She started going out with friends and drinking more than was healthy. And one day, she told me she couldn't do it, anymore, and she didn't *want* the life we had planned."

"Why?" asked Harper.

"Because, she didn't think she could be a good wife and a mother. Ellie was so little and needed more from her than she was capable of giving. She said she wanted to "rewind"—and that meant asking me for a divorce," he said. Caleb looked down at his feet for a minute. "It was so hard to understand. She didn't even want *partial* custody of Ellie."

"Wow! So, she hasn't seen her since then? So, how long had it been, before last night?"

"Mariah spent time with Ellie on her third birthday, and on a few Christmases at Bill and Kate's house, but only for a few hours. Ellie didn't really remember her, and Mariah didn't seem to connect with her, either. It broke my heart."

"And this time?" Harper asked. "What was it like?"

Caleb shrugged. "This time seems...*different*. I mean, I was pretty pissed to see her there, showing up without any warning. Even Bill and Kate didn't seem all that thrilled, at first. But this time Mariah was good with Ellie—*really* good. She took her time to get to know her, and she didn't make Ellie do all the work, either. My daughter has pretty good social skills for a four-and-a-half-year-old, and I promise you, she didn't get them from me: that's all Mariah. When I fell in love with her, she was sweet and happy, most of the time. And then, for a while, it was like she became a different person. I didn't know that giving birth and all the hormone changes women go through could do that to a person." Caleb shook his head. "How could you ever prepare for it? How do you even know who's at risk?"

"I'm so sorry, Caleb." Harper took a breath, swallowed. "So, now? Do you have a plan? And am *I* a part of it?" Harper had always been direct, and she needed to know: her still-bruised heart was in no shape to take another hit.

"Mariah wants to come home. She's willing to agree to whatever terms I want, as long as she can have regular time with Ellie, and eventually, work toward a reconciliation. *With me.* Mariah wants to try to be a family again." He folded his arms across his chest and met her eyes, directly.

"Well, fine. That's what *Mariah* wants—and that might be what *Ellie* wants. But don't *you* get a vote?" Harper asked.

"Actually, no. I can't think about what I want," Caleb said. "Ellie seemed so happy to spend time with her mother. You should have seen her. She was absolutely glowing! Even Kate and Bill are starting to come around—I can already see it. From what I can tell, they believe Mariah has changed, that she's in a better place, now. And she looked good—healthy and whole—although she could stand to gain some weight." Caleb shook his head. "And to see her and Ellie together again? Honestly, I *never* expected to see that."

When she heard the rumble of a heavy-duty truck engine coming up the driveway, Harper sighed in frustration. *Some days, timing was everything.*

"Well, good luck, then. Let me know how it turns out. Thank you for dinner—but I guess I won't be able to return the favor," she said, lifting one shoulder. "But Caleb? Can you just...be careful? I don't want to see *either* you or Ellie get hurt again."

He nodded. "I don't want that, either." He smiled, but it didn't come close to reaching his eyes. "Well, I see two, big, strong guys over there, waiting to help you plant your trees. You don't need me." He turned and began to walk away. Glancing back at her, he called out, "They're going to look great, Harper. You're doing something good, here."

She nodded her thanks. "Don't be a stranger," she called after him. Caleb was an amazing guy and he deserved a happy ending. *So, why did she feel like he wasn't going to get one?* And he was dead wrong about her not needing him—but that ship had apparently sailed without her ever setting foot on board.

CHAPTER TWELVE

*H*arper glimpsed Paige striding toward the passenger "meet and greet," a wide smile on her pale, indoor face. *Good Lord, her sister was in for a few changes—and a major reality check.* The harsh New Mexico sun had already darkened Harper's skin, lightened her hair, and added a cluster of brand-new horizontal lines to her forehead. But she loved her life here and she hoped her sister would grow to love life on the ranch, too. For starters, she'd be buying Paige a giant bottle of SPF-60 sunscreen.

"Hey, you! It is so good that you're finally here!" Harper said, hugging her sister, hard.

"It's great to be here! I'm so excited and I have a *ton* of ideas. But mostly, I'm dying to see what you've done. I mean, pictures are one thing, but it's the feel you get when you walk into a place that's really important. Let's go pick up my bags and get out of here. And please, can we go someplace that's *not* New Mexican for lunch? I need you to break me in easy, this time," Paige said.

"I know just the place." Since they were passing through Santa Fe, Harper took her sister to the chic café where she'd met Cherie Gonzalez a few weeks earlier—which reminded her that she was overdue to check-in with the attorney. "Salads, fresh-squeezed lavender lemonade, and little patio tables with umbrellas."

"Perfect. So, how is it, working with Caleb, *after...*"

"It's fine," Harper said, cutting Paige short. "*We're* fine. You know, friends. There's an attraction, for sure. He probably looks at my butt, sometimes, when I'm walking away, and I definitely look at his. But no more kisses. He's trying to make this work for Ellie. And, you know, he *did* love Mariah once—maybe he wants to rekindle that, or whatever. I try not to get too personal."

"Well, maybe it's time to move on, then. Is there anyone else in the picture, for you?"

Harper shook her head. "Hah! No, there's a very small pool of single, available men in rural New Mexico—and, anyway, I'm not interested. Obviously, I jumped in way too quickly with Caleb, but that was a total coincidence. I wasn't *looking*. I'm still less than six months out from my divorce, and I have a ton of work to do on the ranch. I've just been keeping myself busy, Paige, and I really hope you'll like the new and improved chicken ranch."

"I'm looking forward to seeing it—but enough with that name! We have to come up with a better one, and I'll even spring for a nice, new sign so we can start the branding phase of this enterprise, already, and I am all over that!" Paige said.

Harper had no doubts.

After a pleasant lunch, they headed out of Santa Fe and made the turn toward Verde Springs, then followed the winding county road to the ranch. She would give Paige the tour, let her rest in the warmth of the afternoon, and then take her to Maggie's for dinner so she could introduce Paige to the locals.

The truck rolled to a stop in the newly designated parking area, and Harper stayed silent. She wanted to give Paige a minute to take it all in before opening the door and stepping out.

"Oh. My. God. You did it! Harper, it's amazing. Truly. We'll be attracting repeat guests out the wazoo!"

Harper smiled, pleased with her sister's reaction and justifiably proud of herself.

The home's entryway was now flanked by two, gorgeous, fifteen-foot desert willow trees covered with showy magenta blossoms in full bloom. Surrounding them were lush but low-water plantings in every hue of blue, green, gray, and rose. In the center of a large circular space, Caleb had installed a fountain in an old stone birdbath. The soft sound of falling water enhanced the ambience and was popular with the local wildlife.

The landscaped grounds continued around the corner of the house, merging with a fledgling kitchen garden that bordered the covered patio. Harper had recently discovered that the sandy soil, once amended, turned out to be perfect for growing herbs and vegetables of all types. She'd even planted starts of tomatoes, peppers, and tomatillos that she could use in the kitchen. Or, rather, her sister could.

Harper had invested nearly half of her proceeds from the sale of her former Gig Harbor house in the rehabilitation of the ranch house and gardens, and she'd chosen wisely. Colorful and durable outdoor cushions now scattered the *bancos* that lined the patio, and small tables and chairs graced the space, perfect for coffee in the morning or wine in the evening. In the fall, she planned to add long strings of red chili ristras as soon as they came into season. Maybe, someday, they'd grow and dry their own. She'd moved to New Mexico, determined to make a fresh start, and she was all in.

Paige gasped when they entered the central hallway. "I can't believe this is the same place! And the smell is gone. I want to thank this contractor, or maybe, kiss him! Where *is* Mr. Toolbelt?"

Harper pretended that was a rhetorical question.

Moving on, she'd designated one of the two "salons" for personal use and had set the other up for their B&B guests to use. The central hallway between them was now lined with rustic benches topped with colorful, hand-crafted pillows. A marble-topped table stood against one wall, holding an exuberant flower arrangement, and a 1940's guestbook with a leather cover stamped with a Ford tractor. Further back, Harper had created a breakfast room at one end of the large, sunny kitchen, and it was now her absolute favorite space in the house.

She'd spent a bundle on a long, antique farmhouse table that fit the space perfectly, and she'd surrounded it with mix-and-match chairs that seemed to work: some Windsor-backs stripped of paint, some local New Mexico hand-crafted pieces, some simple farmhouse chairs. The natural aged furniture and softer white-washed tones worked well together. Marguerite, the "quilt lady" of Farmington had designed and quilted a custom table runner for the center of the table. A blue enameled pitcher that Harper had found in an antique market held another bouquet of flowers, and her aunt's hammered copper candlesticks held golden, beeswax candles. She'd hung some portraits of early New Mexico family members in oval frames on the walls, from Sabina's personal collection. Ruth Watkins had been very cooperative, allowing Harper to go through the Arroyo Seco house and pull out some personal items, like books of family photographs and some handmade pottery pieces their Aunt Sabina had especially treasured.

Caleb had worked hard to salvage the existing kitchen counter, which now glowed with a natural oil finish, and he'd cleaned and regrouted the original blue-and-white patterned Mexican tile backsplash. Through the bank of windows, Paige looked out at the view beyond the patio, a combination of thriving gardens and the natural high desert landscape.

"Oh, it's gorgeous, Harper. *I* want to be a guest here!" Paige said, softly. "Take me to my room. Take me to see *all* the bedrooms."

As the tour moved on, Harper watched her sister fall a little more in love with the house and its spectacular natural setting. Marguerite's colorful geometric quilts, the freshly waxed hardwood floors, and the off-white walls made for a calm, restive atmosphere. Relocating the bats to their new outdoor home had helped to eliminate the peculiar ammonia-like odor the house had once held. *Bat removal—there was one aspect of home remodeling best left to the experts.*

"I'm going to get horizontal for a few minutes and soak it all in," Paige said, testing out her new bed. "Wow, Richmond to Albuquerque is a *long* flight."

Harper sat in the plush, sage-green chair in the corner and propped her feet up on the bed. "I'm glad you're here, Paige. It's been a little lonely, but I've been so busy working that I haven't had time to reach out and make very many friends. I think we should throw a party. You know, so we can get to know the locals, and they can get to know us."

"Yeah. Like a big reveal, so people know what we've been up to out here! Well, I shouldn't say *we*, since you've done all the work so far. With the help of Mr. Toolbelt, of course. So, speaking of, have you met *her?*"

"No, I just saw her once from a distance in town. Ellie spotted me and waved. She looked over, but she didn't react or come over to say hi. Mariah is definitely pretty. Shoulder-length, light-brown hair. Cute, heart-shaped face. Ellie looks almost exactly like her mom, except for those huge blue eyes the kid has. It must be impossible for Caleb to look at Ellie every day and not think of his wife."

"*Ex*-wife. And you and Caleb? Are you guys still on good terms?" Paige asked.

"So far. And I've been working myself ragged, trying not to think about him. He comes and goes and does the work we agreed on, but we don't run into each other that often. I don't know—maybe he's purposely avoiding me?"

"If he is, that might mean he still has feelings for you," Paige said.

"You think?" Harper asked.

"I don't know for sure, but you can bet I'll be observing you two whenever I get the chance, and I promise to give you my full assessment," her sister said.

"Well. It's nice to have *that* to look forward to," Harper said, dryly. "Okay, why don't you chill for a while, and come find me when you're up. We'll go into town and have dinner at Maggie's."

Paige yawned. "Sounds good. I need to close my eyes for a while. Catch you later. But, good job, Sis. This place is amazing."

Harper and her sister sat at a window booth in Maggie's. Harper stuck to enchiladas with *mole* sauce, and Paige ordered the tortilla soup with a side salad. "Let's think about the name. And I agree, no references to chickens." Harper said.

"I'm with you," Paige said, between bites.

"And from a branding perspective, I agree that it's important to keep it simple, memorable, and meaningful," Harper said, repeating what Paige had explained.

Paige nodded. "It's so beautiful now! Truly stunning. It's so far from the chicken ranch it once was—and you'd never mistake it for a bordello. It's...like a classy inn where you'd want to take your lover for a weekend, or hold an amazing outdoor wedding, or launch a top-secret tech start-up. Have you thought of all those options in your business plan?"

"Nope. Marketing is *your* jam, and part of your contribution, remember? I'm the one with the green thumb," Harper said. "And the checkbook, at least until my money runs out. Then it'll be your turn."

"Your money *isn't* going to run out, because the two of us are going to make this a brilliant success," Paige said, her green eyes shining with entrepreneurial spirit.

Harper smirked. *Her sister didn't seem to get this excited about teaching business law at the university in Richmond.* "Okay. The name, Paige. Focus."

"Well, it's very simple and completely obvious," her sister said. "Let's call it The Inn at Verde Springs. That way, we get the *location* in there, and it's good publicity for the whole town. All we need now is a sign," Paige said.

"I think it's perfect, too." Harper nodded. "So, are we really going to do this? Let's order a round of margaritas to celebrate."

"You read my mind," Paige said, smiling.

Harper smiled, too—until she saw the cozy family of three sitting together in a booth on the opposite wall. The little girl with the light-brown curls and big, blue eyes was sitting close to her look-alike mom. Mariah leaned forward to say something, and the dad laughed. *Caleb's* pleasant laugh. What a beautiful, little family they made. "Shoot. I didn't know they'd be here, together," she muttered, nodding politely in their direction.

Paige followed her gaze, commenting, "Is that him? Geez, does he have a type, or what? I think you have a sexier vibe, though. Someone needs to *feed* that poor girl, bless her heart. She's lost all her curves."

Harper rolled her eyes, then excused herself to go to the lady's room. While she was in there getting things done, she heard the door open and another person enter, go directly into a stall, and throw up. *Unpleasant, but it happened.* It wasn't anything to do with the food—it was always top-notch or it didn't leave Maggie's kitchen.

Harper flushed the toilet and moved to the concrete countertop to wash her hands. The door opened behind her and Mariah Johansson emerged to join her at the sinks, her hazel eyes huge in a heart-shaped face that was much too thin. *Paige was precisely right.*

Harper nodded in a silent greeting.

"Sorry about that. I've had a little stomach bug," Mariah said. "Guess I'm not over it, yet."

"I'm sorry. I hope you're feeling better soon," Harper responded, anxious to get out of the small bathroom and back to her enchiladas. Surprisingly, it was Mariah who stopped her.

"Um…aren't you the one redoing the old chicken ranch? My daughter's pointed you out to me a couple of times. I'm Mariah

Johansson. My husband said he's done some work out there. I'm also looking for a job. Do you think you might have anything available?"

Darn! She wasn't getting out of it, now.

Harper nodded and smiled, "Yes. I'm Harper Crawley. I'm here having dinner with my sister, Paige, who is my business partner. It's just the two of us for now—we've barely gotten started. But if something comes up, I'll let you know."

"Thanks. I can do just about anything. I'm even thinking of starting a business of my own. It makes me happy to see some new life in this sleepy town," she said.

Mariah had smiled to take any sting out of it, but the offhand remark rubbed Harper the wrong way. She already loved the little town of Verde Springs—it was completely charming, and the people she'd met here had been nothing but welcoming from the beginning. Anyway, she *preferred* the slow pace of small-town life over the alternative—but she didn't want to get into an in-depth discussion with Caleb's wife—or offer her a job—in Maggie's bathroom.

"Well, I'd better get back," Mariah said, smiling shyly, and Harper followed her out the door."

Paige came up with the idea of holding a soft open for their first guests the last two weeks of June, so they could get any kinks out before the upcoming Fourth of July weekend. Her sister had jumped in with both feet, unveiling the new website she'd been secretly working on while she was in Virginia. Nearly complete, it had only been waiting for a name. Now that they had it, the plan began to feel more real for both of them. *And the clock was ticking.*

Paige, the consummate online shopper, ordered custom merchandise with The Inn at Verde Springs name and their new logo, featuring a desert willow blossom framed by slender green leaves. The colors were perfectly on-point for their brand: a rich blue green, and a deeper orchid color, on a creamy white background. Boxes of custom coffee mugs, coasters, and waffle-knit cotton bathrobes soon arrived, all sporting their distinctive logo. Caleb had asked a woodcarver friend to make a large, custom sign for the entrance garden and a slightly smaller plaque that would sit on a post along the county road, marking the turn into the ranch drive. Harper couldn't wait to see both signs set in place.

With the house well in hand, her focus moved to the old chicken coops. She and Caleb had assessed the sturdiness of all seven coops and selected the two that would be torn down in a single day, and repurposed by a specialty lumber company in Santa Fe. That left five large, empty spaces that could become *something*. Caleb worked hard to shore up the exteriors, while Harper spent nearly a week cleaning the interiors, removing the nesting boxes and perches, and with Caleb's help, wracking her brain to try to re-envision what the remaining coops could become.

Each structure was sixteen-feet wide and thirty-two feet long. Times five, it added up to a lot of real estate, and Harper was determined to make the most of it. She'd scoured an architectural supply for old windows to let light into the coops, and Caleb was now busy installing them. The high, narrow windows brought in morning light, but no direct sun in the heat of the afternoon. Harper had also purchased five "half-light" doors to place on the coop-fronts, and she'd asked Caleb to slice them horizontally, creating "Dutch doors" that could be left open on the top, but still allow light in when firmly closed.

The floors were a mess, though, uneven and wobbly, with some areas damaged by carpenter ants and termites. After they'd been properly treated, Caleb firmed up the floors with three-quarter-inch plywood sheeting, which Harper then coated with two thick coats of polyurethane. When the floors had dried, she covered them with plastic and hired a painting crew to spray-coat the inside walls and the ceilings with the same shade of warm white—"Spanish Villa"—that they'd used in the main ranch house. Only after *all* of this work had been completed could she possibly envision what five empty white boxes could become. Her imagination could only carry her so far—some results she had to see with her own eyes.

"Caleb, can I ask you a question?" she asked, painting the trim around the newly installed windows a rich barn-red. She'd decided to leave the silvery exterior wood intact, after a light sanding, followed by a coating of water-proofing preservative.

"Uh, sure."

"What did Mariah do? You know, before Ellie was born?" Harper asked.

"She was pretty young when we met. She'd worked in a few different fields, but nothing stuck. She's a pretty good cook, though. If you think *my* lasagna was good, you should try hers. And Mariah's a *great* baker. Maybe she can do something with that."

Harper nodded, taking it all in, but she had no interest in trying Caleb's wife's lasagna anytime soon.

"Why do you ask?" Caleb said, glancing at her.

"Oh. Well, I ran into Mariah at Maggie's the other night, when the three of you were having dinner," Harper added. "She said she was looking for a job, and she asked me to let her know if anything came up, here at the ranch."

"Hmm…she didn't mention it to me. But I think it would be good for her to have something to do, especially when Ellie's in preschool."

"What's Ellie's school schedule this summer? Does she go every day?" she asked. Being a busy working single dad, Caleb had opted for year-round preschool, and Ellie chattered about her friends and adventures there, constantly.

"No, just three days a week, for now," he explained. "I didn't want to overwhelm her. I didn't want to overwhelm Mariah, either, on Ellie's days off. But so far, she seems to be coping alright. Ellie can be a handful. She's a good kid but she has a lot of energy, and there are some days when she can't seem to stop asking questions. Mariah's still getting used to being around Ellie again, to being responsible for her. So, I'm keeping a close eye on the situation."

"Caleb. Do you *want* me to find her something to do, here? Paige and I can handle most of it for now—but I suppose I could find something for Mariah to do, after we begin bringing in paying guests. *If* it would help."

"I couldn't ask you to do that, Harper. Really, I couldn't," Caleb said.

She nodded. Well, no obligation, but she'd keep it in mind. Anything to help keep Mariah's stress, and therefore Caleb's stress, at a manageable level. *Because sometimes, she was crazy like that—she really needed to work on her boundaries.*

CHAPTER THIRTEEN

*H*arper sat with Paige on the comfortable overstuffed sofa, feet up on an old trunk, intermittently watching *Must Love Dogs*. They both knew the movie would end with the star-crossed couple getting wet and falling in love, so Harper didn't feel guilty about talking during the middle.

"I love dogs. Kevin hated them, so we never had one. But I'm thinking seriously of getting one," Harper said. "A ranch needs a dog."

Paige shook her head.

"No? Why not?" Harper asked, perplexed. Her sister *loved* dogs.

"Because the ranch needs *two* dogs," Paige replied. "And I get to help pick them out." Tuning out the movie completely, she picked up her phone and Googled 'Pet Finder New Mexico.' In less than a minute, she was oohing, and ahhing, and turning the screen so Harper could join her. "But I want a puppy, or at least one that's less than a year old. Housebroken would be good, too—but that's probably unrealistic. Anyway, with fifty-six acres to roam, they're probably going to be outdoor dogs," Paige said.

"But not when they're *puppies*," Harper exclaimed, in horror. "They need TLC, and they need to *bond* with us. They'd probably get eaten by coyotes, anyway. So, we'll keep them indoors, mostly, until they're fully grown. But they're going to be confined to areas they can't destroy. I've paid a fortune—literally, nearly *all* of my fortune—to rehab this place. And I don't want it chewed to bits by puppies, no matter how adorable they are," Harper said.

"That's a fair point. Okay, let's go look at some pups, tomorrow," her sister said.

"So, what are we looking *for?*" Harper asked.

"Littermates. Two sisters like us need two sister puppies," Paige said, with an abundance of feeling.

"I think you should stop looking at pictures of puppies, Paige. You might be getting overly sentimental."

"No, I'm not. Being here with you is the most fun I've had in years."

"Yeah, me too. I'm glad you're here." Harper turned the movie off since neither of them was really watching it—and she was feeling restless and irritable. "But this May supermoon is driving me crazy! When I see Caleb doing manly things, I want to rip his clothes off and climb him like a tree. And from the lack of spring in his step, I'd say *he's* not getting any either."

"Maybe the lovely Mariah no longer floats his boat?" Paige suggested.

"Or maybe the lovely Mariah doesn't put out." Harper replied.

"Eww! You can be really crude sometimes, you know that?" Paige said. "Most likely, they're just working through things. It's got to be a tough situation for both of them."

"Sorry. Yes, I'm aware, and I'm working on it. But I'm going upstairs to not sleep, now. The puppy search begins tomorrow. 'Night, Paige."

※

"Coffee," Harper croaked the next morning.

"Well, good morning to you," replied Paige, busy in the kitchen. "Sleep well?"

"No. That damn moon! I didn't sleep more than a few hours. Coffee."

Paige handed her a filled mug with the Inn's logo, then returned to making huevos rancheros using the excellent salsa she'd picked up at Maggie's last week. "So, maybe *I* should drive when we head into town?"

"Lucy's pretty particular. Can you even drive a stick?" Harper asked, after she'd had a few sips of caffeine.

"Not well—but, hey, what better place to learn than on a country road? I'm game," Paige said, with way too much enthusiasm for this early in the morning, especially after Harper's nearly sleepless night.

"Okay. *After* you feed me, I may feel up to giving you a lesson on manual transmissions. And then we can spend the morning looking at dogs."

"*Puppies.*"

"Canines," said Harper, ending the debate. "But our signs are being delivered around four-thirty, and I want to be back here by then. Caleb's already dug the holes, and he left a bag of ready-mix concrete for us to mix up to set the posts."

"Wow, a man that's both handy *and* irresistible. Does he have a brother?" Paige asked.

"Not that I know of. Why? Are you in the market? You know… New Mexico *would* be the perfect place to have a summer fling before you go back to your respectable professor job. Think about it."

As Paige quietly digested this possible encouragement, along with her huevos, a Mona Lisa smile lit her face. "You know, maybe there *is* something about this supermoon."

After breakfast, Harper went over the game plan with her small crew of recently-hired helpers, and then left with her sister driving Lucy on a loosely organized puppy prowl.

They visited the animal shelter in Santa Fe and a smaller dog rescue halfway between Santa Fe and Verde Springs, and then they headed back to town. On the return trip, Caleb called and Harper put her phone on speaker.

"What's up? Aren't you off today?" she asked him.

"I got an emergency job for a friend in Dixon—that's why I called. I wanted to know if you could watch Ellie for me, just for a few hours." He paused. "Mariah's been pretty reliable, but this morning, she said she had something important she needed to do. I couldn't take Ellie with me—I'm going to be up on a ladder all day."

"Sorry, Caleb, I'm not home right now, and neither is Paige. We spent the morning in Santa Fe, looking for a couple of dogs to adopt. We should be home in less than an hour though, if that helps."

"Oh, well. I'm hoping Mariah's made other arrangements by now. She probably has. No sweat. Catch you later," he said.

"Sorry I couldn't help you out. I'd love to, next time," she said. Before she could disconnect, Caleb spoke again.

"I might know somebody who has pups. What kind of dogs are you looking for?"

"Just, you know, ranch dogs. Not too big, not too small, but friendly. Paige and I want to adopt two littermates, preferably females."

"Ah, sister dogs for sisters," Caleb said, earning a thumbs up from Paige.

"Something like that. Know of any we should look at?" Harper asked.

"Try Desert Dawgs—it's a shelter that rehomes unwanted dogs from some of the pueblos. They're usually heeler and shepherd mixes; kind of scrappy, but also sweet. I heard someone brought in a big litter a few weeks ago, eight or nine pups, so they might still have a couple of them left. Good luck with the search. I've gotta get back to it."

"Yep. Later." She ended the call and Googled Desert Dawgs, which, being new to the area, she hadn't heard of. Sure enough, there were some cute pups, and a pretty, female shepherd-heeler mix caught her eye right away. But she'd have to read through the descriptions to see if any of them were littermates. And with Paige driving a stick for the first time, that would best be done sitting motionless at a table at Maggie's.

Paige parked with more determination than skill, and they entered through Maggie's double doors. Scanning the booths, Harper noticed Ellie sitting alone, coloring on a paper placemat. *Where was her mother?*

Of course, they had to go over and say hello. "Hey, Ellie. Long time, no see. How've you been?"

Shrug. "Okay. You know, one day at a time," Ellie said, with a dramatic sigh.

It sounded hilarious coming from the preschooler, and Harper suspected she'd overheard it from one of her parents. "Are you here by yourself?"

She shook her head. "Mama had a doctor's appointment. So, she said to stay right here until she got back." Ellie took a bite out of her grilled cheese sandwich and a small sip of her root beer.

"Well, until your Mama comes back, would it be okay if we sat with you? This is my sister. Her name is Paige."

"Yeah, that would be cool," said Ellie, reverting to her usually stellar social skills. "Nice to meet you. My name is Ellie."

Harper slid into the booth beside Ellie, and Paige took the opposite bench seat. At least she knew an effective way to occupy Caleb's daughter while they waited for her mother to return. As she pulled out her phone, she caught a grateful look from Maggie, who had her hands full with the lunch rush. Apparently, she'd been keeping an eye on the little girl.

"So, guess what Paige and I did this morning?" Harper asked.

"What?"

"We went to look at puppies. We want to adopt two sisters from the same litter," Harper told the little girl.

"Did you get them? Can I see them? Do you think *I'll* ever get a puppy?" Ellie asked, all in one breath. "Daddy says maybe 'someday,' and Mama says 'let's wait and see.'"

Harper smiled, but said only, "Not yet." She brought up the Desert Dawgs website and showed Ellie the dogs currently available for adoption, focusing on the younger dogs and puppies, of which there were only a few.

"They are SO cute! I want all of them!" Ellie squealed. "No, not all. Just one of my very own. But which dogs are *you* going to get?"

"We're not sure," Harper said. "Can help us decide?"

"Yes, I will. I *will* help you decide. I can help you name them, too. I'm good at naming things!"

"Okay, deal. But we have to find just the right pups. Let's keep looking. Paige, maybe you can order for both of us? Maggie knows what I like." If enchiladas with *mole* sauce wasn't the special of the day, Harper always got a green chili cheeseburger and fries. *It's a good thing her days were long, and her work, strenuous.*

"Ooh, *this* one! Is it a girl?" Ellie asked, pointing to one of the little shepherd mixes that had already caught Harper's eye. "She's SO pretty!"

Reading the description, she had to agree. Bertie was a four-month-old female shepherd-heeler mix, although Harper suspected there might be some bird-dog lurking in there, with her soft jowly mouth and alert golden eyes. "Yep," she said, nodding, "I like her, too. Now, let's see if she has a sister."

The shelter's description contained the pup's approximate birth-date, so, searching by birthdates, Harper found three additional entries. Similar in appearance, they had to be littermates. *Perfect.* Two males and one female, named Tilly. She looked substantially more like a German shepherd in coloring, but she had the same overall shape and size as her sister. She had a happy, silly expression, rather than her sister's vaguely worried look, courtesy of the cluster of loose frown lines running vertically up the middle of her forehead. *Where did they come up with the name Tilly?* Obviously, the pup would have to be renamed. And she knew who would have some ideas about that…

Paige returned from placing their orders and joined in the puppy-naming discussion. "Oh, yeah, these are some sweet little girls that look like they'd fit right in on the ranch! I mean, at the Inn. Ellie, can you think of any good names if we brought these two girls home?"

"Of course, I can." She frowned in concentration. "This one," she said, pointing at the pup with the worried face, should be Bluebird."

That could work. They could call her Birdy for short. Dogs didn't care about spelling.

"And this one," Ellie pointed at the happy-silly pup, "we should name Sunflower. Bluebird and Sunflower," she said, happy with her decision.

They'd shorten that one to Sunny. "I think those are some pretty good names, Ell. But first, we have to apply to adopt them. Paige, can you call the shelter and let them know we're interested? Let's adopt them together, if it's alright with you. I'm going to take this girl to the restroom. Judging by the size of that root beer you drank, young lady, I bet you have to go."

"Maybe. I can try. Mama says that even if I don't *think* I have to go, I should try."

"That's excellent advice," Harper agreed. "Alright. You ready?" They slid out of the booth and she took Ellie by the hand, stopping to say hello to Maggie, who was presiding over the grill.

"Hey. How are things going?" Harper asked.

"Good. Busy. Mariah brought Ellie in and ordered her lunch, then said she had an important medical appointment and she'd be back soon. She asked me to keep an eye on Ellie. I don't mind, and of course, we'd all look out for her. But lunch time is pretty busy in the summer. I'm glad you and your sister showed up when you did. Hey, there, Miss Ellie? Did you eat all your grilled cheese?"

"Yes, Miss Maggie. But I have to *go* now," she said, starting to squirm.

Harper got the message. "Onward to the lady's room. Don't give it another thought, Maggie, Paige and I can stay until Mariah gets back."

In the bathroom, Ellie functioned independently, other than not being able to lock the door properly. Harper put her hand over the seam at the top, held it shut, and waited to see if Ellie needed any help.

"You doing okay in there, sweetie?"

"Uh huh. I don't need any help. But you're still in front of the door, right?"

"You got it. I'm not going anywhere. So, Bluebird and Sunflower! Those are some pretty great names. I'm sure by now Paige is already on the phone with the shelter, getting all the details. Maybe we can go see them in person, tomorrow."

"Can I come with you?" Ellie asked.

It was important to keep in mind the cardinal rule of dog adoption: *never visit the shelter unless you want to come home with a dog.* Harper doubted that Mariah and Caleb were in a place to take on a new puppy, and she didn't want Ellie to be disappointed if, for some reason, "Bluebird" and "Sunflower" didn't check out.

"I think it would be best if you meet the puppies when we bring them home to the ranch, sweetie," she said, as Ellie made her way out of the stall.

"Alright. But I get to be the first one to see them. Deal?" Ellie said.

"Deal. Hey, sweetie, is your mama feeling okay?" Harper asked, sticking her nose so, so firmly where it didn't belong. *But, Ellie. But, Caleb…*

"Most of the time," Ellie said.

That wasn't exactly clarifying. Maybe it was just a checkup, not a return of Mariah's serious depression. Harper helped Ellie get the water running at the right temperature, find the soap dispenser, and wash and dry her hands.

"Except mornings," said Ellie over her shoulder as she headed toward the door.

"Um…hold on a second, sweetie. What happens in the mornings?" she asked, digging herself in deeper. *Was Mariah having trouble getting out of bed, getting Ellie ready for preschool? Dropping her off on time?* Difficulty getting started with her day could be a sign of serious depression.

"You know," Ellie said, making a gagging sound, complete with her tongue sticking out nearly to her chin. At that precise moment, the door opened and Mariah walked in with a panicky expression on her pale face, no doubt searching for her daughter. *Paige was right. The woman was scary-thin.*

"*There* you are! I asked you to stay in the booth, Ellie!" she said, with only a cursory glance at Harper.

"Oh, that's *my* fault," Harper spoke up. "I thought that after drinking that big glass of root beer, Ellie might need to use the restroom. Didn't my sister Paige tell you where we were?"

"Well, yes. But I don't even *know* her. All I know is that my daughter wasn't where I left her," Mariah said, not yet sounding relieved, and definitely not calm.

"I'm fine, Mama. I ate my grilled cheese, and Maggie came by to say hello, and then Harper and Paige came and we looked at pictures of puppies."

"I hope you didn't get Ellie excited over something that's not going to happen," Mariah said, quietly. "I know she really wants a dog, but we just can't get one right now. And I'm sorry, I *shouldn't* have snapped. Thanks for keeping an eye on her," Mariah said, ruffling Ellie's hair.

"Of course. We were happy to. As far as the puppies go, we're getting them for the ranch—my sister and I are adopting two—and Ellie is welcome to come out and play with them anytime. You're welcome, too, of course," Harper added, hoping to keep things on an even keel.

"I might be too busy. I haven't found a job yet, but I'm looking," said Mariah, finally calming down enough to be civil to Harper.

They'd reached the booth, and so had their enormous plates of food.

"Come on, Ellie, let's go, sweetie," Mariah said. "These ladies are going to have lunch now, and you've already had yours. Besides, it's nap-time." She smiled belatedly at Harper and Paige, holding her hand out for her daughter.

"But I'm too big to take a nap," protested Ellie, sounding more perplexed than defiant.

"Well, I'd like you to try to take a nap today, please," Mariah said, taking her daughter gently in hand. As they headed out the door, Ellie turned back to wave at Harper.

Ellie looked a little lost. But a lot of things had changed in her young life, in a very short span of time. To be fair, a lot of things had changed in Mariah's life, too. And Caleb's. From the outside, Harper thought parenting looked pretty challenging, even without throwing in additional complications. It might be summertime, but she doubted the living was easy these days in the reunited Johansson household.

Paige met her eyes. "*So, that's* who Mr. Toolbelt is married to?"

Harper shook her head. "*Was* married to. But I have a suspicion Mariah would like to think they still *are*. And I think I might know why."

"What's your theory?" Paige asked.

Harper debated. Although it was none of her business, it was very much Caleb's business, and he was her friend. Besides, she never kept secrets from her sister, and visa-versa. "In the bathroom, I got nosy and asked Ellie if her mom was feeling okay. I thought her doctor's appointment might be depression-related. Then…Ellie mentioned that her mom has been throwing up in the mornings—of course, not in those exact words."

"The plot thickens," said Paige. "So, I guess you're going to be keeping a close eye on that situation?"

"You bet I am. And that little girl is for sure going to come out to the ranch and play with our puppies. It's the least we can do for her."

CHAPTER FOURTEEN

*D*esert Dawgs required a home visit, three letters of recommendation, *and* a hefty fee—but after their visit on Saturday, Harper and Paige had fallen in love with both of the young female pups. Their adoption was approved, and on Sunday, they were able to bring their sweet girls home.

They'd fixed comfy beds for them in the utility room off the kitchen and set up a baby gate for the bottom of the steep staircase. The pantry now held a veritable feast of dog biscuits, training treats, puppy kibble, and canned food. And they'd invested in toys, brushes, and matching collars and leashes. These pups were going to live the life they deserved—happy, healthy, and, eventually, roaming free on the ranch's fifty-six acres.

In the truck, Paige held both of the pups in her arms and yelled at Harper to be careful around every curve, and somehow, they made it home without a canine catastrophe. By coincidence, or not, Caleb was busy unloading some building materials up near the coops, and he 'just happened' to have Ellie with him.

"Hey, I hope you don't mind that we're here. Mariah wasn't feeling well, so I thought Ellie and I would get out of her hair for a bit."

Harper grinned at Caleb. "And...you thought we *might* be bringing the puppies to their new home, and Ellie *might* want to be part of the welcoming committee?"

Caleb gave them his 'ah, shucks, you caught me' smile. "Mm... something like that. Hey, Ellie. Come and see what Harper and Paige brought home!"

Ellie ran over from the little patch of sunflowers coming up in the border surrounding the coops. "Can I see? Can I see? Daddy, lift me up!"

She peered over the passenger door, where Paige was untangling her seatbelt while holding two wriggling pups, and wondering how to get out of the truck with them in one piece.

"Hold on, Ellie. May I?" Caleb asked, reaching over the door to grab the pup nearest him, which he handed gently to his daughter. "Now keep one hand under his bottom and try not to strangle him, honey."

"*Her*," Paige corrected him. "They're sisters." She handed the other puppy to Caleb and finally exited the truck. "Let's not do *that* again, Harper, at least until you get a different vehicle. I'm in favor of a roomy SUV with a heavy-duty screen between the lick monsters and my face."

"Done! Just write me a check for thirty grand," Harper agreed.

"Not unless I sell both of my kidneys," Paige said, before slapping a hand over her mouth. "Sorry. Harper and I get kind of mouthy. I didn't mean to say that in front of your lovely daughter."

"No worries. She's a little distracted at the moment. These girls are pretty cute! How old?" he asked.

"Four months, maybe a tad older. They're from one of the pueblos south of Santa Fe. They seem to be in good health, but we'll have to get them spayed when they're old enough, and micro-chipped," Paige said.

"Ellie, do you want to give the puppies some treats?" Harper invited. "Paige bought out the entire store!"

"Daddy, can I?"

"May I?"

"Daddy, may I?"

"Yes, as long as Harper is there to help you."

"So, do these girls have names yet?" Caleb asked Paige.

"Funny you should ask. Your daughter named them when we first found them on the adoption website and thought we might want them to be ours. Ellie is holding Sunflower, and *you're* holding Blue-bird. Sunny and Birdy for short. I think they're excellent names."

"That would be right," said Caleb. "She's nuts about sunflowers. Harper helped her plant some seeds on the ranch, and she brought her some seedlings for our place in town," Caleb said, before abruptly losing his train of thought. His eyes had locked on Harper and Ellie as they sat together in the grass, playing with the new puppy. He had a fascinating expression on his face: longing, mixed with amusement.

"She's nuts about Ellie," Paige said, taking in Caleb's reaction.

"Ellie is nuts about Harper, too. She's always asking if she can come to work with me. But the project here is almost wrapped up—I'm just doing some finish work on the coops."

"Well, that's good, because they've got to start earning their keep. Harper thinks they'll work well as studios and workshop spaces. And our future guests, of course, will have the option of staying in the Inn's more deluxe accommodations," she said, "while only a stone's throw from their work and meeting spaces."

Caleb nodded. "It's a great set up you have here, Paige. I envy you. And Harper's done an incredible job with the gardens. They're a real showpiece—and I can't wait to see how they'll grow and mature in the years to come. Your sister has a real knack for design, even though she only claims to have a green thumb," he said.

Paige could both relate and agree—she couldn't be prouder of her sister.

"Do you think you'll be ready for your first guests next week?" he asked.

"Yes, I do. We're also thinking of having a small party next Thursday, if we kick it into gear. It'll be a housewarming, and a chance to let locals know what we've been up to. And, as Harper tells me, she couldn't have done it without *you*. Paige thought about adding, 'you and Harper make a good team,' but that would be a little tacky, considering that he was once again living with his *ex*-wife—who continued to avoid using the appropriate prefix. Pausing just short of rudeness, she finally said, "you and Ellie and Mariah are all welcome to come."

Caleb would be such an excellent addition to her sister's life, and having Ellie in the picture would make it that much sweeter. *If only Mariah wasn't in the picture at all.* But she shut that thought down fast because it was, undeniably, incredibly selfish. Every little girl needed her mother. God knows, she'd never stopped missing her own.

Later that night, Harper and Paige sat out on the patio enjoying the warm evening air, two tired puppies asleep in their arms. They were already a good addition: Sunny, open and curious, Birdy, shy and comically suspicious, always watching the world around her with discerning eyes. These pups belonged together, just like she and Paige.

"So, at the risk of opening a can of worms, I think Caleb still has feelings for you. And I *know* you have feelings for him. What are you going to do about that?" Paige asked.

"There's nothing I *can* do. He's trying to make things work with Mariah, who is *not* his wife, for Ellie's sake. I can't get in the way of that. *Unless.*"

"Unless she's trying to pull a fast one on him," Harper said. "You know—what Ellie said. What if Mariah is pregnant by someone else, and *that's* why she turned up out of the blue to reconcile with her ex-husband? After all, Caleb is a caring, responsible man whom she trusted to care for her daughter when she walked out two years ago."

"That's a strong accusation, if you're making one, Harper, and you have no proof! People *do* get the stomach flu, and migraines, and food poisoning. They do, even, sometimes experience nausea from anxiety. Maybe, struggling to make things work with your husband and young daughter, after being away for two years, is really freaking hard," Paige said.

"He's not her husband."

"That's your takeaway?" Page looked skeptical. "Well, he's fulfilling that role, isn't he? He's providing a home for her, and trusting her to take care of Ellie, while he's climbing up on roof tops bringing home the bacon."

"Yeah, I *get* that he has to try to accept Mariah back into Ellie's life. But has he accepted her back into *his?* I think *he's* frustrated, too," Harper said.

"Well, it's undoubtedly a frustrating situation."

"It's not only the frustration of readjustment. Sometimes…I catch him looking at me in…*that* way. And I want him so damn much that I'd be willing to climb up on a roof to have him—I want him a*lmost* so much that I'd shut myself in a closet full of bats with him," Harper said, with a shudder.

Paige grimaced. "Wow, that's a serious amount of want—and I get it. But I don't need you to give me the heebie-jeebies this close to bedtime. Speaking of, are you going to let Birdy sleep with you? Or are you going to leave her in her bed in the utility room, tonight?"

Harper looked at her sister like she'd lost her mind. "Bite your tongue! She's just a *baby* who's been kidnapped from her mama and plunked into a strange new environment. Of course, I'm going to let her sleep with me," she said. "What about you and Sunny?"

"Same. We're suckers, aren't we?" Paige said.

"Well, there *is* one born every day," she agreed without a trace of regret.

CHAPTER FIFTEEN

*P*roactive by nature, Harper carried a roll of paper towels upstairs, because she was sure to have a puddle of puppy pee to clean up in the morning. Then she could look forward to lying awake staring at the waning moon, thinking of Caleb Johansson and his adorable daughter. She could send up a prayer to the patron saint of puppy rescuers that the three of them could somehow end up happily together, but where would that leave Mariah? The woman had carried and given birth to Ellie, changed her diapers, fed her, and probably nursed her for the first two years of her life—and then suffered a serious, long-lasting, postpartum depression. *Didn't she deserve to be happy, too?*

Sighing, Harper closed her eyes and held Birdy close, her hand resting on the puppy's plump, warm belly. *Thank God for baby dogs, nature's pacifier.*

At the crack of dawn, Paige was already up and functional when Harper came downstairs to take Birdy out to pee. "How did Sunny do last night?" she asked, with a yawn.

"Fine. Sunny is a Zen dog," Paige said. "Nothing seems to worry her or frighten her. I slept like a baby, and so did she."

"Lucky *you*. Birdy kept bolting upright every time she heard a coyote howl. Then she'd let out this low rumbly baby-growl, like she'd be willing to take on the whole pack. She wouldn't even be a snack for them."

Birdy and Sunny peed and sniffed and peed again and finally took to playing together like the littermates they were, tumbling around in the grass that Harper cared for on a daily basis. Growing a healthy lawn in northern New Mexico was not for the faint of heart.

"I'll watch the girls if you want to make us some breakfast, or visa-versa."

"I'm on it. Coffee first?" Paige asked.

"Thanks. That would be a life saver. I didn't get much sleep. Again," Harper grumbled.

In a miraculous ten minutes, Paige returned with plates piled high with *chilaquiles*, one of her new southwestern specialties, topped with Maggie's addictive salsa. She'd made fresh-squeezed orange juice, too. The world would be a much happier place if everybody had a Paige.

"Have I told you lately that I love you?" Harper asked her sister.

"Why, thank you, Rod Stewart," said Paige. After taking a couple of bites, she brought up the obvious. "If we're going to throw a party in a couple of days, we should probably start inviting people. And, we need music. Enough of the wide-open spaces and the coyotes howling all night long—they varmints act like they own the place. I'm ready to party!"

"I can't argue with you. I'll ask The-Man-Who-Knows-All-Things if he knows anybody who could provide music for us," Harper said.

"Otherwise known as Mr. Toolbelt? It's hard to keep track," said Paige. "Hey, I could ask him if you'd rather not. Isn't it...kind of awkward?"

Harper shook her head. "No, it's not awkward. Heart-wrenching, yes—awkward, no. Caleb and I were friends before, and I thought we might be *more* than that, until Mariah showed up."

"Lighten up! You need to listen to some music and dance your ass off, not that you actually *have* much of one. All this hard work has you seriously toned and tanned. You look like an ad for luxury southwestern wear, minus the nice clothing, and you don't wear enough turquoise."

"Thanks, I think? Sometimes I'm not sure with you. You need to work on your compliments. *You've* changed, too. You're looking a little less pale and office-y," Harper said, returning the compliment.

"Pale and office-y? Oh, my God, we need to sign you up for a basic English course. Or manners. Or both," Paige said, nearly coughing up her *chilaquiles*. "I'll be generous and blame it on your lack of sleep. So, what are we doing today?"

"You still haven't seen most of the ranch. So, today, we're walking the property with the puppies, finding natural treasures to display all over our gorgeous Inn, and then, maybe, having lunch at Maggie's. That about covers it."

"*And* planning a party. We can toss some ideas around while we're treasure hunting. I'll handle the logistics. Regardless of your desire to avoid Mr. Toolbelt and his domestic problems, you two still have finish work to do on the coops, and I want to make sure you follow through," Paige said.

"Yes, Ma'am, Boss Lady. Alright, you cooked; I'll wash up. Wear boots. You *did* bring boots, didn't you? There might be snakes—or other crawly things." She'd vowed to avoid mentioning scorpions to her sister unless absolutely necessary.

"Dammit! I wish you hadn't said that. In that case, don't forget to bring your snakebite kit," Paige said, as she headed upstairs to change out of her designer floral pajamas.

Well, I would if I had one, Harper made a mental note. She'd read somewhere that taking a popular antihistamine helped if you took it right away, but she didn't have any antihistamines, either. They'd just have to take their chances with the resident reptiles.

Harper hadn't walked the entire boundary since the day she'd helped Caleb find the property pins and had left a lot of flagging behind. She grabbed another roll in case the ridiculously strong spring winds had taken her flagging with them. She thought she'd remember where the pins were, in any case. After all, there were only four of them. *How hard could it be?*

Birdy and Sunny walked side-by-side on their leashes, Sunny with her smiling face in the air, Birdy with her nose to the ground like a trained bloodhound. So far, Birdy was all work and Sunny was all play, but Harper hoped they'd eventually rub off on each other. Everyone needed to learn balance, even dogs.

The brightly colored tape had mostly remained in place, and Harper left a little more, just in case. She found the pins and pointed them out to her sister, Then, they walked a meandering route of the property that led them to several derelict outbuildings, and to what might or might not be an older ruin. Made of native stone, it had sunk low into the ground. Nearby, on a large boulder, they found a large spiral scratched into the stone, which they both thought was pretty cool. Neither of them found anything exciting like potsherds or flakes of stone from chipping arrow-heads, but then again, they didn't exactly know what to look for. *The-Man-Who-Knows-All-Things* probably did.

Her crafty sister found the odd skeletons of cholla cactus, some interesting and colorful rocks, and the tall stocks of dried yucca seed pods. The entire circumnavigation of the property took a few hours at a brisk pace, but they stopped to let the pups sniff everything their little hearts desired. Thankfully, it was a comfortable day, not too warm, and only lightly overcast.

"Home sweet home," Harper said, leading the way into the house from the back door that led onto the patio. "God, I'm ready for something cold and frosty. Does kombucha count? I bought some at the Sprouts in Santa Fe last week." She continued into the kitchen and had a heart attack.

"Hello, Harper. Nice place you've got here. I like what you've done with it," said a voice she'd hoped to never hear again.

"Kevin, what are you doing here?" *It was exactly like finding a serpent in their paradise.*

"I wanted to see what you were up to, since you haven't been very chatty, lately. Hello, Paige. Nice to see you, again. You're looking well," he said, smoothly.

"Go screw yourself, Kevin. I'll be upstairs, Harper. Yell if you need anything." Paige grabbed both dogs, glared at Kevin as if he were a well-known puppy killer, and headed upstairs.

"Care for a drink? Kombucha, beer, cyanide?" Harper offered.

"Water would be just fine. Thanks for offering. Why don't you grab a drink and join me?"

Harper didn't have much choice: playing nice might be the only way to find out what the snake wanted.

"Here you go, rural New Mexico's finest well water. It comes from the earth, naturally chilled. Now speak," she said.

"Well, I guess I'm a little surprised. You didn't tell me you'd inherited a ranch, and it's a pretty substantial chunk of property. What's it worth? Plus, this house. Three thousand square feet? Historic, and totally tricked out? Of course, you'll never make it running a B&B. Erica and I have stayed in quite a few of them, and you're not cut out for the hostess thing. You might want to stick to gardening.

"Now…if you wanted to make some *real* money, I could help you with that. We could subdivide, sell the parcels, create an upscale resort here. On the high end—the mountain views here would make that possible. We could develop it together: I could design the houses; you could design the grounds. We made a pretty good team, once," Kevin said. "You should think about it."

"Over my dead body," said Harper.

"Mine, too," said Paige, from the doorway, dogs now safely secured. "Or yours. I'm not that choosy."

"We don't need, or want, your help, Kevin. You can't possibly imagine I'd fall for it. Now, why are you *really* here. Did Erica already kick you to the curb?" Harper asked, not smiling.

He dropped his eyelids and blinked, looking uncannily like a pit viper— and by now she'd seen a few rattlers on the rockier reaches of the property.

"Of course, not. You know me, Harper. What can I say? I have a great head for business. I'm always looking to develop valuable properties in respectful and sustainable ways, and I'd hoped you'd want to do this together. Both of us could make some real money."

"I don't need *you* to help me make some 'real money.' I'm more interested in creating a 'real community' here. Paige and I have plans, and you will never be part of them," Harper said, folding her arms across her chest.

Kevin rose, jingling the keys in his pants pocket, a habit she'd always detested. He looked around, assessing the property's strengths and weaknesses. She could see the wheels turning in his head, calculating what she and Paige could make, if they were lucky. And how much more *he* could make if he got his greedy little hands on it. For a moment, she wished he'd been able to see the property before four months of relentless labor and half of all her personal assets had completely transformed it. *Just for a moment, she wanted him to be proud of her. It was silly, really. Kevin's soul only sensed dollar signs.*

"You're opening next week? Let me know how it goes. I'm… intrigued. I think I'll stick around for a while. Maybe we could have coffee?"

"Not if hell froze over and I was hypothermic. It's time for you to leave!" Harper heard a menacing little baby growl coming from upstairs and smiled. *Go, Birdy! The dog had great instincts.*

Kevin jingled his keys once more, sauntered out to his luxury Humvee, and headed down the long drive and out of sight.

"Sheesh! You're pretty good with the clap backs," Paige said, from the shadows. "I could learn something from you."

Harper nodded, accepting the compliment. "Stick around and you just might, she said, suddenly feeling the physical exhaustion that tended to follow Kevin-related drama.

"That settles it—I think this qualifies as a chocolate emergency," her sister pronounced. "Do we still have ice cream? Give me ten minutes, and I'll whip up hot fudge sundaes and a pitcher of sweet tea. Go on out on the patio and put your feet up."

Harper nodded and shuffled out to a comfy chaise lounge, reclined her head, and closed her eyes. Quiet returned to their little patch of high desert. At the moment, even the cicadas in the locust trees were silent.

CHAPTER SIXTEEN

*T*hey prepped all day Wednesday, and by Thursday mid-afternoon, they were ready. Towering thunderheads billowed overhead, but so far, the rain hadn't made it all the way to the ground, one of New Mexico's strangest weather quirks. It was so dry here that the rain often evaporated mid-air.

Word of their housewarming party had gone out on the grapevine, which hadn't taken long in a town the size of Verde Springs. Maggie would be catering, and at Caleb's suggestion, Paige had recruited a string band willing to make the trip up from Albuquerque. They were bringing their spouses and would stay the night as the sisters' first official guests.

Caleb and his construction crew had banged together trestle tables to hold food, flowers, and the Inn at Verde Springs merchandise. Paige had gone all out, ordering two extra cases of mugs with the Inn's logo, and at the last minute, Harper had filled them with bouquets of herbs, flowers, and wild sage, all grown on the property. *Hierbas de olor*—aromatic herbs—they were called in Spanish. Traditionally, a mixture of thyme, marjoram, bay leaves, and Mexican oregano.

Fortunately, oregano was easy to grow in the high-desert climate, and she'd planted heaps.

Stacks of brochures were held in place by heavy rocks, so they wouldn't take off in the late afternoon wind. And Caleb had strung flickering white lights along the roofline of the recently christened Coop Studios, hoping to entice visitors to make the stroll up to check out the new live/work spaces. They were pretty much ready to go, with the exception of the beds, which were on order.

With the large desert willows flanking the entry in full bloom, the Inn had never looked better. Harper thought of it that way now. *The Inn. Not only her home and Paige's. And definitely, no longer The Chicken Ranch.* The lovely lady looked glorious in her transformation, and Harper knew her Aunt Sabina would be pretty damned happy with the way everything had turned out.

They'd finally found the perfect spot for Aunt Sabina, too, in her place of honor on the mantel piece, resting in eternity. Harper had briefly thought of scattering her aunt's ashes somewhere on the ranch, but no particular place had spoken to her, or to Paige. Winters could be brutal here, and summers scorching in the direct sun. She suspected Aunt Sabina would be happiest in the house, right in the middle of everything, watching over them like a benign presence. She hoped so—and, sometimes, she even believed it.

Wearing an adorable sundress and miniature jean jacket, Ellie had taken responsibility for Sunny, while Birdy had taken to following Caleb around like he was her daddy. That left Harper free to play casual hostess, a role she hoped to grow accustomed to, while her big sister played killer businesswoman. Harper watched Paige putting out subtle feelers, making connections, and actually shining like a beam of light, completely in her element.

The coffee-mug bouquets, or *hierbas de olor*, were a big hit: putting their two noggins together, she and Paige had come up with a winner. The Inn at Verde Springs would be unforgettable, the flowers and herb bouquets would evoke good memories and come in handy in the kitchen. Plus, the bouquets were a nod to a local cultural tradition.

The string band musicians were great, and the locals were dancing up a storm. Harper wanted to join them, but she couldn't take her eye off the ball. At that moment, Caleb came up and handed her the leashes of the two pups. "Hey, nice gathering. I hope you and Paige are happy with the turnout. Can you hold onto these two mutts for a minute? I promised Ellie a dance."

"Absolutely." She sat on the grass with the two pups in her lap, smiling, as Caleb danced with his daughter standing on his feet, never letting go of her hands. Ellie never took her eyes off her daddy's face. *What a lucky little girl.* If Harper hadn't already been halfway in love with Caleb, watching him dance with his daughter would definitely have tipped her over the edge.

They returned to join Harper on the grass, and Ellie ran off with both dogs. "May I have this dance?" Caleb asked, holding out his hand.

"Do you think we should?" she asked, even though she wanted to, more than anything.

"I'm asking for *one* dance. It's okay if the hostess and her contractor have a dance together. And, frankly, we deserve it. We've both worked our asses off for this."

"Alright. One dance." She nodded. "And in case I haven't thanked you properly, thanks. Really. I couldn't have done any of this without you."

"You would have found a way. I've never seen anyone so determined. Don't underestimate yourself, Harper. You could do anything you wanted."

Her heart caught in her throat for a moment—then reality asserted itself. "How is your wife, Caleb?" she asked, softly.

"Please, don't. One dance—that's all I asked for," he said.

"Okay. I guess that's fair." She leaned into him, feeling his heart beating steadily in his chest, smelling the particular scent of the man she'd already become addicted to: wood shavings, hard work, a hint of piñon soap. *She could happily stay here, holding him forever.*

"She's *not* my wife," he said, softly. "She *was*, once. Then she left, taking part of my heart with her. Now, she seems to want it back—but it's not mine to give. Not anymore."

"What does that mean?" she asked, looking up at him.

Caleb shook his head. "I've said too much, already. Except this, Harper. I'm so proud of you. Now, I'd better get Ellie home, before it gets too late."

"Can I ask why Mariah didn't come tonight?" she asked, stepping back from him. "Paige said she invited her."

"I don't know for sure. She said she wasn't feeling well. She's been kind of off her food lately. Maybe a bug, or something."

Harper would put her money on "or something."

※

As she stood beside the driveway waving goodnight to Ellie and Caleb, she watched Kevin's Humvee pull up the drive. *No one in Verde Springs drove a Humvee—the parking lot was more or less full of pickup trucks, several were vintage.*

"You should have told me you were throwing a party," he said. "I could have helped you host," he said, with smug arrogance.

"You weren't invited," she said, plainly. "What are you doing here?"

"This is a pretty good turnout," Kevin said, ignoring her question. "And the gardens look very nice—I can see your handiwork everywhere, Harper. But my offer still stands—we should develop this venture together. Your little attempt at a B&B will never succeed."

"What my sister and I choose to do, or not do, with the ranch is none of your business."

"I can *make* it my business," he said, his voice cold.

"Why are you bothering?" she couldn't help asking. "Are you really that annoyed that I've moved on with my life? Can't you stand to see me happy? What did you expect me to do after Erica, and how many other women that I never knew about? If you'd wanted an open marriage, you could have just asked, Kevin. And then I could have said *no*. You didn't have to go behind my back and lie about it, repeatedly."

"Yeah, well, I'm not the only one who lied, Harper. I agreed to pay spousal support based on your previous income and financial circumstances. And what a coincidence! The minute we divorce, you suddenly inherit a windfall that you decide to keep all to yourself."

Harper sunk her hands deep in her jeans pockets so she couldn't punch his lights out, then counted slowly to five: "I can guess how much that must annoy someone like you, but it's not like I asked my aunt to jump off a cliff so I could inherit her estate on a specific date.

And I didn't inherit it *all*—I inherited *half.* The ranch didn't look any-thing like this when we first set foot on the place: what you see is four months of eighty-hour weeks, blood, sweat, and tears." She paused, looking around for reinforcements, or distractions, and finding none. "Here," she said, picking up a coffee-mug bouquet. "Take this back to your lonely hotel room, book your flight back to Seattle, and stay the hell out of my life, permanently. I mean it!"

"Okay. If that's the way you want it. You'll be hearing from my lawyer," he said, giving her a shrug and climbing back into his ridicu-lous Humvee and driving into the darkness.

Close to midnight, the dogs were fast asleep, and Paige and Harper were debriefing on the patio.

"How do you think it went?" Paige asked, her voice happy and relaxed.

"Everything was going just fine until Kevin showed up. He is *such* a prick—as in, bursting *all* of my balloons. The guy's an expert. He's been doing it for years, and he seems to take such pleasure in it!"

"Can I ask you something?" Paige said.

"Shoot. My brain is pretty fried, but I'll try to answer."

"Can we get by if Kevin messes with your spousal support? Tell me the truth."

"I don't know, Paige. It would depend on how much it changes, and it would depend on what bookings we bring in. We might have to consider selling something to pay this year's property taxes in Novem-ber, because that's not such a long way off. Could we save enough, between us, in only four months? I don't know. One thing's for sure: we need to generate some hefty cash flow, and soon."

"Maybe we could ask for an extension?" Paige asked.

"After the property's been behind on taxes for the past few years? I don't think so," Harper said, shaking her head. "They'd never go for it."

"Well, I guess there's only one thing to do," Paige said.

"What's that?" Harper was almost afraid to hear the answer.

"Market the heck out of early fall weddings. It's too bad June was a bust—we just didn't have enough time to get ready. People book weddings *way* in advance," she said, knowledgeably. "I've been doing a lot of research on wedding venues."

"Well, then, I guess I'll start putting in some fall blooming annuals," Harper said, making a list in her head.

"You *do* know you're more than a green thumb, don't you? I mean, the gardens *are* spectacular, and it's only their first year. But Caleb and I both think you've done an incredible job, all around."

"When did you talk to Caleb about me?" Harper asked.

"I don't know, it just came up. He thinks you're amazing. You know that, right?" Paige said.

Harper gave her sister a tired smile. "He said something tonight—when we were dancing."

"You danced with him?" Paige's mouth formed a perfect "O."

"Will you let me tell my story? We were dancing, and I asked how his wife was doing—I know, dumb idea—and he shut me down. Then, a few minutes later, when we were *still* dancing, he whispered something in my ear."

"Well don't keep me in suspense!" Paige demanded.

Harper paused. "He said, 'She's not my wife.'"

CHAPTER SEVENTEEN

*O*n Monday afternoon, Harper received a call from Heather Diamond, the Tacoma attorney who had represented her in her divorce.

"Harper. I'm sorry to be the bearer of bad news. But I had a call from Fred Kohn, Kevin's attorney. They're arguing that with the change in your overall financial circumstances, your settlement should be revisited." She sighed. "Because it's really their only option, Fred's going to make an argument aimed at adjusting your spousal support. Although you may not be making money *yet*, your potential to make money, lots of it, has changed, at least according to Kevin."

"Wait—that's it?" Harper asked. "We're not fighting back?"

"Well, of course, you can if you want to," Heather replied, "but it might cost you a fair bit. And I feel…like I've been a little out of the loop—you didn't even tell me about the ranch. I'm still playing catch-up."

"I've had a lot going on, Heather. Dealing with the house in Gig Harbor, and my aunt's death. Not to mention, rehabbing a fifty-six-acre ranch. I've sold the car I inherited from my aunt to help with remodeling expenses, and I've put my entire life savings into this place."

"I'm sorry it's been such a struggle for you—and I guess you have some thinking to do. Let me know what you'd like to do, and I'll proceed accordingly. And don't forget to send me your current address—I might need to follow up with you. Look, I have another client soon. Stay in touch, okay?"

Life was about to get very real, very quickly.

"Are we set for the soft open? I mean, *really* set? We can't afford any bad reviews, and we need to start bringing in the big bucks, pronto," Harper said, the next morning. She'd tracked her sister down in the breakfast room off the kitchen. Paige's laptop was open and she was wearing her serious, girl-boss expression.

"Why do you suddenly have ants in your pants? Has something changed in the last twenty-four hours?" Paige asked. "Talk to me."

"Yes, as a matter of fact." Harper sat down across from her sister. "Kevin's attorney is petitioning the court to modify my spousal support. If I decide to fight back, Heather is willing to represent me, but it'll cost me money that I don't currently have. I think…I'm not willing to fight it, at this point. I don't have the energy. I'm one-hundred-percent sick of dealing with Kevin, and I want everything to be over. So, I think…I'm just going to put my head down and push through."

"Yikes! Are you sure? What about the ranch? Does Heather think he has any case there?" Paige asked.

"No, none. He just wanted to rattle my cage. Kevin has zero claim to an inheritance that came to me after our divorce was final. If anyone deserves to gain from it, it sure isn't Kevin. He only met Sabina once, at our wedding— even though I'd asked him multiple times to come down with me when I visited her. Kevin always said it was good for both of us to have some 'alone' time. And I guess it's pretty clear how he liked spending *his* 'alone' time."

Paige gave a wave of her hand. "Water under the bridge, Harper. Let's focus on making an impression that will bring us fantastic reviews and repeat guests. We're already getting a few bookings for the Fourth of July weekend. We've had some interest from a couple of groups of artists and writers looking for retreat spaces in August and September—that's your department. I want to pivot into making the Inn a destination for weddings and receptions, as well as for wedding guests who want to stay over for a few days. *That's* where we'll bring in the big bucks. I know you were set on a B&B, but in the grand scheme of things, weddings are going to be a *much* better source of revenue for us, so I hope you can get on board with this."

"I'm actually glad you came up with this plan, Paige. You know, I really didn't like the idea of having strangers sleeping in my house *all* the time. Occasional guests are okay, though. I've kind of gotten attached to it just the way it is, with you, me, and the pups," Harper said. "It'll be better this way."

"Holy cow, Harper! You couldn't have figured that out *before* you decided to launch a B&B? You are so lucky that I'm in this up to the neck, with you! Geez!"

"I'm sorry—I guess I'm just a little quirky, that way. But I'm totally on-board with a pivot—and I have *big* ideas for the Coop Studios. All *kinds* of creative retreats and workshops, classes and demonstrations, and short-term rentals to people who are starting over, like us. And if you really think the wedding direction is the best way to go, I'm behind you one hundred percent, Paige. Just let me know what you need me to do." Harper said.

Paige sighed. "Well at least the new plan will make the gardens even more important, right? All these happy couples are going to need excellent photo opps," Paige said. "So, you know, go a little crazy if you want to, within reason. I trust you. And maybe we can sponsor a few low-cost weddings, and find us a good photographer who doesn't charge an arm and a leg," Paige suggested.

"I'll ask The-Man-Who-Knows-All-Things, and Maggie. There's also a community board at the Pecos library—I'll see if I can find any brochures or business cards from local photographers," Harper said. "If I do, I'll give them a call and set up some meet-and-greets."

"Thanks. And I like your idea of planting lots of fall-blooming annuals, if it's not too late. What are you thinking of? You know, so I have some idea of the color palette," Paige clarified.

"It's not too late if we keep them watered and we mulch well." Harper had been doing this so long she didn't need notes. "The *Caryopteris* should still be blooming, so we should have a range of nice blues with gray-green foliage. I bought two of the biggest climbing roses I could find and planted them in partial sun along the patio wall—they love that eastern light. The blooms are white, kind of like an 'Iceberg.' Throughout the beds in the front garden, there are lots of lovely little grasses that will be coming into fall color, in a variety of golds and greens. Plenty of sage, both planted and naturally growing in the landscape. Then there are the fall mainstays: the asters, the goldenrods, plus, a cool Amaranth called 'Hopi Red Dye.' Along the main walkway, I planted clumps of the tallest showiest perennials I could find, including 'Sahin's Early-Flowering' Helenium. That burnt orange will be gorgeous. And over by the Coop Studios, some miscanthus grass and clumps of willow-leaved sunflower, *Helianthus salicifolius*," Harper said, pulling up a photo on Google Images to show Paige.

"Um, Harper? I don't need their complete pedigree, just the color palette. So, to simplify: greens, blues, grays, and whites, some rose and lavender color-spots, with gold, red, and orange as your gardens come into autumn," Paige summarized.

"Girl, your mind is like a meat cleaver, with Intel Core processing. I'm seriously impressed!" Harper said. "You should really find a way to market that skill!

"I know," Paige said, not modestly. "I call my brain the EliteBook. I used to have one—best darn workhorse I've ever had. But one night, in the midst of our divorce, I got drunk and spilled a glass of Malbec on my laptop. Sadly, it wasn't recoverable, no matter how long I buried it in rice. On the other hand, *I* don't have a green thumb and you *do*. So, how can I help?"

"Well, I need to finish planting the last of the gardens, so you can photograph them for PR purposes. The sooner the better. Feel like getting your hands dirty?" Harper asked.

"I think that's beneath my managerial capabilities," Paige informed her, in her MBA voice. "Let's farm it out."

"Speaking of…Caleb's *not*-wife hinted that she might be looking for a job," Harper said. "You know, when we were at Maggie's, the other day."

"And?"

"And…I said I'd keep my eye out. Let her know if anything came up," Harper said, while mentally preparing her defense.

"Well, that's opening a can of worms. What could you possibly be thinking?" Paige asked her.

"I was thinking it might be a nice day job to offer to Mariah. Let's see if she's got any skills. Maybe she'd be willing to help us out, on a part-time basis. People haven't exactly been storming the gates, begging for jobs."

"Do you know her background? Like, what kind of work has she done in the past?" asked Paige.

"According to Caleb, pre-Ellie, Mariah did a little of this and a little of that."

Paige shook her head and made that "tsk, tsk" sound like a retired school teacher.

Sometimes her sister sounded a lot older than the age on her driver's license.

"'This and that' will never get you where you want to go. So, what's Mariah like? She barely said 'boo' to me when we met at Maggie's, and not so much as a 'thank you' on her way out," Paige huffed.

"To be fair, when we were in the restroom, she did thank *me* for keeping an eye on Ellie. Mariah is…hard to pin down. I don't get a *bad* vibe. I know she's had some mental health issues that seemed to be brought on by her pregnancy with Ellie—but I wouldn't say she seems depressed, now. She kind of seems…more anxious, or worried. And, according to Ellie, there's the barfing thing. I wonder what *that's* about?"

"*Morning sickness* is the technical term, Harper. You're going to have to clean up your act when we have guests paying a lot of money to stay here. You know that, right?"

"I'll work on it. So, should I give her a call?" Harper asked, to confirm.

"No…let me. I want to feel her out myself," Paige said, surprising Harper. "Anyway, I think I should handle all the human resources for the Inn, so that we have some consistency. I might even want to hold a small job fair—we could ask Maggie if we could use the diner on a Sunday."

"Okay, the ball is in your court. Whoever runs into Caleb first can get Mariah's details. Maybe it'll be a win-win for all of the parties involved. Well, I'm off to that big native plant nursery in Santa Fe, and I probably won't be back until late afternoon. You okay to hold down the fort?"

Paige simply nodded, already deep into her spreadsheet.

When Caleb stopped in the house looking for Harper, Paige asked him if Mariah might want to help them out, part-time.

"Yeah, I think she'd be stoked. She might need some direction, at first, but Mariah has a pretty strong creative streak. She can turn her hand to almost anything like that. Do you want me to talk to her?"

"No, I'd like to meet with her myself. Would you mind sharing Mariah's cell phone number?"

"No problem. I'll text it to you right now, Paige. Thanks."

"It was actually Harper's idea," she told him. "But I'll tell her you said thanks."

Paige sat in a booth at Maggie's sipping iced green tea and waiting for her meeting with Caleb's ex-wife. At this point, she didn't have much to offer, other than a few days helping Harper finish her plantings so they could photograph the gardens. But she'd feel Mariah out and see what skills she had to offer. For sure, if things went as planned, they'd need plenty of help in the near future, and Mariah needed a job.

Maggie's door opened and Mariah walked in. The younger woman was thin to a point of gauntness. Although she was still lovely in an ethereal way, her cheeks were hollow, her eyes deeply shadowed, and her color nonexistent.

Paige stood up and waved a hand. "Hi, Mariah. Thanks for coming. I thought Maggie's would be the easiest."

"Of course. Thank you for taking the time to meet with me," the younger woman said, slipping into the opposite side of the booth.

"How's your day going so far?" Paige asked, hoping to put Mariah at ease. She had a lovely natural smile and the same big round eyes as her daughter, but in a warm hazel rather than Ellie's bold blue.

"Well, we had a bit of a slow start, getting Ellie up and ready this morning. But it's all good now. I brought you my resume, so you can see some of the things I've done in the last few years," Mariah said shyly.

Paige browsed it quickly but would look at it more thoroughly when she returned to the ranch. Mariah had done a combination of cashiering and waitressing, and then had taken a job as a caterer's assistant. *Interesting that they had the food thing in common—Paige had worked her way through college in restaurant kitchens.* And Mariah had also taken two semesters of business classes at a community college in Albuquerque, during her years away, on top of her previous associate's degree in fine arts from Santa Fe Community College.

"It sounds like we have some things in common. I'm pretty comfortable around kitchens, too. This looks good Mariah. Have you ever been fired from a job, or let go?" Paige asked.

"No, never. I admit, I've moved around a bit, which has meant changing jobs, frequently. But there were extenuating circumstances: I had severe postpartum depression for almost two years, which led to my inability to…follow through with my commitments. But I got some help on my own. I even went back to school for a while." Mariah's narrative seemed to stop and hang in mid-air. She took a breath and continued on. "And then, when I began feeling more like myself, I realized I needed to work on making amends and repairing my relationships—with Caleb, after everything I put him through. With my parents, and especially, with Ellie."

Well, that was brutally honest. "It sounds like you've been through a lot. Are you sure you're feeling up to taking on a job right now, even part-time?" she asked.

Mariah nodded. "My daughter is turning five, soon, and after Ellie starts kindergarten in the fall, I'll have the freedom to work outside the home. Full-time, if needed. I *do* want to build something for myself—not just a way to get by, but a real *career*. I like being creative, and I'm a hard worker. I know I'll find my niche—and I have lots of ideas."

Paige took another sip of her iced green tea. "Starting over can't be easy, and I admire your honesty. Alright, I'll be honest, too. Harper and I are really hoping to build something exciting at the ranch, and ultimately, to turn it into a wedding venue, as well as a destination for creatives to hold workshops and retreats. At this point, we don't have much concrete to offer you at this point. Harper does have a couple of days of work for you, but before I get to that, I'd like to hear more about your skillset."

Mariah's pretty eyes lit up. "I love being creative, especially in the kitchen. I've probably most competent in baking. In fact, I brought you something." Shyly, she pulled a small box out of her purse and handed it to Paige. "Go ahead, open it. I thought, you know, with weddings coming up, hopefully, you might be in need of some specialty baking."

Paige opened the box to reveal four, perfectly uniform French macarons, each delicate meringue-and-almond-flour cookie filled with luscious-looking buttercream. The jewel-toned colors would coordinate perfectly with her hoped-for fall weddings. "These are amazing, Mariah! How thoughtful of you to bring them." *Smart, too, from an entrepreneurial standpoint.* "I think we can definitely use something like this when we get a few weddings booked, and I'll keep you in mind. Have you made any wedding cakes? They're usually at the top of the bride-to-be's list when planning her wedding."

"I've done a few for my cousins' weddings, and a small one for a high school friend, but I'm really not a professional baker," she said. "I'm just freelancing, for now, and working on improving my skills. Ellie's always happy to be my sampler."

Time to put Mariah's words to the test. Paige selected a macaron with raspberry buttercream and bit into it, then offered the box to Mariah. She savored the crispness of the meringue cookies and the silkiness of the buttercream. "Yum! If *this* is any indication of the quality of your work, there's no reason you couldn't go pro. In fact, I'd love to help you set up a business plan: start slow, build up a customer base, then eventually, go for your own shop. I really wish I could put you to work right away, doing what you love, Mariah, but Harper and I are just getting our own business off the ground."

"No worries, I get it. And thanks for your encouragement. In my wildest dreams, I'd have my own bakery and a huge following of loyal customers! But I'm willing to start slow and see how it goes. So, you mentioned that your sister might have some work for me?" Mariah asked.

"Yes, she does, but I'll definitely keep you in mind as we go forward. Harper's transforming the ranch with some spectacular gardens, but it's a ton of work for one person. She could use some help getting the last of the plantings in. We're in a time crunch, because we need to photograph the gardens for PR purposes while they're looking their best. I think it would only be a couple of days work, but she's willing to pay well, if you're up for it," Paige explained. "I know it's really short notice, but would you be available in the next few days?"

"Absolutely. I'm not a super-early morning person, but I'm happy to work as late in the day as it takes."

"I think that could work, but I'll check with Harper, and she'll give you a call."

Mariah nodded. "I'm happy to be joining the team, even if it's just a temporary job. And I'd really appreciate you keeping me in mind for some custom baking, after you start booking some weddings."

"Great! It sounds like this is going to work out well. I'll have Harper give you a call to arrange the time. While you're out at the ranch, I'll give you a tour," Paige said, smiling. "And thanks so much for these," she said, closing up the box of French macarons. "I'm going to be nice and share them with my sister."

Mariah reminded Paige of a younger, less-confident version of herself—and they both seemed to be comfortable in the kitchen. Despite the sticky situation with Caleb and Harper, she liked the young woman and had a sense that they could work well together. *But time would tell.*

CHAPTER EIGHTEEN

"*W*e have no place to marry people!" Paige shouted, taking the stairs two at a time.

Harper stood in the kitchen, cooking breakfast, the easiest meal. She hoped it was edible because Maggie's stayed closed on Sundays. "I thought we had fifty-six scenic acres of high desert in which to marry people. What on earth are you talking about?"

"We need a *designated place*, as in, a charming little grove of trees, a rock arch overlooking a canyon, or a pond with two, charming weeping willows," Paige said. "But I guess we'll have to settle for a rustic gazebo. Maybe we'll add twinkle lights or—no, wait—those ornate Mexican stars made out of punched tin. It will be beautiful! We'll leave the wood to weather naturally, and you'll plant some of those white shrub roses around it, pronto. Icepick, or whatever. Now, where should we do that? We don't have any time to waste!"

"You mean, 'Iceberg?' Yes, they're my favorite variety of shrub roses. In fact, I just placed an order for half-a-dozen more. I don't know, Paige. I'm late to the wedding venue idea—I haven't spent a lot of time thinking about it. But if you think it's kind of urgent, I can ask Caleb if he's free this afternoon. The three of us could do a walkaround, and put our heads together after."

"Yes, please. We need to make this a priority," Paige said, firmly.

"Can I eat first? Want some of my omelet?" Harper offered.

"Hard pass, Harper. When business slows down this fall, I'm giving you cooking lessons."

"You won't be here, remember? Aren't you obligated to teach business law to a bunch of college students in Virginia this fall?"

"Oh. Right. I guess we'll have to use Skype or Zoom. Maybe I'll just buy you a couple of my favorite cookbooks." Paige sighed.

"No one uses real cookbooks anymore. They use their phones right in the kitchen, which is kind of icky if you think about it. How often do those filthy things get sanitized?" Harper asked.

"Can you please try to focus? Call Caleb, okay? I'm going to be online, finding photos of perfect wedding venues that we can use for inspiration." Glancing at Harper's plate, she asked, "Is Maggie's open?" When Harper shook her head because her mouth was full of burned egg, Paige muttered, "Well, you could at least learn how to make good coffee." Walking over to the counter, she dumped out the perfectly good brew that Harper was currently drinking and proceeded to make another pot of her own.

Harper watched her sister carefully to see if there were any tricks she might have missed: water in the reservoir, grounds in the funnel thingy, close the lid, and hit the brew button. Then the little orange light came on. *No, she had it down—her sister was just naturally judgmental.*

An hour-and-fifteen-minutes later, a content Harper, a hangry Paige, and a restless Caleb wandered the ranch looking for a place to build a gazebo or pergola. Harper wasn't sure of the difference. Paige clutched a notebook full of Pinterest clips of couples in wedding finery, gazing deeply into each other's eyes. Caleb held a tape measure, and Harper kept her eyes on their two wandering pups. Sunny stuck close, making the rounds of all three humans, sucking up to all of them for affection. Birdy patrolled in a wide circle, nose to the ground, occasionally emitting a puppy growl, which Harper found adorable.

"Anybody struck with a genius idea yet?" Paige asked.

Harper shook her head. "No. But, I'd like to keep the wedding shenanigans away from the Coop Studios. They're off-limits unless by special arrangement, okay?" For unknown reasons, she'd felt an unnatural attachment to the former chicken coops since she'd first set eyes on them. "As co-heir and Chief Landscaper, I'm claiming the Coop Studios for other purposes. And I have plans and ideas."

Caleb cleared his throat. "Well, I have a couple of suggestions. It might work best to have a few different staging areas. Not every couple has the same taste—and not all of your guests will be capable of tromping around in the high desert, especially on really hot days."

"Yes. Of course, you're right." said Paige. "I'd hate to think we're being ableist, here, at The Inn at Verde Springs."

"Yeah," agreed Harper. "Especially, when we're just ignorant. Neither Paige nor I have ever done something like this before, Caleb. Tell us your ideas." *He truly was The-Man-Who-Knows-All-Things.*

He did the adorable chin-stroking thing again, scanning the property with a practiced eye. One hand on his hip, Caleb stood and raised his arm to point into the distance, and Harper followed it with her eyes like a well-trained bird dog. "Can you see where the grass is greener and a little thicker? There used to be an old watercourse there. It probably dried up when the water table dropped during the drought. We could pick one of the flatter spots there, not too far from the house, and create a circular lawn maybe thirty feet in diameter. And we could slope the sides, gently, using the leftover soil from level-ling the circle—that would allow for seated guests to have a good view of the action."

Paige nodded, "Okay, I like where you're going with this."

"Then, Harper, you could plant a wide border all around the circle. I can kind of see it surrounded by aspens, but you could also keep it open and just use low shrubs and herbs to delineate the space."

"I love that idea, and aspens are really fast growing. But it will take a lot of work, and we don't have much time or money left," Harper said.

"But it's an investment that will continue to pay off, *and* it can be part of our branding message: 'Get Married in the Grove,' or some-thing like that. I like it, Caleb," Paige said. She raised two hands and double high-fived him.

"It's kind of a haul from the main house," said Harper. "What about the not-wanting-to-be-ableist part—how are we going to make it accessible?"

"Well, that brings us to location number two: the main entrance. The garden you've created there, with the two desert willows the frame the house, and the climbing roses along the adobe walls—it'll all look fantastic in people's wedding photos. And you already *have* a central circle there—all we would have to do is move the fountain closer to the patio to create more of an open space in the middle."

"Oh, *that's* all? You couldn't have come up with this brilliant idea *before* we spent a thousand dollars on outdoor plumbing?" Harper asked. "I agree that it ticks a lot of boxes, and it solves the mobility problem for guests using walkers and wheelchairs—but isn't it gonna cost too much to dig it all up, move the fountain, and add plumbing in the new location?"

Caleb nodded. "I'll do all the work. There's already plumbing on the other side of the adobe wall, in the kitchen. I don't know why we didn't think of it in the first place—it's the most logical place to put the fountain!"

"I love it! Problem solved. But I *still* want a gazebo, or a pergola," said Paige. "With custom outdoor lighting."

"What's the difference between a gazebo and a pergola?" Harper asked. "I need to know what I should be picturing in my mind, so I can get the plantings right."

Caleb answered her. "A gazebo has a fixed roof, so the space below is permanently covered—a pergola is a partial shade structure that allows sunlight to come through. I'll put together a drawing for you. But any structure we build will have to go in Harper's soon-to-be aspen grove, because anything I built in the entrance garden would block the view of the main house, and that's your money shot."

"I agree, Paige, it would ruin the branding you've already done," said Harper, fully on board now. "Caleb, let me know if you need me for anything. I'll come up with a good design and a plant list."

After they'd all finished a round of high-fives, Paige headed inside, excited and full of plans, leaving Harper alone with Caleb.

"So, how are things?" she asked, politely attempting to be non-specific.

"Weird." He put his tape measure away, and they walked slowly toward his truck.

"Are you and Mariah connecting, or is it still mostly about Ellie?" she asked, even though it was none of her business.

He shook his head. "It's awkward—and I feel really awkward talking about it to you."

"Well, you have to talk to someone. I'm willing to listen, Caleb. We're friends. Good friends."

"Okay. Okay. I can *see* her trying, too hard, sometimes. But it's like I'm watching a movie, or something. I'm not connecting with Mariah, I think, because it doesn't feel *real*. But I love seeing Mariah engage with Ellie, and they're really bonding. There's still a trust issue—even without me saying a word, I know Ellie sometimes wonders how long her mom will stick around. So, we're not out of the woods, yet."

"I'm sorry—it sounds so stressful. Have you talked about marriage counseling? Or maybe family counseling? I imagine it would be hard for any couple to reunite after a two-year separation, without some help and guidance," Harper said. "You don't have to do this all on your own—there are people who can help."

Where was this coming from? She wanted Caleb more than she'd ever wanted anyone. But she also wanted him to be happy—whatever that meant for him. What was up next on her bingo card, sainthood?

"Believe it or not, I've suggested it. But Mariah doesn't want to, at least not yet. She worked with a lot of counselors when she was being treated for postpartum depression," he said, as if that explained everything. "I think she just wants to take it one day at a time, and see what happens."

Harper pondered that for a minute. "What does Mariah seem to want, other than a chance to reconnect with Ellie?"

Caleb smiled. "Well, she came home the other day, pretty gung-ho about Paige's job offer. Part-time, no guarantee of the number of hours, she said—but it's the idea of the work itself that excited her. I guess she *did* do something with her life when we were apart: she saw a counselor on and off, went back to school, had a job she liked, maybe more. But in the end, she said, she was just overwhelmed with guilt about how she'd left things with me, and especially, with Ellie. She says it's important for her to make amends. Like I said, she's trying."

"Well, that's something. I hope she likes working with us. I don't think she and I got off to the best start, but I promise to do better," Harper said. "It sounds like Mariah's been through a lot. Everyone deserves a break, now and then." But before Caleb left, she had one more question. "Caleb, how's Mariah's health? Does she seem okay to you?"

He shrugged. "She's pretty low energy, sometimes, and she sleeps a lot. According to Ellie, Mariah's a little slow going in the mornings. But she's been following through on everything she says she's going to do, so far, so no real concerns. Why?"

"I was just…hoping she's not showing signs of depression, again. I think that would be hard on Ellie, and on you, too."

"No," he said, shaking his head. "She's not at all like she was, before. If that was the case, I wouldn't feel comfortable having her spend so much time with Ellie. Mariah may be stressed—but she's not out of control. Well, I've gotta run. It'll be nice to be working with you again, Harper." He gave her that little half-smile that she couldn't quite read. *Half happy? Or half sad?*

Harper went back in the house and headed up to her bedroom. In addition to their office downstairs, she'd set up a little work area in the corner of her room, with a view out the window into the patio-garden. It was her favorite place for thinking private thoughts, usually with a dog or two snoozing at her feet.

This would be a busy week, working side by side with Caleb. It would be a matter of practicing love without attachment or expectation. *She loved him.* Even without the chance to see what might have happened, after a single night of his heart-melting kisses, she found it completely impossible not to. From the beginning, she'd appreciated a man whose word you could take to the bank—*with one understandable exception.* With his authentic mix of rugged sexiness and absolute reliability, he'd gotten under her skin—and she had to hope that meant things between them weren't finished.

CHAPTER NINETEEN

*P*aige welcomed their first paying guests at the Inn—the Salazars and the Garcias, visiting from Colorado—preparing elaborate breakfasts and generally being the hostess with the mostess. Meanwhile, Harper and Caleb spent three days marking out, clearing, and leveling a wide spot in the high desert landscape. Then, Caleb dug a series of twelve large holes to hold their young, fast-growing aspen trees. Harper had arranged them in groups of six, with a wide gap at both ends of the circle. According to her sister, six was a sacred number, offering "love, warmth, and security, with an ultimate outcome of harmony, companionship, and adaptation." *Google was full of useful esoteric information…*

Thirty feet in diameter, the circle's wide opening faced the Inn, and Caleb had marked out a path that would connect the aspen grove to the entry garden and parking area; at its opposite end, he'd used his front-end loader to position a large, picturesque boulder he'd found on a different part of the property. The smooth reddish sandstone would make a nice backdrop for wedding parties, and it would look distinctive in wedding photographs. Paige was over the moon and already deep into ideas for branding.

This morning, Harper had the fun job of picking out a baker's dozen of healthy, straight-trunked aspen trees to be delivered by Thursday, and she'd selected the rest of the perennials, grasses, and shrubs that would be installed in the surrounding border. From her favorite plant nursery in Santa Fe, she'd chosen ten, rosy *Penstemon palmeri* specimens to plant in between the aspens. In optimal conditions, meaning enough moisture, the elegant perennials could shoot up to five feet in height, and nearly the same in width. Showy and fragrant, with a scent reminiscent of honeysuckle, they'd pair well with the lamb's ears, Russel lupines, black-eyed Susans, and some more of her favorite fall perennial, 'Sahin's Early-Flowering' Helenium. This hardy floral abundance was more than enough to get the ball started. New to gardening in this cooler, higher, and dryer plant zone, she figured she'd lose a few plants, even with the best of care. Still, she didn't want any of their prospective brides and grooms to be disappointed, and now, she was confident they wouldn't be.

Harper drove home in silence, giving her brain time to decompress before Paige bombarded her with questions. Her sister could best be described as dynamic, ambitious, and driven. Paige, of all people on their little team, needed to adopt New Mexico's unofficial motto, *carpe diem, mañana*—seize the day, tomorrow. It was okay, occasionally, just to chill and appreciate life—but only if the two of them could manage to hold onto the ranch until their venture had a chance to succeed.

Together, Harper and Caleb rototilled the sandy ground, incorporated two entire truckloads of aged chicken manure, and added fine gravel for good drainage. Automatic irrigation would be installed once all the plantings were in. It was utterly exhausting work, and if they recovered, they'd begin planting tomorrow: first the aspens, which had yet to be delivered, then the larger shrubs like mountain mahogany and oak leaf hydrangea. *Every garden needed hydrangeas.* Then she'd need to plant the ten Palmer penstemons and the smaller perennials and grasses.

Caleb needed to complete his finish work on the Coop Studios, and since she could use a hand, she decided to call Mariah Johannson, after all. The work wasn't necessarily creative—but it was good, honest labor that paid a fair wage.

"Sure, I could help you out. I haven't done a lot of gardening, but I'm pretty good at following directions. And I *love* flowers."

"Okay, Mariah, that would be great! But the forecast says it's going to be hot out tomorrow, so make sure you hydrate and bring a hat. And I always have an Igloo cooler full of water in my truck, and some Gatorade packets in my glove compartment."

"I'll be fine. I was born and raised in Santa Fe," Mariah reminded her. "I've lived in the area all my life."

"Okay, then. Try to get here as early as you can, before the sun gets too high."

"I'll try to be there by eight-fifteen or so," said Mariah. "I'll ask Caleb to take the early shift with Ellie."

True to her word, Mariah arrived at eight-fifteen sharp, driving Caleb's truck over from the Coops where he would be working on the finish carpentry. Harper spotted Ellie crouched beside the sunflowers, with both puppies at her side, another sweet Hallmark-card moment.

Mariah slammed the truck door and joined Harper. "Okay, boss. Put me to work." She was dressed in faded jeans and a baggy Albuquerque Balloon Festival t-shirt, with her hair tucked through the back of one of Caleb's ball caps. She looked even thinner and more drawn, but, like it or not, ready to work. Glancing at the sun, which was still fairly low in the sky, Harper hoped Mariah was up to the task at hand.

"Good. Caleb's drilled all the holes for these two-gallon Palmer penstemons. We'll need to amend the soil, then pop them into place and give them a good drink of water. I have a tank on the back of my truck, so let's use that."

They worked companionably, Harper on one side of the circle, Mariah on the other. From time to time, Mariah would glance at her, either to see how she was doing something or trying to keep pace. When they finished planting the penstemons, Harper went to get shovels from the bed of the truck and handed one to Mariah. "Sorry, but from here on out, we'll need to dig by hand, and mostly you. I'll lay out the larger perennials where I want them placed, and when I'm done, I'll join you. I don't expect you to do all the digging yourself. And grab a pair of work gloves from the truck, Mariah—I don't want you getting blisters."

Mariah pulled on gloves and Harper handed her two one-gallon pots of lamb's ears. The local bees loved them. She grabbed two more, and they headed out. Harper placed the plants in a naturalistic way along both sides of the circle, evenly distributed but not precisely symmetrical. Even with her experienced-designer's eye, it was tricky. She went back for two more lamb's ears, then moved on to the lupines and black-eyed Susans. By the time she'd carefully placed all of the larger perennials and joined Mariah, the poor woman had dug nearly a dozen holes. The sun hovered vertically over their heads, and it had to be in the high eighties, hot for this elevation.

"Mariah, you might want to slow down a little. Drink some water, maybe take a break. It's okay to work at your own pace. Go on, take a break," she said, in what she thought was her friendliest, least-authoritative voice.

"If you don't mind, I'd rather keep working. I want to get the job done and help you and Paige get this wedding venue off the ground." Mariah paused, wiping a gloved hand across her forehead. "*I'm* depending on it succeeding, too. I really want a chance to start over, and there's something about this ranch. I've always thought...it's just the coolest place." Turning to face Harper, she said, "Besides, I've let too many people down in the last few years, most of all myself. But, yeah, some water sounds good."

She grabbed a bottle of water out of the Igloo cooler. Unscrewing the cap, Mariah lifted her water bottle, tilted her head, and...continued over backward, hitting the ground with an audible *thunk*. She was out cold and down for the count.

Shit, shit, shit. Pulling off her leather gloves, Harper placed a wet bandana on Mariah's forehead, felt for the pulse in her neck, which was rapid and thready, and simultaneously pulled out her cell phone.

"Caleb, how fast can you get over here? Mariah's passed out. But first, take Ellie into the house and ask Paige to watch her for a while. I don't know what's going on and I don't want to scare her."

Harper watched from a distance as Caleb high-tailed it to the house, carrying Ellie in his arms. Less than a minute later, he was running toward the aspen grove.

"Harper, what the hell have you done to her?" he asked. "You can't expect Mariah to keep up with you—no one could! You've been working non-stop for four months. You should have told her to take it easy!"

"I *did* tell her to take it easy—just before she fainted. She tilted her head back to take a drink and just kept going over. Her pulse is fast and thready, so she's probably dehydrated, and there's no shade, here. Let's get her moved to the main house and lay her on one of the loungers on the patio. It's nice and cool there. But if she doesn't come around right away, you'll need to take her into the ER. Paige and I can watch Ellie."

"Yeah, alright. We'll try that." He stooped and picked her still form up in his arms and sat in the bed of his truck, with Mariah's head in his lap while Harper drove. She parked as close as she could to the Inn's shaded patio.

Unfortunately, Paige and Ellie were sitting at the kitchen table eating a snack, when Caleb carried Mariah and laid her down on one of the patio loungers. Of course, they heard the commotion and came to check outside what was going on.

"Mama! It's Mama!" Ellie cried, reaching for Mariah.

Caleb scooped his daughter up in his arms. "Mama will be alright. She's just had too much sun. That happens, sometimes, honey. Can you go ask Paige for a glass of cold water and a couple of bags of frozen peas, sweetie? And some tea towels. Can you remember all that?" Keeping her busy would be a distraction.

Ellie nodded and ran inside.

"What can I do, Caleb? I didn't mean for this to happen," Harper said. "Mariah was just working really hard, and it's so hot. She wasn't drinking enough, and I guess I was too focused on my work to notice. I'm so sorry."

Caleb nodded, staring at Mariah's pale face. "I know you are. I know you didn't do this on purpose."

Mariah was breathing shallowly, but still out cold. She had a bump where her head had struck a small rock, but Harper doubted that was the essential problem. She'd likely passed out *before* she'd hit the ground.

Paige returned with two bags of frozen peas wrapped in tea towels, and a glass of water. She already had her phone out, opened to "treating sunstroke," and intently read out the suggestions:

"Place the patient in a cool, shady environment out of the direct sun," she read.

Check.

"Offer small sips of fluids."

"Can't, not until she's fully awake," Caleb said.

"IV fluids may be necessary," Paige continued reading.

A muscle twitched in Caleb's jaw. "Can you watch Ellie and keep her until I know what's going on with Mariah?"

Harper nodded, and Paige said, "Of course we will. You go."

Caleb scooped Mariah up like she was weightless and walked the short distance toward his truck. Then he roared down the drive headed for Verde Springs, which had both an urgent care and a small emergency clinic.

Harper considered following him, but Ellie crawled into her lap and laid her head on Harper's chest. Harper's arms naturally surrounded her and held the little girl tight. Her head rested for a moment on

Ellie's, breathing in the clean scent of baby shampoo, and she said, in a soft voice, "Everything's going to be okay, sweetheart."

CHAPTER TWENTY

Caleb headed straight for the small emergency clinic, which had transport on standby for direct transfers to hospitals in Española and Santa Fe. After explaining what had happened, he watched as the doctor on duty began barking out orders. Within minutes, Mariah was hooked up to IV fluids and placed on a cooling mat, with an oxygen mask over her pale face. The nurses attending her pricked her finger to check a quick blood sugar, and then drew labs for the stat hemoglobin and hematocrit the doctor had ordered.

"Has your wife been in ill health, recently?" the doctor asked.

"A little under the weather, yes," Caleb replied, not seeing the immediate necessity of explaining their somewhat complicated marital history.

"We'll know more when we get results from the bloodwork," the doctor said. "It shouldn't take too long. Try not to worry."

"There's one more thing you should know," Caleb said. "Mariah's been throwing up, a lot. My daughter says that it's been happening in the mornings."

The doctor stopped entering his notes and turned to look at Caleb. "Is there a chance your wife might be pregnant, Mr. Johansson," he asked.

Caleb was silent a moment, then gave a shrug. "I wouldn't know."

The doctor looked at him strangely. "Well, then. We'll see what her bloodwork shows. With a woman her age, it's standard practice to include a pregnancy test."

Caleb nodded once but said nothing. He just wished Mariah would wake up. Meanwhile, he sat quietly in the upright, faux leather chair, waiting.

After an entire liter of fluids had been administered and the nurse was reaching up to hang liter number two, Mariah's eyes fluttered open and she turned her head to look at Caleb. "What's going on?" she asked.

"You passed out and hit your head. When we couldn't wake you up, I brought you to the emergency clinic in Verde Springs."

"Where's Ellie?"

"Paige and Harper are with her. In the house, not outside. It was too damn hot to work so hard today—I don't know what Harper was thinking," he growled.

"It wasn't her fault," Mariah said, closing her eyes again. "What's happening, now?"

"The doctor is running tests." *Including a pregnancy test. There was no time like the present, and it could be important.* "Mariah, could you be pregnant?" Caleb asked. *Hated to ask.*

She hesitated for about the longest ten seconds of his life, eyes still closed, then said, "I'm not."

"How do you know for sure?" he asked, not really wanting to know the answer.

"I went to the doctor's the other day...when I said I had something I needed to do. The day that I asked you to watch Ellie, but you had a job that couldn't wait."

Caleb sat digesting this simple piece of information and its profound implications for a full five minutes, while Mariah lay silently on the stretcher, the color slowly returning to her face. *So, she might have been pregnant, and she hadn't said anything to him.* Suddenly, a lot of pieces were fitting together, beginning with Mariah's abrupt reappearance and request for reconciliation. There were so many more questions to be asked, but now wasn't the time, and this definitely wasn't the place.

The curtains slid open and the doctor returned. He nodded at the now-awake patient, pulled up the e-chart, and began reading from his notes: "Mrs. Johansson, you were extremely dehydrated and your blood chemistry is *way* off, much more than we'd expect to see from simple sunstroke. Your husband says you've experienced some vomiting. *Excessive* vomiting, especially if prolonged, can lead to electrolyte imbalances, and that's what we're probably seeing here. Your hematocrit and hemoglobin also read low, and today your blood sugar was low as well—although that might have been a temporary situation attributed to your vigorous activity. And, Mrs. Johansson, I have to add—although we haven't gotten a weight on you yet—you appear to be underweight, and possibly, malnourished. Do you feel comfortable speaking freely in front of your husband? Or would you like him to leave the room and wait for you outside?"

Mariah shook her head. "No, Caleb can stay."

"The good news, from a medical perspective, is that your pregnancy test was negative. I only say this because, in your current physical state, it would be very difficult to sustain a pregnancy full-term."

Mariah nodded but said nothing.

"Are you experiencing regular cycles?" the doctor asked.

Eyes closed, Mariah shook her head.

"Can you remember when you had your last menstrual period?"

"Four or five months ago? Before that, I'd been pretty regular."

"Is there anything else you want to tell me, Mrs. Johansson? We're still running a tox screen because it's standard practice with any loss of consciousness—but it would be helpful to know if you've been engaged in any substance abuse."

Mariah opened her eyes and struggled to sit up. "No, *nothing* like that. I would *never*. Just some…well, I get anxious sometimes. A *lot*, actually."

"And what *do* you do when you get anxious, Mrs. Johansson."

"Sometimes…sometimes, I seem to throw up," she said, in a quiet voice. "I don't even know why. And for some reason, I don't feel well in the mornings."

The doctor nodded. "You may be chronically dehydrated, which can lead to headaches and fatigue. But it's also likely that you're experiencing some significant acid reflux, which can cause lead to morning nausea. It's not uncommon. Would you prefer to speak to me privately?" the doctor asked, again. "Or I could ask my nurse to join us."

"No. I just want to go home. Caleb?" she said, turning to look at him. "I'm feeling much better now. It's all good."

"Mrs. Johansson, I'd like you to stay for a few more hours. I'd like to run a few more precise tests. And I'd like to have you speak with our social worker—she's on-call and she can be here in under an hour."

"Not today, please. I just need to rest. I promise I'll follow up with my new primary care doctor, Dr. Fuentes, here in Verde Springs. I saw him a few weeks ago, and I'll call and make another appointment."

"Alright, then. Go ahead and get dressed. With your permission, I'd like to speak with your husband. It's a routine matter, just to clear up a few questions."

Mariah nodded and lay back, exhausted. "That's fine with me. Just promise me, Caleb, that you'll take me home. Maybe you can ask Paige and Harper if Ellie can spend the night at the ranch, or you could call my parents. I don't have any energy left for her today. I'm sorry."

She slowly sat up and dangled her legs off the bed. Then the nurse came back in to disconnect the IV and help Mariah out of the hospital gown and into her own clothes. As Mariah leaned forward, she began to heave, and the nurse held out a pink emesis basin.

The doctor turned back, "Get a Gastroccult on that emesis and be sure to let me know the results," he said, before motioning for Caleb to follow him down the hallway. Once inside his office, the doctor closed the heavy door and gestured for Caleb to take a seat across from him.

"Mr. Johansson. I understand you'll be taking care of Mariah. I'm not going to beat around the bush: Your wife is very ill. I strongly suspect she has a severe case of GERD brought on by an eating disorder. It would account for nearly all of her symptoms, both acute and chronic. Were you ever aware that your wife might have an eating disorder?"

"No, I wasn't," Caleb said, stunned. "I thought, I *suspected*, that Mariah might be pregnant."

"I'm sorry, but I don't understand. When I asked if you thought she *might* be pregnant, you said, 'I have no idea.' What am I missing, here?" the doctor asked, bluntly.

"My wife—*ex*-wife actually—and I have been estranged for the last two years. She only recently expressed an interest in reconciliation, and but our reconciliation hasn't yet…advanced to marital relations."

"Oh, I see. That *would* be an awkward situation, then." After a quick knock on the door, the nurse opened it to hand the doctor a small, white, cardboard square, then left.

He opened a flap on the square and frowned. "Well, Mariah is experiencing other symptoms that are triggering her frequent nausea and vomiting—and as a result, she's likely experiencing some bleeding in her esophagus—her Gastroccult rapid test is positive," he said, turning the cardboard square to face Caleb. "We apply a developer to the gastric contents to indicate the presence of blood; as you can see by the blue color, it's positive. I recommend that Mariah schedule an upper endoscopy as soon as possible. I can help facilitate that, of course, if she agrees, and I think she should," the doctor finished.

"Alright, I'll pass that on when she's feeling up to talking. But I'm confused. If she's *not* pregnant, why hasn't she had a period for three months?"

The doctor explained, "a woman in Mariah's physical condition would likely be unable to sustain a pregnancy; and she isn't getting a period because she isn't ovulating. We see this in some serious endurance athletes, and sometimes in women who are severely malnourished and underweight, like your wife."

"Ex-wife."

"Sorry. In any case, Mariah is going to need a lot of support until she regains her health. If you're not prepared to give her that support, then perhaps you can help her find additional resources. This was quite a wake-up call, Mr. Johansson, for both of you. This is a seriously ill young woman."

"Of course, I'll do what I can to help. And I know Mariah's parents will, too. I'll call them as soon as I get her settled at home."

"Fine. Now, you'd better take her home, as that's where she appears to want to be. Good luck, and please call me if you'd like the name of a good gastroenterologist in Santa Fe or Albuquerque. I'll be happy to make a referral. She shouldn't wait—it can take a while to get an appointment with a specialist. And if she has any signs of active bleeding, she'll need to go straight to the ER."

"Thank you, doctor."

Caleb called Harper from the waiting room before taking Mariah home. Watching Ellie was no problem, she assured him, and he trusted her. "Tell Ellie that her mom will be fine—she just needed to rest."

Caleb was quiet on the drive home. Given the enormity of the situation they now faced, it was impossible to make small talk. Mariah was seriously ill, and her wellbeing had to be his priority. But the fact that she'd approached him asking for reconciliation *while* suspecting she might be pregnant was impossible to ignore. *There just was no easy way to swallow that bitter pill.*

At the house, he helped his ex-wife inside and to the bedroom, then stood leaning against the door jam, arms folded across his chest, unsure of what to say—and knowing that he *couldn't* say what he wanted to say. Not now.

"I'm sorry. I'm sorry about everything," Mariah said, after a long uncomfortable silence. "I'd gotten myself into a horrible situation, so bad that I can't talk about it, yet. And when I thought I might be... well, I just...panicked. I was in a really bad place, and I needed to feel safe, again. Can you understand that?"

Caleb simply nodded and left the room. He'd sleep elsewhere tonight, and tomorrow he'd make other arrangements. *Whatever it took to see this through.*

CHAPTER TWENTY-ONE

*W*hen evening came, Caleb called Bill and Kate, not especially concerned about any unwritten rule he might be breaking. Mariah's parents loved her, and of course, they'd want to know. Everyone in his family needed the extra support, right now, but especially Ellie. She loved spending time with her grandparents, who hadn't hesitated for a moment to fill the breach when Mariah had taken off two years ago.

"Kate, it's Caleb. How are you? Yes, well, there have been some developments. Mariah's sick. No, not like before—but I think you should come and spend some time with her. You and Bill can stay at the house, and I'll find another place to stay. Yeah, if you can get here by tomorrow afternoon, that would be great. The five of us can have dinner together, then I'll leave and let you guys talk. No, she'll stay here. They're just beginning to bond, and I don't want to take Ellie away from Mariah unless I really need to, as long as you're here to keep an eye on things. Okay, see you tomorrow. And Kate, thank you."

Next, he called Harper. "Hey. Mind if I come over and tuck my little girl in? I think it would help reassure her. Maybe we could have a beer together on the patio? I…need someone to talk to. And you did offer."

Caleb checked on Mariah, who was sleeping soundly, her breathing soft and regular. He left a note by her phone on the bedside stand, saying he'd gone to take Ellie her toothbrush and favorite softie animal and that he'd be back soon.

"Daddy! I'm happy to see you. And you brought Raggles." Ellie's stuffed dog of uncertain parentage was the only real comfort item she still slept with. "And my toofbrush!"

"Yep, I don't want to get on the bad side of the Tooth Fairy. Now, go brush your teeth, then I'll tuck you in and say goodnight. Mama's going to be fine. She's just getting a good night's sleep, and you'll see her tomorrow. Guess who *else* you'll see tomorrow?"

"I dunno."

"Grandma Kate!"

"And Grandpa Bill?"

"Maybe so. We'll have to wait and see."

Caleb tucked his daughter into bed in the guest room beside Harper's, with Paige right across the hall. Ellie was in good hands. Stopping to splash water on his face in the downstairs bathroom, his hands shook with fatigue. He needed to talk to someone, and he needed a cold beer. But mostly, he needed Harper.

"Well, *you* look like fifty miles of hard road," Harper said, not unkindly. She popped the top off a Modelo and placed the bottle in his hand. "I'm so sorry about today. How's Mariah feeling?"

"You think *I* look like fifty miles of hard road, you should see *her*," he said without a trace of a smile. "She's ill, Harper. I knew she'd lost weight, and I suspected that something might be wrong. But I don't know why I didn't allow myself to see how sick she really was, a whole lot sooner. I guess I was just focused on making sure that she and Ellie were in a good place."

"What did the doctor say? That is, if you're free to talk about it."

"Well, she's *not* pregnant. That's the first thing," he said, taking a swallow.

"She's not?" Harper asked. "I guess that's good, considering."

Caleb ran a frustrated hand through his dark hair. "You mean, *you* thought she was, and you didn't say anything? Geez, Harper, I thought you had my back!"

"Don't bite *my* head off. *You* live with the woman. Surely, you suspected that possibility," she said, sitting down beside him.

Caleb said nothing, just took a long swallow from his beer. "Well, she's not. But…she might have *thought* she was—and that might've been why she wanted to reconcile. Which completely sucks. Am I missing anything here?"

Harper shook her head.

"Yeah. I can't even wrap my head around it, because now, she's really sick. Her parents are coming tomorrow, and I hope that all of us together can map out a plan to take care of Mariah, and Ellie, and still allow me to continue working. This is my busiest time of the year,

Harper, when I make most of my income—and on top of that, there will be medical bills coming in."

"Well, is it serious? Like the 'C' word?" Harper asked.

"Not that I know of. But the doctor said everything's off—her blood work, her body chemistry, even her blood sugar, today. Put together with her anxiety, nausea, vomiting, and malnutrition, he suspects Mariah might have an eating disorder. My wife has *malnutrition*—can you believe that? And she has to have some diagnostic work done right away, in the hospital, because he says she's probably bleeding inside, somewhere." He shook his head, looked down at his feet, then took another pull from the bottle.

"God, Caleb, that's terrible! I'm so sorry, for all three of you," she said, reaching out to touch his forearm. "So, what's the next step?"

"Kate and Bill, Mariah's parents, are coming tomorrow from Santa Fe. They'll stay at the house and help her with whatever she needs, and with taking care of Ellie, for as long as is needed. They're rock solid, and we're all lucky to have them."

"And what's next for you?" Harper asked.

"I need some time and space—although I'll still be involved and I'll help out financially. Harper, could I possibly take over one of the Coop Studios? Maybe for a few weeks, maybe for the rest of the summer? I don't want to take Ellie away from her mom right now, and I need to be close by. It would give everybody breathing room. I really don't want to sign a long-term lease for an apartment right now when everything's so uncertain, and there aren't any hotels in town."

"I should probably run it by Paige, but it's fine with me. You're here a lot of the time, anyway, and Ellie is always welcome."

"So, here's an idea, and you can say no. If we set up one of the Coop Studios as a fully-outfitted living space, for me, you could rent it out as a separate unit after I'm gone," he said, shrugging.

"Yeah, that could work. We hadn't really decided what each space would ultimately be used for, anyway. And the fact that you encouraged me to put in bathrooms is going to come in handy," she said. "They haven't finished tiling the showers, yet, though. You'll have to use the one in the main house."

"Yeah, or I can rig up an outdoor shower," he said. "It's summer."

"As long as you don't show your naked buns to any of our guests," she said, giving him a hint of a smile. "Okay, we've got this. Bring your stuff over tomorrow evening, and let me know what you need from me to make this happen."

"Harper, I don't know how to thank you. You've been so great through all of this. I don't want to take advantage of our friendship."

"You're not. It's just problem-solving. I know Paige would do the same for you. It'll be fine, and I'm available anytime you want to talk. Hug?" she asked.

Although he wanted to go there, he shook his head. "Better not. I've got to get home in case Mariah wakes up and needs anything. So, tomorrow then? I can text you when I'm on my way over."

Caleb drove his truck home in the darkness, feeling disoriented and beyond exhausted. Thankfully, it wasn't a long drive, and he took it at a snail's pace. *Had he eaten anything today? He couldn't seem to remember.*

The house was quiet when he walked in. He checked on Mariah and found her sleeping peacefully. Then, he tiptoed into the kitchen and made himself a big bowl of Ellie's cocoa-puffs drowned in milk. He poured a glass of orange juice and headed to sleep in Ellie's room, just for tonight. That way, the guest room would remain ready for Kate and Bill to use, tomorrow.

The room smelled sweet, just like his daughter. It was her little pink haven, the place where she felt safe and loved and wanted. He finished the cereal, chugged the juice, and lay back on the mattress. Thank God, Ellie had graduated to a regular twin bed, last year. He'd only be here for one night. Then Ellie could sleep in her own bed and not have her life disrupted, Kate and Bill would arrive to look after Mariah, and he could hide out in an old chicken coop, where the woman he loved was beyond reach until he could get his life together. Then, they'd see. He sure hoped Harper was patient.

CHAPTER TWENTY-TWO

*S*itting at the big farmhouse table in the breakfast room, Harper made a list of everything a man like Caleb needed to camp out in a refurbished chicken coop for the duration. *She could be nice, sometimes.* He had so much on his plate, right now. The least she could do was make this easy for him.

She'd stock up on TP, hand towels, and toiletries. She'd shop for a comfortable chair, a futon couch that could double as a bed, a refrigerator to hold his beer, and maybe a rug to make it feel less like a chicken coop and more like a Coop Studio. She'd splurge on comfortable bedding—especially as she hoped to be sharing it at some point in the future—and a big laundry hamper with handles that he could carry to the main house whenever he needed to do his laundry. That's where she would draw the line. She wasn't doing laundry for a man she was not even currently allowed to sleep with, because of the sick wife/ex-wife thing. It was complicated, and she could do complicated. But she would not do 'complicated's' laundry for him.

Harper heard her sister puttering around the kitchen. "What are you doing in there?" she asked.

"I'm putting some food together for Caleb: fruit, breakfast stuff, and manly snacks," Paige said. "Beef jerky and smoked almonds. I don't mind if he comes over for regular meals with us—but if there's food available, it'll make the Coop seem a little more like home."

You nitwit, Harper, you forgot to feed him! Men like food—*you like food.*

"I guess I'll get him a gift certificate for Maggie's," Harper said, feeling completely lame. She added "silverware, plates, paper towels, and napkins" to her list. *God, she was so bad at this.* She should have put Paige in charge. One thing she could handle was filling his refrigerator with his beer of choice: *Modelo, dark, in the squatty bottles.*

Harper and Paige sorted through odds and ends of furniture, loaded it all into Lucy, and drove it over to the Coops. While Paige arranged things in her usual competent manner, Harper made a run into the Santa Fe Savers store, on Cerillos, where she picked up a used futon couch, a dorm-size refrigerator, and some unbreakable dinnerware. At the Home Goods store, she found a pair of matching Adirondack chairs to put out in front of the Coop Studio. Next, she stopped at the home goods store where she bought discounted sheets (400-thread count), a foam topper, in case sleeping on the futon was like sleeping on a rock, and a designer comforter that was one-hundred-percent cotton and fifty percent off.

With Lucy fully loaded, she stopped in the diner to purchase a gift certificate. Maggie loaded her up with lots of extra goodies, including chips and her famous salsa, which should kick off Caleb's first night at the Coops with at least a mouthful of joy. Last stop was the local Verde Springs market, where she bought a case of *Modelo* from the cooler. There was little more she could do to make Caleb comfortable with less than twenty-four hours' notice, but she'd tried her best. Just the essentials, nothing over-the-top that would make Caleb feel uncomfortable. She had to wait until the man she'd grown to love was officially unencumbered and had made her aware of that fact, before she made any official moves. Which she definitely planned to do at some point, hopefully before they both faced a cold and lonely winter.

Caleb sat in one of the Adirondack chairs and Harper in the other. Half an overturned whiskey barrel held a bowl of chips and a widemouth jar of Maggie's salsa conveniently between them. In the lavender sky, stars had begun to appear over the horizon of the distant mountains. Fortunately, they'd tucked both puppies away for the night, safe from the coyote families yipping and howling in the distance.

Caleb had choked up a little when he'd walked into the last Coop Studio on the right, the one shaded by a grove of New Mexico locust growing to the southwest. "Harper, this is above and beyond. I'd already killed all the creepy-crawlies, laid a new floor, and sealed all the cracks. I was just planning to throw a mattress and sleeping bag on the floor. But this? *This'll* do."

He hoped Harper read that as high praise. Now they were sharing a much-needed nightcap. There had been dead silence when he'd told Mariah he'd be moving out, followed by an understandable tantrum from Ellie. Although she'd perked up when he'd said he'd be staying at the ranch, and she could spend overnights with him on weekends whenever she wanted—but not tonight. Tonight, Mommy needed Ellie to be there, and her grandparents wanted to read her bedtime stories. Not for the first time, Caleb coaxed his daughter into good humor by saying she could come over tomorrow afternoon and play with Birdy and Sunny.

"So," Harper said. "We've both come a long way from closets filled with roosting bats."

"And roofs that needed work and chicken coops full of chicken shit. *All* of it, Harper. It's been a labor of love, and I am blown away by your vision and how hard you and Paige have worked to make it come true," he told her, every word the truth.

"And *you*. Don't sell yourself short, Mr. Johansson."

"Is that what you and Paige call me behind my back?"

"Um, no," Harper said, blushing, or it might have been the light from the setting sun. "I call you The-Man-Who-Knows-All-Things, and Paige calls you—now don't get all huffy, but, Mr. Toolbelt. That way, we have all the bases covered."

Caleb laughed. "Yikes. Well, I'm definitely not the *first* one—I didn't even know my ex-wife *wasn't* pregnant with someone else's child. Or, that she was throwing up to the point that she was bleeding internally." A scary thought. *How did things go from happy and hopeful—to extreme angst from a life he no longer recognized? And the summer wasn't even over...*

"There's a lot more to it than that, Caleb," Harper said. "Eating disorders are serious, just like depression is serious, and Mariah's had to deal with both. We don't know what's been going through her head, or what kind of support she's had, if any. She probably just panicked, for some reason."

"Funny, 'panicked' is exactly the word *she* used. I *do* get that—and I'm learning everything I can so I can help her. But, you know, I'd just like to point out that I *definitely* don't have all the answers. So, 'Mr. Toolbelt,' huh? Maybe it's your big sister who has a thing for me?"

"Think whatever you like," Harper said, her tone neutral. "Paige is single and available, too, if you're interested." She set down her empty bottle. "I'm heading back to the house. Enjoy your first night in the Coops, and don't forget to rate your stay."

"Thanks, Harper. 'Night. I'm giving you five stars on Yelp."

Harper was busy finalizing the work on the wedding circle, or the aspen grove, or whatever Paige had branded their latest project, which seemed to change daily. It was looking good, but without the extra manpower she'd counted on from Mariah, it had taken a few days longer than she'd expected. Her five-minute walk back to the house would have to count as her afternoon break. Paige was busy elsewhere, so Harper poured a glass of iced tea, sat at the table in the breakfast room, and checked her messages.

There were two from Heather Diamond. The first said, without preamble, "There's some news. Call me." It had come in at ten o'clock this morning, or nine o'clock Pacific time. The second message left at three-thirty said, "Since you're not picking up or returning my calls, I'll give you the news over the phone. Surprisingly, the court has decided in Kevin's favor: they reduced spousal support, effective immediately. Who knows? Maybe he plays racquetball with the judge. Kevin still owes you the full amount for last month, and his attorney will probably tell him to cough up so he can leave a clean record. But after that, you'll be receiving a reduced payout. I'm sure the court will notify you of the details, or Fred Kohn will, if he has your current address."

Heather paused, briefly. "Well, good luck with your New Mexico adventure. I really hope things work out for you and your sister."

Swallowing her irritation, Harper set her phone down and took another sip of iced tea. She could fight this, maybe even hire a different attorney, if she wanted to. But either way, it would cost money she didn't currently have. More than that, *she just wanted it to be over*, to put her struggles with Kevin completely behind her and make a fresh start. *And she knew she could*. She was willing to work hard, and she'd have to. To make up the difference in income, she'd need to resurrect her landscaping business and hope she could make some money from fall garden clean-ups. Maybe she could pick up some end-of-season jobs at one of the nearby resorts in Santa Fe and Taos. But Paige was also counting on her to keep the gardens in top shape for the weddings she was sure she'd be able to book—although she hadn't definitively booked one, *yet*. None of the prospective couples that Paige had met with had fully committed with a cash down payment—probably because they were new and unproven. When it came to weddings, even couples in love were unwilling to take the risk.

Harper hadn't seen Paige all day. Pretending that it was five o'clock, rather than four, and quitting time, she rinsed her glass out at the sink. Then she refilled it with pink summer wine and headed up to her room to take a shower and listen to her The Head and The Heart playlist. She'd shave her legs and put on some of the lavender-scented lotion Paige had given her for her birthday, and indulge in feeling female for a few hours. And Caleb's presence on the ranch had absolutely nothing to do with it.

Passing by Paige's room, she noticed that her door was closed. Paige usually left it open, filling the hallway with lovely light all day long, and setting an example of the neatly made bed and tidy room she hoped Harper would follow. *Not a chance. There was a good reason she kept her own bedroom door permanently closed.*

Pausing outside Paige's door, her hand on the knob, Harper felt compelled to knock, which was weird, too. She and Paige never bothered to knock—something that would have to change if either of them managed to find a partner before their expiration dates. *Stop wasting time.* She knocked twice on the door, and when there was no answer, she opened it. "Paige, you wouldn't believe what—"

Harper stopped short. Her sister was curled up in the fetal position on her unmade bed watching a decade-old Nicholas Sparks movie, a giant wad of tissues in her fist. Paige glanced up at Harper with tears in her eyes.

"Hey, hey. What on earth happened? Did someone die? As far as I know, we don't even have any other living relatives." Setting her pink wine carefully on the antique dresser, Harper laid down on the bed and spooned her big sister, wrapping a none-too-clean arm around her waist. She gave her a squeeze, then said, gently, "Talk to me."

"I...I got fired. Well, terminated. Not for performance—I've always had excellent student reviews. But it doesn't matter, anyway, because the university is shutting down the entire department."

"Oh, no! I'm so sorry, Paige. I know how much you depended on that job—and you were so close to getting tenure. What are you going to do?"

"Well, I'll stay here, I guess, at least for a while. There's no reason for me to go home anytime soon. I can try to look for a job at one of the colleges in Santa Fe—maybe St. John's—but it might be too late to apply to teach this year. So, I guess *this* will be the gap in my resume that I'll have to find a positive way to reframe. Something like, 'CEO of Operations and Branding' at the new and exclusive Inn at Verde Springs. And—of course, relocating to New Mexico to be with my sister."

"What about your money situation? Don't you have school loans that you're still paying back? And what about your condo in Richmond?" she asked.

Paige sat up and took a deep breath. "Harper, the call came in early this morning, so I've had about eight hours to think about it. I'm going to have to sell the condo. I've been considering selling it, anyway."

"Are you sure? Maybe you should take a few days to think about it."

Paige shook her head. "I've never really been in love with it—it was just convenient when I was first starting out on my own. I bought it for a steal after the market crashed in '08. Thank God, Dan didn't want it in the divorce, because it's gone up in price in the past few years. Selling it could temporarily solve our money problems. But if I put it *all* back into the Inn, I'll lose my nest egg, and at my age, I can't afford to do that. So far, we haven't had more than a handful of B&B guests, and only on weekends. So, we'll have to think of something else—or at least something additional—until we book some weddings. What about *you?* Were you coming in to tell me something?"

Harper lay back on the pillows, crossed her arms behind her head, and spilled the beans. "Heather called—the court decided in Kevin's favor and they've agreed to reduced spousal support. I'll get one more check for the full amount we'd agreed on. After that the amount will be reduced—Heather's sending me the details. Somehow, I'll need to make up the difference."

"Well, *that's* terrible timing. So much for our ability to cover monthly expenses. Honestly, my brain is too fried to come up with a solution right now, and I haven't eaten all day. I'm going to head into Maggie's, treat myself to an espresso, and grab an early dinner. Wanna come with me?"

"No, I still need to meet with Caleb about the gazebo situation. I realize he's had a lot on his plate. But if he's not done with it yet, he needs to *get* done."

"Oh, is that what we're calling it now? Meeting about the gazebo? I would think it would be meeting *at* the gazebo," Paige teased.

Harper rolled her eyes. "Hah—I wish. Nothing's happening. Nothing *can* happen. I get it, I do. But I'm not happy about it."

"I know, and I'm sorry about that. But you *do* know you two are meant to be together, right?" Paige asked.

"I think that's what they say about all star-crossed lovers." Harper said.

CHAPTER TWENTY-THREE

*P*aige headed into town, proud of the fact that her sister now trusted her to drive Lucy—but she'd really need to get her own set of wheels. She relaxed her jaw, aware that she'd been clamping down hard. *Stress.* With no spaces left in front of the diner, she circled slowly around the tree-lined square, looking for an opening. She found one between two hippie-vans, a common sight in the 1970s and still popular in New Mexico.

Walking diagonally across the square, she noticed a group of jugglers, stilt-walkers, and belly-dancers in elaborate costumes and stopped to watch. The talent wasn't half bad and the colorful costumes were striking, but Paige was stumped over the period costumes. *Early Victorian? No, that didn't seem right.* As she stood to watch for a moment, one of the men—tall, bearded, and big as a bear—came over to check her out.

"Hi there. I haven't seen you in town, before. I'm Ed," he said, holding out a hand the size of a catcher's mitt.

He had nice brown eyes, though, deep and soulful. He might possibly be hitting on her, but she was so out of practice that she wasn't really sure. Maybe he was just the friendly type? She couldn't think of anything to do but take his catcher's mitt hand in hers. "Hi, Ed. I'm Paige. I have no idea what I'm watching. Can you clue me in?"

"Sure. We're Renaissance performers. Some people would call us actors. We make our own costumes, and everyone gravitates to a skill or a craft they want to learn. A couple of times a year, we get together at a Renaissance fair somewhere. Even though being a Renny performer only attracts a select few diehards, people love to come out and watch us, gnaw on a turkey leg or a meat pie, and listen to troubadours sing some ballads. Good times," he said, with a shrug of his massive shoulders.

Paige thought that this New Mexico 'Renaissance Man' would look perfectly at home storming a castle in Scotland. "Wow! Sounds like fun. Do you have a brochure, or a card, or something? When are you holding your next fair? My sister and I might want to attend." Crowds were a great place to schmooze, and they weren't in a position to let their business grow by word-of-mouth alone.

"Oh, *we* aren't the ones that *hold* the fairs—we're the performers or players—some of us are volunteers, some are paid. But we all have other jobs, including me. This is just a sideline, but an important one: Renaissance reenactment is more of a calling than a hobby," Ed explained, handing her an ornate business card from his wallet.

"So, how do you find places to perform? I mean, how does one get invited to participate in a Renaissance fair?" Paige asked, tucking his card in her purse.

"There's an association—I'm one of the state's chapter delegates. And sometimes the ski resorts or wineries bring a fair in at the opening or closing of the season. We tend to draw a good crowd," Ed said. "I guess people like something that's a little different, now and then."

"That's good to know. So, do you know of any specific plans for a fair around here this summer or fall?" she asked, a tingle of an idea working its way into her EliteBook brain.

"Not until the big one in Santa Fe in September. But we practice here in the square, once a month. Gotta keep the skills sharp, and we enjoy connecting with each other. The bigger events tend to come up later in the fall. Sometimes things do come up spontaneously—and if we can make it work, we usually do."

"Thanks for talking with me, Ed," she said, reaching out to offer her own hand, again. "I...may be in touch."

Paige crossed the square, deep in thought, but any serious planning could only happen after Maggie fed her. She hadn't had a bite to eat since the College Provost had dropped a bomb on her teaching career. Maybe it was time for a change from business law—or at least, a professional gap year. For certain, it was turning out to be an interesting summer of reinvention for both of the Crawley sisters.

In the privacy of Maggie's back booth, Paige initiated a quick Google Search. Apparently, Renaissance fairs were a legitimate thing, and they could be big moneymakers as long as the weather cooperated. In northern New Mexico, that meant after monsoon season had passed, so most Renaissance fairs here took place in the late summer or early fall. Harvest time, more or less. And the annual Santa Fe Renaissance Faire, the one Ed had referred to, was traditionally scheduled for the third week of September.

Well, September was still a few months away. If she and Paige hosted a Renaissance fair in August, it might bring in enough spectators to pay for itself, advertise everything the Inn had to offer, and in her wildest dreams, entice a few happily engaged couples to hold their fall weddings at The Inn at Verde Springs. They'd just have to take their chances with the weather and hope for a good turnout.

Word of mouth advertising was critical—and she couldn't think of a better way to get the word out, cover their expenses, and help the Renaissance cause. *Of course, you might also have some fun,* her sister's voice whispered in her ear, almost like Harper was right there looking over her shoulder.

Paige finished her burger, minus the green chili, and swallowed the last of her espresso. Then she walked back across the park to her car, anxious to hurry home and share her unexpected news. The performers had already packed up their gear and gone home, probably to more ordinary lives. But she admired them—they'd found something they were passionate about, and through it, they'd built a community.

It was a shame she'd missed the chance to talk to Ed again—he seemed like a good resource—but she had his card and would give him a call. She could already imagine the high-desert grounds of The Inn at Verde Springs covered with colorful tents, crowds of lords and ladies, dancers and jesters. She was in danger of straying miles from her former career—teaching business law to marginally interested college students—and it hadn't even been twenty-four hours.

"Hi honey, I'm home," Paige called out gayly.

"How many of Maggie's margaritas did you drink? You left here in tears!" Harper said, coming down the staircase and meeting her sister in the hallway.

"Zero. I stuck to espresso, my fuel of choice. Let's go sit in our private living room, which we never seem to use, even though you fixed it up so nicely for us. I've thought of a way to get a jump on our finances, until we're able to book some weddings. *Maybe*."

Paige was right, they hardly ever used this beautiful room. *La Sala*, in Spanish. It had a fireplace that drew just fine, so maybe they'd use it more in the winter when it would likely be just the two of them. *Two sisters and their scruffy rescue dogs—at least it was better than a houseful of cats.* "Well, you've got my ears perked up. What's noodling around in your brain?"

"We, you and I, are going to host a Renaissance fair, and I am going to advertise the hell out of it in three states, and we are going to get lots and lots of PR out of it for the Inn. Are you with me?" Paige asked, her green eyes sparkling with excitement.

"Give me a minute—that is a *lot* to digest. When would you like to hold this event, and do we even have time to plan it?" Harper asked.

"As soon as we have a weekend without too many other bookings, which shouldn't be hard since we're just getting started. And, as soon as possible, so all the people who fall in love with the ranch will have time to book their late-summer and autumn weddings. Other events, too, but I'm still counting on the weddings to bring us through the end of the year."

"You're the one maintaining the calendar, so you pick the dates and I'll get on board. Just don't make me dress up as a clown or a jester, or something."

"No, of course, not. Although that's not a bad idea."

Harper left to take Birdy and Sunny for a walk before she could get roped into something she'd regret. They came quickly to her whistle now, and they were turning out to be good dogs in all ways. A fortunate thing, because if Paige had her way, a couple of hundred people would be turning up on the ranch very soon.

She headed up toward the Coops, hoping to meet with Caleb for a progress update—and to be honest, to get her daily fix. She couldn't *touch*, but that didn't mean she couldn't *look* once in a while. And she hadn't seen him up close and personal in almost twenty-four hours.

"Knock, knock—howdy, howdy. You up for a beer? And have you still got two in your fridge?" She'd supplied them, so he might as well share.

"Don't you know I'd never let you down?" he said, popping his handsome head over the Dutch door, and handing her a *Modelo* with the top already off. Chips and salsa?"

"Do you even need to ask? Come out and join me," she invited.

They each gravitated to "their" Adirondack chair and settled in, almost like they were a real couple.

"So, any news?" Caleb asked.

"Paige just lost her teaching job, but she thinks she's found a way to make some money while we wait for the wedding venue idea to take off."

"Cool. I mean, not the losing her job part, but the new way to make money part."

"How about you?" she asked.

"Good news, actually. Mariah's parents have offered to pay for inpatient treatment, and she's leaving for a rehab center that specializes in eating disorders early next week," Caleb replied. "She didn't fight us on any of it, thank God. I think she knew she needed help but was afraid to reach out—afraid of everything that she's had to deal with."

"That's really good, Caleb. So, will you be moving back to your house, then?"

Caleb nodded. "For a while. That's what's best for Ellie with all the changes—like Mariah coming and then leaving again. I'm sure my little girl is feeling pretty scared."

"I'm so sorry, Caleb. Mariah's been through the wringer, but so have you and Ellie. Let me know if there's anything I can do," Harper said.

"I will. Maybe, spend a little extra time with Ellie?" he asked.

"Absolutely. I'll reach out, I promise," Harper said, and she meant it.

"So, I guess you, and especially Paige, want to know how the pergola thing is coming along," Caleb said, reading her mind.

Harper nodded and took a sip of her *Modelo*. "I'm still stumped as to whether it's a gazebo or a pergola, but what I *really* want to know is, when is it going to be finished?"

"Tomorrow. I'm planning a big reveal. And, maybe, fixing you two hard-working sisters a picnic supper, right in the center of the aspen grove. How do you like them apples?" he said, a smile lighting his deep-set gray eyes.

"Cool! That gives us both something to look forward to. We deserve it—the three of us make a great team." *And they did.* Harper was beyond thrilled that Paige seemed every bit as smitten with Caleb as she was. Whether wearing a toolbelt or driving a front-end loader, Caleb had come through for them in a big way. She admired his positive attitude and his ability to think outside the box. Both of these fine qualities existed in the 'safe' zone. Her other feelings had to be put on the back burner, for now.

"So, tomorrow night, around seven-thirty? I want it to be late enough to show you and Paige the outdoor lights," Caleb said, holding out his beer.

Harper reached over and clinked bottle necks with Caleb. Tonight, they both wore their usual Carhartts and flannel shirts, two peas in a pod. But tomorrow, she might want to dress up for the big reveal. *How long had it been since she'd had anything approaching a date?* It was a little hard to remember.

Harper and Paige were eating breakfast together, her sister's excellent *chilaquiles*. "Caleb says he's throwing us a picnic tonight in the aspen grove as part of his big reveal. Seven-thirty. Let's dress up, give ourselves a treat. Are you in, Paige?"

"Wow, is this my sister talking? I have to admit, it sounds like a lot of fun, and I wish I could. But I'm meeting Ed at Maggie's to go over the details of our Renaissance Faire and get him to sign the contract. He's bringing a couple of other performers along, so it would be hard to reschedule. But please tell Caleb I'm sorry I can't make it."

Harper nodded. "Sure, I will. Good luck tonight, Paige. I hope it all works out the way you're imagining it will."

She carried her breakfast plate to the sink, rinsed it, and left it in the stack. Paige was now in charge of all domestic duties, and it was almost like having a wife. "I'm off to…," Harper started to say, out of force of habit, but she didn't have any immediate plans. It helped a lot that she'd finished installing the automatic watering system. "Hey, I don't have anything that I absolutely have to do today. I don't think that's happened since I set foot on the chicken ranch! And it's been, what, over four months?"

"Whoo-hoo! A day off. I want one of those!" Paige said, sticking her lip out.

"No pouting—and no days off for *you* until after our Renaissance Faire. This is your deal," Harper pointed out.

"Okay, but afterwards, if we make some money, we should do something. Some activity that does not involve my sister wearing Carhartts. Maybe dancing? Or a spa weekend?"

"Uh, yeah, dream on. I'm heading into town, and if I don't find exactly what I'm looking for in Verde Springs, I might head into Santa Fe."

"You're going clothes shopping, aren't you? To try to impress Mr. Toolbelt," Paige said, using her sister's intuition. "And without me, traitor. I hope everything you try on makes you look a little bit fat."

"Not a chance. I'm tanned, and toned, and ready to picnic," Harper drawled.

Paige waved her out the door, already opening her laptop.

Almost giddy inside, Harper was secretly relieved that Paige had other plans, tonight. Maybe now she and Caleb might make some plans of their own. She was dying for another one of his kisses, which she could remember with startling clarity, even though it had been months. *Was that so wrong?* The man *was* divorced—had been for more than two years—and so far, the sudden reappearance of his former spouse had not brought a mountain of joy into his life. *Something had to give, didn't it?*

CHAPTER TWENTY-FOUR

*H*arper showered, shaved her legs, and applied half a bottle of lotion to her desert-dry skin. Then she dressed in a casual cotton sundress, now that the weather had grown reliably warm. She stopped in at Maggie's for a cup of coffee and a blueberry muffin, and since it was after the breakfast rush, she sat at the counter and chatted with Maggie.

"I'm looking for something kind of special to wear tonight. A certain person of the male variety has pretty much only seen me wearing work clothes—mostly, dirty, smelly work clothes."

Maggie paused as she sorted silverware into neat little piles, before rolling them in paper napkins. "Okay. What's the occasion?"

"A picnic. Outdoors, private, in the evening. I'm hoping kissing might be involved," Harper said, unusually forthcoming. But she and Maggie had recently moved into the 'close friends' phase of their relationship, despite their considerable age gap. *It was nice to have friends.*

"Catelyn's Closet has some cute summer things, and nothing too pricey. If you want to knock someone's socks off, you might have to make the run into Santa Fe. I usually avoid it in the summer if I can help it," Maggie said. "It can be a madhouse, especially during Native

Market Week. But don't let that stop you and Paige from checking it out—you definitely should."

Harper nodded, swallowing the last bite of her muffin. "Well, good, I'll start there. I want a nice relaxing day, not a running-around day. I might even take a nap this afternoon so I'm ready for anything."

Maggie yawned, covering her mouth. "Oh, you did have to say the *nap* word. I didn't get much sleep last night, for some reason. This place wears me out, and I'm not getting any younger." She finished making the silverware roll-ups and poured herself a cup of coffee, before making a face and brewing a fresh pot. "Well, have fun. You've worked hard all spring and half the summer. You deserve a break."

Harper nodded. "I completely agree, and it's been a long time coming. Thanks for the coffee, and the heads-up. I'll head over to Catelyn's Closet right now and see if anything catches my eye."

Maggie gave her a tired smile. "Hey, you let me know how it goes, you hear? I'm living vicariously these days. The dating pool in my age bracket could maybe fill one of my coffee mugs."

Harper laughed. "I will, for sure. Thanks, Maggie." Then she headed back to her truck and picked up her phone. She located it on Google Maps and found her way there in less than two minutes. Verde Springs was *that* small.

"Hi, can I help you?" a friendly voice asked. Once Harper's eyes adjusted to the lower light level, she saw a cute redhead standing behind the counter. Presumably, her name was Catelyn.

"Hi, I'm new in town, and I wanted to take a look at what you have to offer. I'm kind of looking for something special to wear tonight."

"Nice! How fancy? Indoor or outdoor?" she asked, moving out from behind the counter and sharing a friendly smile with Harper.

"Outdoor, but not too fancy, and a cute guy might be involved." That was as close as she could come to expressing her intent, without getting really weird with a total stranger. "We're, um…going on a picnic," she added.

"Got it. You should take a look at some of the cute jumpsuits I just got in. They're a great choice for outdoor events because they stay put. A New Mexico wind can send a skirt or dress up over your face—and *that's* never a good look. The fabric is nice, too. Kind of loose and drapey."

In the five months since her last cut and style in Tacoma, Harper's former pixie cut had grown long enough to touch her collar bones. The sun had bleached the ends of her natural light-brown hair to a tawny gold, and the overall effect was now a medium-length shag a la the 1970s, and currently back in style. With the right jewelry and outfit, she could almost pull off cute, feminine, and on-trend. Plus, Paige had tons of great jewelry and she never minded sharing—one of the perks of having a big sister.

"Okay, sure. Show me what you've got. And, if you can, what kind of jewelry I should wear with it."

"I can do that. I love styling people." *So that's what you called it, thought Harper.*

"Now, with that nice tan you've got going, I think you'd look great in this plum color, or this smoky blue. It's outdoors, right? With the sun going down, these are the colors I'd go for. What size are we looking for?" Catelyn asked.

"We are looking for a size four or six. I used to be a size six, but my sister says I look thinner. I have been working my a—really hard, lately."

"Here you go," Catelyn said, carrying four jumpsuits over to the dressing rooms and hanging them on the wall. She'd pulled the blue and the plum in a four and a six. "Try them on and come out and show me. I always give my honest opinion."

Harper closed the dressing room door and slid off her loose sundress, an excellent choice for clothes shopping on a warm day. She held both colors up against her body, trying to imagine herself through Caleb's eyes. The plum was perky and attention-grabbing, even kind of elegant. But the blue was smokier and sexier and would look fantastic with some of Paige's jewelry. *Blue it is.* In a moment of optimism, Harper slipped on the size four and it fit like a glove. Not a tight glove, either, but a soft, clingy glove that allowed her room to move. She even did a variation of a squat, to mimic sitting on the ground, and she didn't hear any seams rip or feel like she was getting a wedgie. It would more than do for tonight, it was *perfect.* Kudos to Catelyn—she knew her stuff.

Harper could pair the jumpsuit with a brushed-denim jean jacket already hanging in her closet and Paige's jewelry. *And perfume?* Something light and not too floral. She didn't want to overdo it and have Caleb die of shock—she wanted him alive and kicking. *Shoes? Damn. She'd forgotten shoes.* She turned the truck around and headed back to the cafe. "I forgot about shoes!" she said, bursting into the door. Thank God the lunch rush hadn't come in yet.

"Taos Footwear makes great sandals. Anyway, you should have a pair for all-purpose events, you know, when you don't want to wear your work boots," Maggie teased. "The market carries a small supply in the back—in towns like Verde Springs, it pays to diversify. If they don't have your size or the style you want, you'll have to run into Santa Fe or Taos, though."

"Thanks, you're a lifesaver."

Harper was happy to possess a strong, slim, athletic build and petite, feminine feet. She found a pair of thin, strappy, 100%-leather sandals in a navy color that would work for tonight, and they'd look great with her usual jeans and t-shirts, too. The store even had a women's size eight in stock. *It seemed to be her lucky day.*

She returned home in time to catch Paige before she left for her own evening out. "Paige, I need help. Look what I bought," she said, pulling out the jumpsuit and sandals. Now I need you to style me. And can I borrow some jewelry?"

"Well, you're lucky I'm still here, because with that gorgeous v-neck jumpsuit you'll definitely need the perfect necklace." Paige opened her dresser and brought out a rectangular wooden box.

Inside, Harper saw a collection of small, sealed plastic bags. "You keep your pretty things in zip-lock baggies? Why?" she asked.

"It prevents the necklaces from getting tangled when I'm traveling, and it helps prevent the silver from tarnishing. But don't worry, it won't take me long to find what I'm looking for," Paige assured her.

What she was looking for turned out to be a chunky, two-strand necklace of sterling silver and lapis that would play well with the color of the jumpsuit. Harper already had a pair of silver-and-lapis earrings she'd picked up on one of her visits to Aunt Sabina in Santa Fe. *Good golly, she felt like Cinderella getting ready for the ball, minus the helpful mice.*

Apparently reading her mind, Paige waived her away with a flick of her hand. "Go away, now, my pretty. Your prince awaits. And Ed awaits at Maggie's, with a handful of other Renaissance folks. I have to go play nice and land us the gig."

Caleb texted that he'd be at the main house at seven-fifteen, and they'd walk over to the aspen grove together. Harper couldn't wait. She was dressed, sandaled, and perfumed. Paige's necklace lay lightly against her tanned chest, and the silver-and-lapis earrings emphasized her firm jaw and dark-blue eyes. She thought, no, she *knew*, she had never looked better. Not even on her...*well, she didn't want to go there tonight. Or possibly, ever again.*

When she heard Caleb's truck pull up, her sense of anticipation rose even higher—and then came crashing down, hard. *Oh, God, what if she'd read it all wrong? What if it wasn't a date? He hadn't said it was a date, and he'd invited her sister to join them! She'd probably misread the entire situation.*

She should go change into her Carhartts and a clean t-shirt, right this minute. As she turned the corner to sprint up the stairs, Caleb walked in with a big wicker picnic basket in one hand. "Hey, where you going, pretty lady? Ready for your picnic dinner?"

"I um, I'm here. Paige isn't. And I don't know what I'm doing," Harper said, turning to face him.

"Well, I think you're coming with me to go sit amongst your aspen trees and eat some good grub. And I have a confession to make: with everything that's been going on, I asked Maggie to pack this for me—so you know it'll be good," he said, holding up the picnic basket, and nicely flexing his bicep.

Caleb looked tall, handsome, and…like a man interested enough to make an effort. He wore a navy-and-white-checked shirt, clean dark jeans, and lace-up suede Oxfords, instead of his usual Carhartts and mud-encrusted work boots. Maybe this *was* a date. At any rate, they both cleaned up pretty well, she was hungry, and there was no time like the present.

Harper came slowly down the stairs. Caleb's hand reached for hers, and they walked out the door and up the garden path that led to the aspen grove. In the early evening light, the tall clumps of ornamental grass looked silvery and shimmery. Puffy cookie-cutter clouds sailed slowly toward the horizon, but the sun still generated a pleasant warmth. As she approached her newly planted border, she caught the warm scents of lavender and rose, amongst the earthier sage and summer grasses. Most of all, she was treated to the sight of the completed pergola, a unique Caleb Johansson design. And he'd completely knocked it out of the park.

Hexagonal in shape, it carried through the theme of 'sixes' that Paige had come up with and Harper had continued. Made of weathered, old, barn beams bleached silver in New Mexico's heat and sunlight, it was massive and elegant. At the moment, the beams overhead were strung with six strands of twinkling white lights radiating like the spokes of a wheel, and at the center was suspended a star-shaped Mexican lantern. It was beyond perfect, and her sister was going to love it. *But it had no roof.*

Caleb set the picnic basket down, pulled out a soft Mexican blanket, and shook it out on the grass. He took Harper's hand and helped her to sit down, then said, "Watch this."

He pulled a fancy remote-control from the wicker basket and pressed a button. Retractable shades began to cover the central portion of the pergola, leaving the other two triangular edges exposed. It was incredibly clever, tailored to their needs, and a work of art.

"Caleb, what? It's incredible! I *love* it. Paige is going to love it, and all of our guests are going to love it, too. How many millions of dollars do we owe you for this work of genius?"

"I'm not gonna lie—the shades cost you a pretty penny. But the wood came from a friend's barn, plus some odds and ends from the two coops that we tore down. The only cost for materials was for transport. I spent some money on the lighting, but I'm giving you a break on labor because I've basically lived here for free for, what, almost a month? You really saved my ass, Harper. This was my way of saying thanks...and that I believe in what you and Paige are doing."

"Well, I guess there's only one thing left to do, then."

"And what's that?" he said.

Come down here and sit beside me on this comfy blanket and I'll show you, she really, really wanted to say. But she had to let Caleb lead the way. *He* was the one with the spontaneously-returning, troubled wife and the newly entangled life—while, for the first time in a decade, *she* was the one with all the freedom. *Harper now intimately understood choosing "it's complicated" as one's relationship status.* Racking her addlepated brain for a response, she settled for, "join me?"

※

Caleb didn't need a more specific invitation. He'd been working side-by-side with Harper all spring and summer, and he hadn't kissed her since Mariah had come back into his life with more baggage than any of them had bargained for. But that didn't mean he hadn't *wanted* to kiss Harper a thousand times in a thousand different places—and he wasn't going to wait any longer.

He sat down across from her, leaned in, and closed the distance. Harper's lips were just as delicious as he remembered, and the painfully long wait made their connection all the sweeter.

"I think we've still got it," Harper said, smiling, when they finally came up for air.

"You think? You're driving me crazy tonight, Harper. You look absolutely gorgeous, and I don't know if I can keep my hands off you."

"Who says I want you to?" she said, sliding her own hands slowly up under the back of his shirt. The touch of her hands on his bare skin was a little bit of heaven, and he groaned in response. Suddenly, Caleb let out a growl and pushed the picnic basket to the side. He gently laid Harper down on the blanket, covering her with his body, one leg on the blanket to take his weight off her. He kissed her face, her neck, her throat, and worked his way slowly south of her collar bones. Then he lifted his head and looked down at her, taking in the beauty of his wildest dream, ready and willing. And he stopped.

Caleb rolled onto his back and stared up at the sky, an impossible shade of blue with the light slowly fading. The protective circle of trees, and scents, and colors, and sounds of the evening turning to night created the perfect setting for making love to the woman he loved. He was beyond ready—but he wasn't *free*—not when the mother of his child was depending on him to be there for her. There had to be a good outcome for Mariah, for Ellie's sake, and *that* had to be his focus. Only then would he be completely able to move forward. *Would Harper wait for him?*

"Harper, God, I want you. *All* of you. But the timing…it isn't right. I can't get… involved right now. Not with Mariah still in rehab, and Ellie not sure when, or if, she'll get her mom back. They both need me right now. You have no idea how sorry I am." Being *caught in a war between his heart and his brain was no place he'd ever wanted to be—and Harper deserved so much more.*

"I know this is really hard. And I know you have to do what you have to do. So, I'll wait for you," Harper told him softly.

For a moment, he could only hold her tight and take in her warmth and her loving heart. He didn't have words for what he felt in this moment.

Like the sensitive, intuitive woman he knew her to be, Harper jumped into the breach. "Well. Now, look at all this food Maggie packed for us. I'm starving. Let's eat," she said, sitting up and turning her attention to the wicker basket. Giving him a moment. *But he didn't need a moment.*

"Hold that thought." Caleb extended his arms, gathering the edges of the blanket to pull over them, surrounding them with a delicious warmth. "We can eat later," he said. "I just want to hold you for a while longer."

CHAPTER TWENTY-FIVE

*C*aleb stopped by the ranch with Ellie the next day, carrying two, large takeout bags from Maggie's. The three of them ate out on the shady patio, Ellie slyly feeding Sunny and Birdy little bites of her hamburger bun under the table.

"So, did you have a good time with your grandparents?" Harper asked Ellie.

"It was alright. Grandpa Bill took me out for ice cream. But… Mama wasn't there. Daddy, how long until she gets back? I miss her."

"Three more weeks. I know, it's a long time to wait, Ellie. We need to be patient," Caleb said, gently.

"But I don't *like* being patient. Why can't I go see her?" Ellie asked.

It seemed impossible to explain why Ellie couldn't see her mother: if he said it was because Mariah was really sick, Ellie would worry; and if Mariah *wasn't* really sick, then why couldn't her family, her daughter, visit her now? He settled for, "because the doctors think that's best, Ellie. We all want Mommy to get better." *Totally lame—and Ellie deserved better.*

"I have an idea, Ellie. My mother was in the hospital for a while when Paige and I were little," Harper said, "about your age, in fact." Their mother had needed to have a hysterectomy and had developed an infection following the surgery. Already a single mother, she was in no shape to take care of two, energetic little girls. "Our grandmother came to stay with us for a whole month. Every afternoon, she'd sit down with us at the kitchen table, and we'd draw, and paint, and stencil, and make "Get Well" messages for our mother."

"That's really sweet," Caleb said, smiling.

"Mom kept them in a manila envelope in her bottom dresser drawer. I don't remember what happened to them," Harper said, thoughtfully.

Ellie went inside to watch an animated show about a fearless, blue-haired girl named Hilda, both dogs in tow. Like most kids of her generation, she'd been technologically proficient since she'd turned three, so they had the patio all to themselves for a while.

"How long ago did she die? I never asked," said Caleb. "But you both must have been pretty young."

Harper nodded. "Yeah, I was still in high school, and Paige was in her last year of college. And that was it—she had to come home to Richmond. Paige had to step up and be the mom, in a way, as well as my big sister. That's why we're so close. We're all we've got—especially now that Sabina is gone."

"Sounds tough. What about your father?" Caleb asked. "Was he ever in the picture?

"Earlier, maybe? I don't remember very much. But he wasn't in the picture at the time Mom died, and neither was my Aunt Sabina. I only got to know my aunt *after* my mother died. According to Sabina, my dad had a hard life and he made some really bad decisions. It sounded like all three of us, my mother and sister and I, were better off without him. And Aunt Sabina agreed—when it came to men, she was a realist."

"It must have been kind of a struggle for your mom, though," Caleb said, shaking his head.

"Yeah, especially when we were little, but by the time we started school, everything seemed to smooth out. My mom was a lot like Paige: smart, ambitious, and creative. She couldn't help but succeed, and we were both lucky to have her as a role model. I miss her so much, and I know Paige does too."

At that moment, they heard the screen door slam, and a grumpy-faced girl came out to plop back down in her chair. Apparently, Hilda hadn't held her interest, tonight.

Turning the focus away from herself and back to Ellie, Harper said, "I'll pick up some art supplies. Maybe you can come over again soon, and we can make your mom some 'Get Well' cards—a whole bunch of 'em."

Ellie nodded, poking a finger at her congealed grilled cheese. She was feeling emotions that would be hard for anyone to process, and a whole lot harder when you'd just turned five.

Harper caught Caleb's eye. *Obviously, the adults had a lot of work to do.* Ellie wasn't in a good place at all, especially with three weeks left to go before Mariah could come home to Verde Springs.

"How about Skyping?" Harper asked. "Or Zoom?

"The Center discouraged it," Caleb said.

"Maybe if you explain that there is another, *little*, person involved, they might make an exception? And maybe it would do Mariah good, too. Anyway, it wouldn't hurt to ask."

Caleb nodded. "Thanks, Harper. I'd better get this girl home and ready for bed."

"Yup. Thanks for coming by. It was so nice to see you, Ellie." Harper gave the little girl a hug, and she clung for a long moment.

"What movie do you want to watch tonight?" she heard Caleb ask, as he picked up a despondent Ellie and carried her in his arms.

"The one about the little gold horse."

"Spirit? Oh, yeah, I like that one, too. Do you want to watch *Riding Free* or *Pony Tails*?

Ellie shrugged and laid her head on Caleb's shoulder, and Harper melted a little inside. As hard as it was, she couldn't help thinking, *he's doing the right thing. Maybe sainthood wasn't out of the question, for either of them.*

After Caleb and Ellie left, Harper retrieved the remote-control he'd given her and called out for her sister. "Paige, put your shoes on and grab a jacket. Then come with me."

"But it's getting dark and there are howling coyotes out there."

"I'll protect you."

"Are you sure about this? Can't it wait until tomorrow?"

"Nope, I have a surprise for you—Caleb and I do. Now, get a move on!"

"I *do* like surprises," Paige said, zipping up her fleece and trailing behind her sister.

Harper led the way to the aspen grove, carrying a propane lantern for atmosphere and personal safety. When they'd nearly reached the aspen grove, she handed the remote-control to Paige. "Here, press this button."

For once, Paige did as she was told, and the grove was instantly flooded with soft, warm light—the kind of light that would look beautiful on a wedding brochure. *And that, as Harper had learned from personal experience, really enhanced the mood...*

"Oh. My. God. It's amazing!" Paige walked around with her mouth hanging open for so long that Harper was afraid the local moths might settle in.

"And that's not all. Press the button on the upper right-hand corner," Harper said.

Paige did, and the retractable shades moved slowly and silently across the expanse, shutting out the stars as well as the possibility of rain. "Caleb says we can add long curtains made from Suncloth fabric at each post, so they can be pulled closed or partially closed if it's windy or raining sideways. What do you think? Is it anything like you imagined?"

Paige shook her head. "It's so much *better* than I imagined. Your boyfriend is a genius."

"I know. He's not my boyfriend—but I think so, too."

CHAPTER TWENTY-SIX

A Renaissance Faire had come to the ranch, complete with colorful, striped tents, an *allée* of craft and food booths, as well as their host booth, prominently featuring The Inn at Verde Springs merchandise. Maggie's Café had contributed a booth as well, which Paige, Harper, and Caleb considered the dietary 'safe zone' of fresh salads and veggie wraps. But, according to Ed, the Faire's patrons tended to gravitate heavily toward barbecued turkey legs, corn on a stick, and savory Cornish pasties. *Apparently, some folks knew how to read the room.* There were a few popular restaurants from nearby towns, offering the usual tacos, enchiladas, and New Mexico's ever-popular Frito pie. And altogether, the cornucopia of scents was indescribably delicious.

Paige held a hand-lettered sign that read, "Seek Ye Your Pleasure." Standing precariously on a step ladder, she hung it above the entrance to the food stalls, then stepped firmly back on the ground. The performers and volunteers had proved to be an energetic work crew, competently erecting most of the tents and booths last night, and finishing up this morning. Now, a group of players and performers practiced their skills in the shade of New Mexico locusts and box elders, getting into character for the evening to come. Juggling pins flew through the air, men with swords sparred in mock duels, and Paige chewed on her bottom lip, wondering if anything could be missing.

"Hey, Paige! Looks like it's going to be a great event!" Ed greeted her, looking majestic in his lordly outfit. Maybe he'd just been born in the wrong century, or she had. He was a world away from her usual type—not that her previous "type" had brought her lasting happiness or security. *So, why had her eyes been searching the grounds for him?* Ed had been extremely helpful throughout the planning and organizing of the Faire, for which she was extremely grateful. Sure, gratitude— that's probably all it was—and she knew what to do.

"Hi, Ed. I wanted to thank you for all the help and guidance you've given me. I wouldn't have even known what a Renaissance fair was without you and your group, and I definitely wouldn't have known how to pull one off."

"Always happy to help," he said, tipping his hat. "Let me know if you need anything. Well, I should probably keep moving. I have quite a few people to check in with." He smiled and moved on, glancing back once to give her a thumb's up. *The man had enormous hands. Would that be a bad thing or a good thing?* Paige gave a little shudder. Maybe she *should* have taken her sister's suggestion and had a summer fling during last month's supermoon, so she could get her ya-yas out and make an exclusively rational decision when it came to the man she wanted in her life.

Her sister appeared to be temporarily hiding out in one of the Coop Studios, dressing the beds with fresh linens for their weekend guests—since Verde Springs still lacked a hotel, most of the perform- ers would be staying onsite. After Caleb had finished wiring the five spaces for electricity, she and Harper had gone on a shopping spree at a small appliance store and an office supply store. Each studio now had its own bar with a variety of coffees and teas and a small, vintage-reproduction refrigerator. In the opposite corner, they'd set up a copier/printer and a linear bar top with plug-ins for charging laptops and phones. Every once in a while, Paige watched Harper poke her head out, then withdraw it again like a turtle. Maybe her sister would be in a more festive mood, tomorrow. But Harper had contributed her green thumb and design skills, which Paige appreciated.

Her sister had claimed one of the booths to use as a flower stall and ordered five-gallon buckets of carnations, daisies, lilies, thornless roses, and stems of eucalyptus and salal. She'd ordered some greenery to make wreaths and garlands and had displayed them both throughout the food court tables. Harper had also spent an entire day planting hundreds of inexpensive marigolds in bright yellow, lining the path from the parking area to the Renaissance grounds. After a ton of work, it was all looking quite a bit like the nicest inspirational photos they'd pulled from Pinterest, and Paige was pleased.

Caleb had mastered the art of outdoor lighting, and they would open tonight with the confidence that disaster in the form of a blackout would not shortly follow. It was all going according to plan—except that Caleb wouldn't be here with his toolbelt, electrical tape, and and Man-Who-Knows-All-Things-skillset, in case anything went wrong.

Mariah was coming home from the treatment center, today, and Caleb was picking her up. Then, he'd need to stay at the house to smooth any bumps between Mariah and her daughter, and make sure that Mariah's mother, Kate Henderson, had everything she needed. Re-entry was always hard—but re-entry with your ex-husband and daughter after only recently reconnecting, must be incredibly stressful, and Caleb and Mariah both had a full helping. Maybe that was another reason her sister was focused on her work, tonight. Harper was no doubt preoccupied with how Caleb and Ellie were handling everything—and, of course, missing them.

Harper and Mr. Toolbelt had seemed nearly inseparable for the last few weeks, despite their current hands-off policy. *Was her sister concerned that Caleb might reconcile with his former wife?* On that score, Paige was sure that Harper had nothing to worry about. She'd never seen two people more suited to each other, or completely crazy about each other. She wasn't jealous—that wouldn't be sisterly—but she was self-aware enough to know that she wanted a strong connection like the one Harper had with Caleb. Now in her late thirties, Paige was beginning to doubt she'd ever find it.

"There you are, Paige. I forgot to ask if you'd mind saving a dance for me at the ball tomorrow night? I promise I won't step on your toes. I'm pretty light on my feet for someone my size." Ed blushed a little, which made both of them feel awkward.

He really was a sweet man—but he towered over her, and she was a little afraid of his lumberjack beard. She'd never met anyone remotely like him in her self-contained university bubble. *Maybe that's why she felt completely off her game around him.*

"Sure, I'd be happy to," Paige smiled. "How do you think it's going so far? Are we on track to open the gates at five?"

"I think so. Based on your advertising efforts, how many people do you think we're going to get tonight?" he asked.

"No idea. We could run out of food, or have too much food, but I did the best I could." Paige had plastered fliers all over Verde

Springs, Española, Taos, and Santa Fe, as well as the smaller, nearby town of Pecos. She'd blitzed social media as well—and Ed had put out the word to all his contacts in the Renaissance Community in New Mexico, Texas, Arizona, and Colorado, via a mass email. Paige hoped they'd get a few more last-minute bookings, even though Harper had promised to take care of things in the main house this weekend, not her usual comfort zone.

Paige wanted and needed the Faire to be a success. It was their first big event, for one thing. And she'd gotten to know some of the Rennies and found them to be good people and a lot of fun. More than anything else, the Faire was a ready-made PR opportunity: they'd have hundreds, or it they were lucky, upwards of a thousand people strolling the grounds and visiting the Inn at Verde Springs booth, asking questions, taking brochures, buying mugs, or wearing their custom t-shirts. Paige wanted at least a few of those people to book their weddings at the Inn. *If she couldn't come up with her own happily-ever-after, she could help someone else find theirs.*

At 4:45, a steady stream of cars began coming up the ranch driveway and pulling into a field that had been mown short to reduce the fire hazard from hot tailpipes encountering dried pasture grass. She watched from her merch booth as they trickled through the gate in twos and threes. Colorful jesters in full Renaissance garb greeted them and pointed out the attractions, and delicious scents emanated from the food court. But Paige hesitated to leave her booth to go grab something for herself. As if anticipating her dilemma, one of the girls from Maggie's came over, a salad and a wrap in hand. She pulled two juice spritzers out of her apron pocket and set everything on the folding table at the back of the booth. "For you and Harper, Maggie said. She figured you might not have taken time to eat."

"Oh, God, how I love that woman! Thank you so much, and please thank Maggie, too. I'll text Harper and let her know. She's up in the Coop Studios. Thanks again."

As if she'd heard the siren's call, or, knowing her sister, smelled food, Harper soon came down and joined her. "Wow, Maggie rocks! Which do you want? The wrap, or the salad?"

"Want to split them?" Paige asked.

"Sure. Whatever you want," Harper said. She sat down, grabbed a spritzer, popped the top off, and downed half of it in a single swallow.

"Are you okay?" Paige asked. "You don't seem very…festive."

Harper nodded. "Yeah. I'm just worried about Caleb and Ellie. And Mariah, of course. I hope she's feeling better and getting back on track. It's such a tough situation for all three of them."

"And for you, too. Hang in there. Caleb loves you."

"He's never said it."

"What?" Paige asked.

"You know—the three little words?" Harper said. "We'd just barely gotten started when he had to put the brakes on, which I understand. Since then, things between us have been tricky. And I guess, after Kevin, I need to hear it just once," Harper said. She finished her meal and headed back up to the Coop Studios to close up shop.

Friday night's Faire was well attended, but Paige and Ed expected even bigger things tomorrow, their first full day. Saturday was the big draw, ending with a formal costume ball in the big tent, in the evening.

And it would be their only full day, as they'd decided to end the Faire at two o'clock on Sunday. Everyone had lives they needed to get back to, participants and spectators alike. Paige closed her eyes and willed her body to sleep. She needed to be "on," one hundred percent—tomorrow would be a very long day.

CHAPTER TWENTY-SEVEN

*T*he crowd streamed continuously through the gate in impressive numbers and ticket sales looked promising. Paige had spoken to dozens of people yesterday, handing out brochures and drawing their attention to large photographs of the aspen grove wedding circle and the entry garden, arranged on table-top easels. She was quick to catch those meaningful glances between couples, and even quicker to hand out her new, personalized, "event planner" business cards. Today, the attendance was sure to be double or triple that of yesterday's total—and Paige wanted to book a wedding so badly she could taste it.

Maggie and her girls hurried to fill food orders, as Harper installed several groups of guests in the main house. The Inn was hosting two couples who'd driven down from Colorado Springs, and a couple of the Renaissance performers who were splurging on cushier digs than the Coop Studios. As of tonight, all of their rooms were full. Beyond food, the Renaissance music venue, as well as strolling minstrels, had turned out to be the biggest draw for the crowds, and Paige made a mental note to add even more musical groups if she and Harper decided to do this again. *Who was she kidding? She was hooked.*

When afternoon rolled around and her growling stomach became audible to random passersby, she gave up her resistance and strode across to the food booth that sold turkey legs. The mouth-watering smell of grilled birds had been driving her crazy for two days, and she wanted a taste almost as much as she wanted to book a wedding—which is why Ed found her walking back to her booth, gnawing on a turkey leg, with corn-on-a-stick in her other hand.

"That's the spirit!" he said, laughing. "Here, let me help you carry something," he said, taking the butter-saturated corn-on-a-stick and walking with her.

When they reached the merch booth, he hung around for a while, chatting. It was cool and shady under the tent, which is why she'd cleverly planned to spend most of her time here.

"How are things going?" he asked. "The draw seems better than I expected. Are you getting any further bookings, or at least interest?"

Paige found it disconcerting to gnaw on a giant turkey leg in front of a man she might possibly be attracted to, so she discreetly covered it with a paper napkin and wiped her mouth with another. "I'm not sure. People are distracted—there's so much to see and do here, in no small part due to you. But I'm pushing the wedding venue idea pretty hard. Fingers crossed I'll get at least a couple of bookings out of this event. At least, that's the plan."

"Nice! I hope so, too. You've worked really hard for this, Paige. This is lovely," he said, gesturing to the blown-up photo of the aspen grove.

"Would you like to see it in person?" she asked. "I could use a walk to stretch my legs. Come on, I'll take you there."

Following her, Ed waggled his head to the beat of silent music. "Ah, the title of a classic Mavis Staples song. I'll take you there…I'll take you there," he sang a few bars in a surprisingly pleasant baritone.

"So, you can play a dozen musical instruments, you can dance and sing, and help organize Renaissance fairs. "And you drive a Porsche," teased Paige. "What aren't you telling me? Do you own an international tech startup? Are you the secret love child of Frank Sinatra?"

Ed smiled mysteriously, "I thought you were going to show me some trees?"

The afternoon slid slowly into evening as only a late-summer day can, and Paige finally began to relax. Spending an hour with Ed had helped—he was good company and startlingly intelligent, qualities she'd always found extremely attractive in a man. Now she was back at the merch booth, finding interest from a few lovebirds, including two in-character Renaissance players, Pippa and Thor, who were so adorably smitten with each other that she could almost hear them cooing.

The ranch's fields glowed golden under clear blue skies, and the scent of sweetgrass and sage in the air added to the heady atmosphere. As Paige finally finished her corn-on-a-stick, Maggie came over for a chat, bringing with her a tall glass of lavender lemonade for Paige, just what she needed. As Harper constantly, well, harped, since relocating to New Mexico, "hydrate, hydrate, hydrate." It was the only way to prevent wrinkles, and in her late thirties, it was something to keep in mind.

At six-thirty, Paige packed up her merchandise and brochures, carefully slipping the blown-up photographs back into their plastic sleeves and storing everything under the skirt of the folding table. Then she headed back to the house to change. *What exactly did a modern businesswoman wear to a Renaissance Ball?*

She settled for a long, multi-color, crinkle skirt, a velvet, scoop-necked tunic blouse in midnight blue, and her suede ankle boots. Then, she paired the outfit with the widest leather belt she had in her closet. *Not half bad.* Her breasts were on the small side, so even wearing the low-cut top, she didn't look like a medieval serving wench. She left her shoulder-length hair loose, but decided that if Harper had any daisies left, she'd tuck some in somewhere. She'd only agreed to one dance with Ed. Then, she'd mingle and schmooze, two activities she'd been born for.

When she entered the main tent, she discovered that a hundred little elves had unleashed their supernatural magic. Tiny white lights hung in the air above the dance floor, and all the garlands and wreathes showed off Harper's botanical handiwork. The musicians were already warming up on the small stage. *Actual* serving wenches strolled by with cups of mead, which had required a pricey, special license from San Miguel County's Liquor Control Board. And tonight, she was going to dance.

Paige gracefully accepted a cup of mead and wandered onto the dance floor, captured by the spell of the warm summer night. As the crowd surged onto the dance floor, the medieval music began in earnest. She should move back to the edge of the crowd and look for Ed—maybe even grab her camera and take some candid shots of all the beautiful people having fun. But, somewhere along the way, "PR-Paige" had left the tent.

When a warm hand touched the small of her back, she turned around to meet Ed's mischievous brown eyes. "Hey, Paige. Let me look at you." Taking her hand, he gave her a twirl. "Ah, you're the loveliest lady at the ball. May I have this dance?"

"Why, yes, kind Sir. You may," she said, swallowing the last of her mead and setting her glass down on an empty tray.

Ed led her into a waltz, and he wasn't blowing smoke—he *was* light on his feet. The waltz turned into a country dance, with men and women taking opposite sides of the dance floor, coming together in the middle, and then whirling away again. Many dances and many glasses of mead later, Ed held her close as they swayed to an old ballad, and Paige felt the warmth of something completely unexpected: *desire.* She looked up at Ed's face, he looked down into her eyes, and something definitely sparky flared between them in the magic of the night. He lowered his head and met her lips in a soft kiss, and Paige clung to him for a moment. *Why did this feel so right? This was Ed, The Renaissance Guy, currently wearing stockings and britches. Ed, the man with the giant hands, who towered over her slight frame. Was it just the mead?*

Suddenly, she had to be sure. Paige placed her hands on the back of his neck and pressed her lips against his. Ed responded, holding her tight in his strong arms, and suddenly, she was floating...

Many, hazy hours later, Paige awoke with a horribly pounding headache. She stretched out a hand and encountered the huge sleeping form of Ed Barrett, naked from the waist up. The man had excellent chest hair, she noted in the soft glow of her bedside lamp, but that was beyond the point. Then came a moment of startling clarity: Paige lifted up the sheet to be sure, and *Dear God*, he was naked there, too. And so was she—she'd had sex with the Renaissance man of her own volition. *She might possibly have even initiated it*, she thought through her mead-induced haze. She remembered…that she'd wanted to show him the main house…then, the second floor…then, her room. And then, her bed. But, after that? Paige's memory went blank. She blamed the mead.

Paige slid quietly out of bed and threw on her light summer robe, then she crept out of the room and tiptoed down the stairs. She needed pain relief in the worst way, the kitchen was black as night, and she didn't know where Harper kept her over-the-counter pain relievers.

Then, out of the murky darkness she heard, "Are you going to make a habit out of sleeping with our business associates, or was this a one-off?"

"Jeezus, Harper! You took ten years off of my life, sitting there in the dark. Shut up and get me some ibuprofen—and don't *ever* let me drink mead again. I am *not* a seasoned drinker of Medieval beverages, and I don't ever plan to become one."

Harper got up from the table and came back with a bottle of ibuprofen and a tall glass of water. "Noted. So, do you want to hear some *good* news?" she asked.

"Only if you can tell me using your indoor voice," Paige whispered, sliding carefully onto a bar stool.

"We have *four* wedding inquiries—and I think three of them could be serious. One is that Renaissance couple that you were talking to forever."

"Pippa and Thor. They're very cute," she replied, without enthusiasm. "No, that's really good—and I'll be ecstatic about it when my brain is working again. Harper, I slept with Ed. ED!"

"Yes, I heard," Harper said. "It seemed like you were enjoying yourself, and visa-versa. Ed's got quite the baritone—it's amazing how well sound travels in an old house."

"*Did I?* I honestly can't remember much. But everything seems to feel okay," Paige said, thoughtfully. "So, *that* happened. Of course, I'll make him a nice breakfast—it's only polite. But *then* what do I do with him?"

"I believe you made *that* bed all on your own. Speaking of, I'm going back to mine," Harper said, with an elaborate yawn. "I'm glad we don't have any cows to milk, because I'm not getting up at the crack of dawn, or anytime soon."

CHAPTER TWENTY-EIGHT

Two weeks later...

*H*arper's foggy pre-dawn brain was jolted into alertness by a sound she hoped was from a receding nightmare. *It wasn't.* Er-er-er-er-errrr!!! ER-ER-ER-ER-ERRRR!!! it screeched. *Whatever happened to a nice, polite cock-a-doodle-doo?* On par in decibels with a pack of rottweilers, the terrible noise of a rooster crowing at an ungodly hour made it impossible for Harper to return to sleep.

Wearing her shamelessly pink *Sleepless in Seattle* night-shirt, she yawned and stared out the window directly into her rosy desert willow. Eye-level with her newly resident noisemaker, Harper had a revelation: apparently, roosters *can* fly.

"Hey, buddy, go back to wherever you came from and I promise not to tell anyone. Seriously, your GPS is off or something. There hasn't been a hen around here in a couple of decades. Now, scram."

"Er-er-er-er-errrr.   ER-ER-ER-ER-   ERRRR," was   the noisemaker's response.

"Are you lost?" she asked the rooster. "I can ask around at Maggie's when I head into town." Harper seriously doubted her colorful alarm clock had arrived as another drive-by drop-off—but just in case, she'd give the closest animal shelter a call and ask if they accepted barnyard animals. *Good God—that would mean she'd have to catch him.* At least the water fountain Caleb had recently reinstalled in the entry garden would keep the rooster from becoming a roast chicken this afternoon in the late-summer heat. *Although, if he didn't knock it off, or he gave a repeat performance, the possibility was mighty tempting..*

While Harper was hand-watering a newly installed border—*Artemisia* 'Powis Castle' and *Helianthemum* 'Henfield Brilliant'—the rooster fluttered down from his perch in the desert willow to peck in the pea gravel at her feet. Reaching into her pocket, she pulled out an oat-and-honey granola bar, tore open the wrapper, and shared some with her early-morning guest. After all, she was in the hospitality business, and he seemed to appreciate her generosity.

She put her spiral-coiled hose away and made her way to the kitchen door. Kicking off her garden clogs, she finished her coffee, drank her quota of spring-water in a conscientious effort to stay hydrated, and pondered the situation at hand. As decorative as the rooster seemed, in an interesting throwback to the old chicken ranch, he didn't belong here. She rinsed out her coffee cup and washed and dried hands. Might as well find out who the fellow belonged to. But first, she needed to snap his mugshot.

Ten minutes later, she sat at her desk in the living room/office and typed out a brief flier advertising a handsome rooster, along with her contact details. After printing a couple of copies—Verde Springs wasn't all that big—she grabbed her purse and keys and headed into town.

"Hey, Maggie. How's it going?" Harper asked, cheerfully.

"Not bad at all. Just finishing the breakfast rush. *You're* up and about early," Maggie said, expertly rolling up a breakfast burrito.

Harper thought it looked uncannily like swaddling a newborn.

"I guess I am. Even got my morning watering done, too. I woke up at the crack of dawn, thanks to an early visitor." Harper held out the flier, which featured the rooster's photo, like a wanted poster.

Maggie peered closely, then smiled. "Oh, yeah, that's *Capitán*. He gets around. Miguel will be thrilled—he loves that rooster like a son. Speaking of, do you want me to give him a call?"

"That would be great. I've already fed and watered him, in a manner of speaking, so I'm guessing he's going to stick around at least for a little while. Last I saw him, he'd flown back up into my desert willow for a snooze."

"Okay. As soon as I finish getting this last ticket out, I'll take a break with you and make the call."

Half an hour later, as Harper and Maggie sat chatting and sipping tall iced-teas, a nice-looking, older, Hispanic man strode in the door and looked around for Maggie. When she waved him over to their table, he nodded to Harper and slid into the booth.

"Good morning. Miguel Rodriguez." He reached out his hand and shook hers. "I hear you have my rooster," he said to Harper. Then, "*Gracias*, Maggie."

"*De nada.* I'd better get back to work. See you all later," she said, heading through the swinging doors into the kitchen.

Picking up the thread, Harper smiled. "Well, that's what I hear, although he didn't tell me his name. I'm Harper Crawley. My sister and I have taken over the old chicken ranch just off the county road. Your 'friend' woke me up this morning. He's taken a liking to my garden—especially the top of my desert willow, which sits right outside my bedroom window. If you'd like to follow me, you're welcome to take him home."

"*Capitán* is a wanderer—it's in his blood. He follows me all over the ranch, but the minute I turn my back, he's off on a little walkabout to keep up with the neighborhood gossip. He usually comes home by sundown, but sometimes, I have to go and get him." Miguel shrugged, seemingly untroubled by his wandering rooster.

"I like the name, *Capitán*," Harper said.

"He's named for where I got him from—in Lincoln County there's a town called *Capitán*, right at the base of the Sacramento Mountains. It's pretty small, but I have an uncle there who raises prize-winning roosters. This *Capitán* is a Java-Phoenix cross. Pretty fancy."

"He is a handsome fellow," Harper agreed. "And he didn't seem aggressive at all."

Miguel shook his head. "My uncle's birds are always friendly and easy to work with, otherwise, they don't have a long life," he said, gesturing a chopping motion. "Well, I'm ready to go if you are—but I won't need to follow you, I know how to get there. As the crow flies, my own ranch isn't too far away. We're almost neighbors."

"Wow! Who knew? It's so nice to meet you, Miguel. Well, I'll head out, now, and I'll see you in a few minutes.."

*

Harper sat on the low adobe wall that flanked the patio, keeping an eye on Miguel's wandering rooster and watching the ranch drive for a vehicle. Soon enough, a turquoise Ford-100 Ranger came slowly up the ranch drive. It slowed, momentarily, near the Coops, but the engine remained idling. Then the truck proceeded toward the house and rolled to a stop.

"I like what you've done with the place," Miguel said, after joining Harper on the patio. When the big bird saw Miguel, it hopped over and circled his feet, clucking in a very un-rooster-like way, obviously pleased to see him.

"There's my *gallito*," Miguel said. "Haven't I told you not to go wandering? Someday, someone's going to make *arroz con pollo* out of you."

Capitán turned his back on Miguel as if offended, and began pecking at her newly planted rock roses. They were almost too easy to pull out of the loose soil, but she could always plant more. "So, you've been here before?" Harper asked, ignoring the rooster. "Come and sit in the shade. We can have some lemonade on the patio."

Miguel followed her and took a seat on the comfortable furniture. "*Que bonita. Gracias.* Actually, you know, I worked for your auntie—my wife and I both did, when we were first married. Alicia and I had a little house in town, but we came out here every day and worked hard. We saved a little money and took over her father's place when he was ready to let it go. It's just to the west of here," he said, pointing with his arm.

"Really? It's so great to meet someone who knew my Aunt Sabina, when she lived here. Did you both work with the poultry operation?" Harper asked.

"Yes, some, when she needed the help. Alicia worked mostly in the house—my wife loved to cook. She's passed on, now."

"I'm sorry. My condolences, Miguel," Harper said.

"*Gracias.*" Miguel nodded. "I handled the general maintenance, and I worked on the small orchard your auntie was trying to bring back." He gestured vaguely in the distance, beyond the house. I did some grafting, but mostly, I planted new trees, trying to find rootstocks that were drought-tolerant and late bloomers that could withstand a spring freeze. But we wanted fruit that tasted good, too."

"This is a pretty big place, but I'm not aware of any orchard," Harper said, frowning. "Maybe it's gone, or overgrown? I'm curious, though—what kinds of trees she had, then."

Miguel nodded. "Peaches, apricots, Santa Rosa plums, and those old Italian plums, the ones that're almost black on the outside. Some heirloom varieties too. Tried pomegranates, but they didn't make it even one season up here. Same with olives," he said, with a shrug. "Too cold in the winter. Climate might be different, now. It's plenty warm, these days."

"That's fascinating. I've been so busy getting the house, the Coops, and the gardens put in, I haven't had too much time to explore everything. Fifty-six acres is a lot of ground to cover, and I've been concentrating on these few acres around the main house. I'm so glad we've connected, Miguel."

"*Capitán* must have had the right idea, coming all the way over here. Maybe, it was meant to be," he said, smiling. "So, you haven't found the peaches yet? Because, by now, the birds have."

"No, I haven't found the peaches. Will you show me?" she asked, excited about the possibility of fresh fruit right in her own backyard.

"Of course. One moment." Miguel went back to his truck and pulled out a couple of plastic shopping bags. "Maybe we'll need these. *Capitán*, you stay put, *gallito*."

Harper went along after Miguel, down the brushy slope behind the main house, not following any discernable path. The lay of the land, in any other climate, would lead naturally toward a water course—and there must be *some* subterranean water because a line of scrappy trees followed the lowest point of the small ravine. Just above the natural streambed, now perpetually dry, a small stand of trees came into view. What Harper had presumed from a distance to be a locust grove turned out to be the remnants of a tiny home orchard, the trees gnarled and full of hundreds of suckers, but still producing fruit.

Their approach startled a flock of hungry birds into flight, probably annoyed to be chased away from the succulent fruit. The warm mid-day air was perfumed with the indescribably sweet scent of drying apricots, from handfuls of small fruits remaining on the trees. Miguel moved to another small tree, reached up and pulled a Santa Rosa plum, and squeezed it with his fingers. "Not quite ripe, yet, but it will come. The Italian plums after that."

The freestone peaches were mostly over-ripe, and probably not good for much more than making jam. Miguel held out a bag to Harper, and kept one for himself. "Do you mind?"

"No, of course not! I'd *love* it if you could pick as much fruit as you want, and come back anytime. We're neighbors—and we wouldn't be here now if you hadn't shown me the orchard. This is amazing!" Harper bit into a blemish-free ripe peach and the juice dripped onto her hand

and ran down her arm as far as the crook of her elbow, but it was worth it. She'd never be able to tolerate a store-bought peach again. A New Mexico ripe peach was pretty much heaven in a stone fruit.

After they walked back to Miguel's truck, they exchanged numbers. "I'll give you a call sometime. I could help you get those old trees into shape, but not now. Winter is pruning time." He paused. "Maybe I can help you out in other ways, whenever you're swamped. I've always been pretty good with plants. You know, I really looked up to your auntie, managing this big place, mostly by herself. Sabina Crawley was a strong woman—*una mujer fuerte*—and a very kind person, too."

"I would love that, Miguel. And thank you for what you said about my aunt. Did you know my Uncle Hugh, too?" Harper asked.

"Only by poor reputation. *Mala.* People didn't think too much of him, leaving his woman like that. She had another fella hanging around here for most of a summer, before he took off, too. But in Verde Springs, we stick by each other. When your auntie was left in a bad way, lots of people helped her out—and she returned the favor plenty of times."

"That's so nice to hear. I didn't know my aunt well when I was growing up. I only got to know her later, as an adult, after she was living in Santa Fe. Believe it or not, my sister and I didn't even know about this place. Sabina had mentioned, a few times, that she and Uncle Hugh had once raised chickens. But neither of us had any idea she'd held onto the ranch all these years—and we *definitely* never thought that *we'd* end up here."

"Maybe that was God's plan. Maybe this is where you need to be." He smiled and turned his attention to the rooster. "Okay, *Capitán,* let's go home." He opened the driver's side door of the truck and the rooster loaded up just like a well-trained dog. "I'll be in touch," Miguel said with a final wave.

Well, that was interesting. Now, she had at least a partial answer to her need for help and advice, and another connection in the small Verde Springs community. *All thanks to a rooster with wanderlust.*

She couldn't wait to tell Paige about Miguel, and to show her the orchard. But with Paige out of town, that would have to wait. She smiled, thinking of the turn her morning had taken—strange, but good. *And who was the 'fella' Sabina had hanging around, long after Hugh left? Her aunt had never mentioned him.* Before all the fruit was spoiled, she should make a peach cobbler and take it to Miguel. Although peach cobbler wasn't in her limited repertoire, there had to be a YouTube video.

CHAPTER TWENTY-NINE

*P*aige had been gone for a few weeks, back to Virginia to pack up and sell her condo, leaving Harper to manage the Inn. Breakfast and lunch were easy. Harper had learned a lot from watching her sister—and from watching *Cook's Country* reruns late at night when Caleb was someplace other than in her bed. Guests were on their own for dinner, although she tried to gently steer them toward Maggie's, or to *Los Olivos* if they wanted something fancier. The best idea she'd come up with, all by herself, was 'The Happy Hour Charcuterie Board,' which was really just a bunch of meats and cheeses, olives, crackers, and fresh New Mexico pecans. She made a mental note to plant a couple of rows of raspberries and blueberries for her guests when she expanded the kitchen garden. *Mora raspberries were culinarily famous, and Mora wasn't far away, as the crow flies.*

Caleb was still spending lots of time with both Mariah and Ellie, he'd said, on the rare occasions when he had time to talk on the phone. He'd finished all of the work at the ranch, and they were waiting for Paige's house to sell and close escrow, before they could pay him in full for the work on the pergola. Paige had it all worked out on a spreadsheet, divided equally between them, fifty-fifty.

As agreed, Caleb was keeping his distance, but she and Paige talked every day. Her sister was a firm believer in micro-managing, which sometimes annoyed the heck out of Harper. But right now, she was depending on Paige's business sense to make their B&B/wedding venue/creative workshop enterprise a success. The Inn's Renaissance Faire had been a Godsend in terms of getting a lot of people out to see their new venture, but renting tents and other equipment, as well as paying the performers, had made it expensive to host. And Paige was still working on the final spreadsheet. Harper knew they hadn't *lost* money, but she wasn't sure how much of a profit they'd made, or what they'd do with the money, if they had it.

Her phone buzzed. *Paige calling again.* "I've wrapped everything up here, arranged for shipping, and am anxious to get back to the ranch. The title company expects it'll close escrow a few days early, so I changed my flight to come home tomorrow."

"That's fan-freaking-tastic. With the three couples from Houston staying at the Inn, and the photographers staying in two of the Coop Studios for a week, I'm just barely coping—so, I will gladly hand my kitchen duties back to you. Do you need me to pick you up?" Harper asked.

"Thanks, but no. I'm renting a car at the airport. I'm going to browse all the used-car lots and spend my real estate windfall on a new set of wheels. If I don't find something in Albuquerque, I might spend the night and then check out cars in Santa Fe the next day. But I'll let you know either way."

"I get it—you're on a mission, so, I guess we'll see you when we see you."

There was only one more loose end—Caleb. Harper hadn't spoken to him for a few days. And, she needed to come up with something for tomorrow's lunch for the Inn's guests. Although as a rule, the Inn didn't provide lunch on-site, her guests had requested a working lunch, and she'd said she'd see what she could do. She'd kill two birds with one stone and beg him, again, for his mother's lasagna recipe.

"Johansson," he answered, somewhat abruptly.

"Caleb, it's *me*."

"Oh, sorry, Harper. I'm out in the shop, working on some custom shelving for a client. How are things at the ranch?"

"Good, so far. But Paige is coming home either tomorrow or the next day. She's flying into Albuquerque, then going car shopping."

"Tell her I wish her luck," Caleb said.

"Okay, I will. So, how are things with you?" she asked.

"Mariah seems to be in a better place. She's eating well and going to a group meeting in Santa Fe three times a week. She checks in with her counselor every day. But, even with all that, she's still finding lots of time to spend with Ellie. Those two really missed each other, and it's good to see them getting back on track."

"That's good. How are the two of you getting along?" she asked.

"We're getting along, and that's a good thing," Caleb said. "Try not to read too much into this, okay? There's only *you*. There are just some things I'm helping Mariah deal with—because she means a lot to me. And I want Ellie and her mom to have the best possible chance for a good relationship."

"I know. I just miss you. And...I really want your lasagna recipe," Harper confessed.

Caleb laughed. "That, you can have. I'll email it to you after I clean up, here. The secret is to scrape up all those crispy bits when you're done browning the meat, and don't skimp on the mozzarella."

"Thanks. I'll save you a piece. Say 'hi' to Ellie for me. Mariah, too," she added.

"Yep. Okay, I'd better get back to it. Speaking of Mariah, she said she feels terrible about what happened, before. She feels like she let you down, and Paige, too."

"Oh, my gosh! Tell her not to worry, Caleb. Seriously. She was dealing with a lot. And, to tell the truth, during the couple of hours we worked together, she did a *great* job. She's a really hard worker."

"Okay, I'll tell her," Caleb said. "I have to go, now, Harper."

Paige looked out the window of the 747 jet as they flew right nearly over the length of the Sangre de Cristos. Then, dropping gradually in altitude, they followed the wide, meandering Rio Grande, flanked by the green path of the Bosque, and descended into Albuquerque. The woman sitting next to her was speaking to someone on the phone in Spanish. Paige's recently adopted state wasn't exactly *new*—and as of the treaty signed in 1848, it was no longer Mexico. It seemed to be some intriguing combination of ancient cultures, south-of-the-border flavor, and a laid-back, creative spirit that she was slowly learning to appreciate. More than that, she could feel it *changing* her. She was no longer the person she used to be.

Besides, there was nothing left for her in Virginia. Dan was happily remarried, and he and his new wife were planning to start a family. Her job was gone, and with it, any chance she had of securing tenure. And now, her former home, the condo she'd lived in since she and Dan had ended their nine-year marriage, was gone, too. It was time to make a fresh start, and part of that was buying a car, something ranchworthy but economical. There was no time like the present, which meant she'd be browsing used-car lots on the slow route back "home." Surprisingly, after such a short time, it *did* feel like home. While some people might argue that, with fifty-six neglected acres, they'd bitten off more than they could chew, Paige thought the ranch was exactly the kind of project that she and her sister needed to carve out a new life. It was almost as if Aunt Sabina had known she and her sister had both needed a new place to call home, and she was beyond grateful.

Google helpfully located several used-car lots clustered along Fourth Street, so she started there.

Several unproductive hours later, Paige found a little hole-in-the-wall taqueria that her sister would be crazy about. Two *al pastor* tacos and a Mexican Coke later, at least her stomach was happy.

But by the end of the afternoon, she was exhausted. It was time to check into a small motel in Bernalillo, just off I-25. After a quick snack at The Range, she'd take a shower, check in with Harper, and head to Santa Fe with fresh eyes in the morning.

Glancing at her phone, she saw several messages from Ed Barrett. She felt some guilt for not responding earlier, but she'd been busy winding down one life and gearing up to start another—and the two-hour time change from Virginia hadn't helped. *Excuses, excuses,* her conscience protested. *She couldn't put him off indefinitely—it wouldn't be right.*

She sighed and pressed his number, which she still had on speed-dial, from their efforts to launch the Renaissance Faire. "Hey, Ed. It's Paige."

"How are you? It's good to hear your voice. When I didn't hear from you, I was worried" he said.

Ed was worried about her? "I'm fine—and I'm sorry I didn't get back to you sooner. I was back in Virginia, signing the final papers to sell my condo. Then, I had some packing up to do. I'm in New Mexico, now, just outside of Albuquerque."

"I'm glad you're alright, and congrats on selling your condo—I guess the money will help take the pressure off you and Harper, at least temporarily. So, are you heading back to the ranch, tonight?"

"Actually, I flew into Albuquerque this morning and spent the whole day looking at used cars. I'm looking for a reliable SUV with low miles, but I didn't find anything I liked in the city so I'm heading up to Santa Fe in the morning. I found a few things online that looked like possibilities, but you never know until you check them out in person."

"I hope you find what you're looking for," he said. There was a slight pause, and then he continued, "I'd love to take you to lunch. Or, I could even come with you to check out a few cars, if you like. And I promise not to mansplain you to death."

Ed lived just outside of Santa Fe, so meeting him wouldn't be out of her way. *Did she want to see him again?* Ed was great company, but sleeping with him had probably been a big mistake. They didn't have very much in common. Besides, she'd made a commitment to her sister, and to herself, to focus on the Inn this fall. She needed to make sure it was bringing in optimal cash flow, because both of their futures depended on it.

"Can I think about it? I'm pretty beat, and I need a good night's sleep. I promise I'll call or text you in the morning."

"Okay, then," he said, "Get some rest."

The next day, after a hot shower and the standard Continental breakfast, Paige was ready to go. After a decent night's sleep, she called Ed and said she was free for lunch, but that she'd tackle car shopping on her own. Single, self-supporting, and now, an entrepreneur, she needed to stand on her own two feet.

The first car lot she approached on the outskirts of Santa Fe didn't have much of a selection. She passed on two hatchbacks without enough clearance for northern New Mexico's rough roads—and anyway, she wanted an SUV with all-wheel drive, automatic transmission, and a high-end sound system. *Was she asking too much?*

Since she'd had a late start, it was nearly time to meet Ed for lunch. She headed into the downtown area and found a parking spot, then headed to the restaurant Ed had recommended. Potted plants overflowed with colorful annuals and a bubbling fountain dominated the courtyard entryway. Stepping inside, Paige was greeted by the host, who was expecting her. Ed wasn't skimping.

When he walked in, Paige very nearly didn't recognize him: summer-weight business suit, crisp white shirt, open at the neck. Nice, expensive loafers. He cleaned up well for a Renaissance player. *Was the effort for her?*

"Hey, there you are!" He enveloped her in a bear hug, then kissed her on the cheek. "I've missed you. I'm so glad you're back. Would you like to sit inside or outside?"

"Outside, if it's in the shade. Otherwise, indoors is fine," Paige said, struggling to find the familiarity she'd once felt with him. *This seemed to be a different Ed.*

"Outside it is. There's plenty of shade. You'll see." With his hand on the small of her back, he smoothly guided her to their table.

The host seated them at a table under a grape arbor, not far from yet another burbling fountain. The menus were bound in real leather, and the selection was Old World Mediterranean, and lovely.

"I feel like I'm under-dressed," Paige whispered. "Or, more accurately, like I've been wandering used-car lots for two days," she said, laughing. "I hope you didn't get all spiffed up for me."

"Well, not that I'd *mind* doing that, but I actually had a business meeting this morning. I'm free for the rest of the afternoon, though. Are you sure you don't want a helping hand? Or a silent observer? And if you wanted to return your rental here, I could give you a lift back to the ranch. It's no problem," he said, generously.

"That's so nice of you to offer, Ed, but I'll be okay. I hope I'll find something this afternoon, but if I have to spend another night in town, I'll have breakfast at my favorite coffee shop in the morning. And it'll be worth it to finally have my own transportation. I've been driving Harper's old work truck, and it's probably going to need a new clutch after the way I've abused it this summer. My sister and I will both be much happier with me driving an automatic." Changing the subject, she said, "So, tell me about this place. Any favorites on the menu?"

"I usually order a mezze plate, which will give you a little taste of quite a few things. Then the grilled artichokes with lemon. If I'm really hungry, an entrée. But today, it's just lunch, not dinner. Would you like to start with the mezze?"

"Yes, that sounds lovely."

"Would you like a glass of wine with lunch?" he asked. "Or I could get us a bottle." He smiled at her and picked up the wine list.

"Just a glass," said Paige. "I need to keep my head on straight, or I might accidentally come home with a lemon and Harper would never let me hear the end of it."

"You two are really close, I can see that," Ed said, waving the waiter over. He ordered two glasses of Pinot Gris from a New Zealand winery he liked, on the South Island. He seemed knowledgeable about so many things she never would have expected.

Paige picked up the conversation. "I guess it's a result of spending a lot of time together as kids. Our mom worked a couple of jobs. I was the big sister, almost six years older. I left for college and made it through my senior year. Then, quite unexpectedly, our mom died in a car accident. Harper was still in high school, so as soon as I got my diploma, I moved back home for a few years to help get her through until she graduated. Harper relocated to the Pacific Northwest for college, but we've stayed close."

"That must have been a big responsibility. Part sister, part friend, part parent," he said.

Perceptive. "That's exactly right. It wasn't what I had in mind, right after graduating from Penn. I guess I've been 'adulting' for a long time."

"I'm sorry. That sounds rough. What did you study at Penn?" he asked.

"Business administration, with a minor in business law. But I needed to stay close to Harper, so, while she was finishing high school, I went back for my MBA at the University of Virginia, specializing in business law."

"And what did you end up doing with it?" he asked.

"I worked in the private sector for three or four years, because I had school loans to pay back. Then I taught for almost six years, first as an adjunct. Then a few months before I'd hoped to be offered tenure, my position was terminated. They're closing the entire business department. I knew the University had some money problems, but I didn't expect to lose my job. I *loved* teaching."

"How long ago was this?" Ed asked.

"Almost two months ago, now. That's why I finally decided to completely uproot myself and make a fresh start in New Mexico. And I wanted to be with my sister. It seemed like there was nothing left for me back in Virginia."

"Or, maybe, there's a brilliant new life waiting for you, *here*," he said, tipping his wine glass toward her. "Let's toast to that," he said, and they did.

Their generous mezze plate arrived, and it was more than enough for the two of them. This one featured warm pita bread, grilled baby eggplant and zucchini, the artichokes Ed had mentioned, fresh, creamy feta, and several dips in colorful bowls, dusted with a hint of sumac and sesame seeds. The meal went down perfectly with the Pinot Gris Ed had chosen.

Paige sat back and groaned with satisfaction. "That was *so* good! There wouldn't have been room for an entrée."

"I'm glad you liked it—but it was only lunch, Paige. I'd like to take you out to a proper dinner sometime. Whenever you're free. No hurry. I know you and your sister have your hands full getting your new business off the ground. But I'd really like to get to know you better."

"Thanks for understanding. It's been great seeing you again, Ed." Taking a breath, she worked up the courage to say something that had been weighing on her conscience: "I feel...like I owe you an apology. I seldom overindulge and...jump anyone like I did. I don't know what got into me that night."

Ed laughed. "*Mead* got into both of us that night, and there's no apology necessary. I enjoyed myself," he said, resting a hand on her arm for a moment. "I hope you did, too."

Damn. He was being so sweet, and she could hardly meet his eyes. It might have been the most spectacular night of her life—but she could scarcely remember anything beyond a couple of sloppy kisses. To be fair, sloppy on *her* part, not his.

"As far as dinner, I'll have to check with Harper to see if the schedule has filled up. She said we were getting a lot of new bookings, but maybe I can work something in." *Work something in?* That sounded like they were business associates—almost worse than an outright rejection. True, they might have started out as business associates, but now they were friends—and it was obvious that Ed would like it to be more. "I'd love to stay longer, but I have some more car shopping to do. Stay in touch. And thank you for the delicious lunch, Ed. I had a wonderful time." *There was absolutely nothing wrong with the man, or with his approach. Just...nice guy, wrong time.*

Almost as if she'd spoken the words out loud, Ed gave a gracious nod and raised his glass. "Here's to finding what you're looking for."

Pretty perceptive herself, she knew he wasn't referring to used cars. The man had a rather incredible amount of dignity. Ed deserved better—the best, even—and she really had not been at her best lately.

CHAPTER THIRTY

*H*arper heard the sound of wheels on gravel. Dropping her weeding tool, she wiped her hands on the seat of her work pants, hoping it was Caleb. She missed him with an intensity that overwhelmed her. But squinting in the bright afternoon sun, she saw someone driving a large, expensive SUV. *An SUV that looked very familiar.*

She wandered over to the parking area and could scarcely believe her eyes.

"Howdy, stranger! Isn't *she* a sight for sore eyes?" her sister said, beaming. Paige climbed out of the driver's seat looking like a cat that had delivered the perfect canary on four shiny wheels.

"How…how did you…I don't understand," said Harper, flummoxed.

"Well, I told you I was going car shopping. I struck out in Albuquerque, yesterday, and at the first lot I went to in Santa Fe. Then I had lunch with Ed. That guy must be good luck for me: after lunch, I went to a second used-car lot and asked to see their higher-end SUVs. And *voila!* Isn't she a beauty?" Paige said, gently patting the driver's side fender."

"A beauty I've *driven*—that's Aunt Sabina's car! I sold her almost five months ago to a dealer in Santa Fe, but I thought she would have moved on by now," Harper said, perplexed.

"I know, but I wanted to surprise you. She's in perfect condition, just like she was when you got her. And she *did* sell, straight away."

"So, what happened? Did the new owner return her for some reason?" Harper asked.

"Yes, in a manner of speaking. Over the Fourth of July weekend he won the big lottery at one of the local casinos, and the prize was a new car. So, he returned her to the lot where he bought her, and now she's mine! Or, ours. After all, she was yours first—Aunt Sabina wanted you to have her."

"It doesn't really matter to me, Paige, as long as I get to drive her once in a while. *And* you have to give her a proper name," Harper said.

"Yeah, about that. I had plenty of time to come up with a name on my drive home from Santa Fe," Paige said, grinning her cheesiest grin.

"Well, what are you calling her?" Harper asked.

"Ethel," Paige said, looking to her sister for confirmation.

Harper grinned and linked arms with her sister. "Yeah, that'll do. Need any help bringing your stuff in?" She glanced into the back of the SUV and gasped. "I take it you paid a whole lot of baggage fees."

"Well, there are a lot of things I've been living without all summer, and I didn't want to wait for them to be delivered, or, get lost in transit. Now are you going to help me or not?" On the way into the house Paige asked, "Any news from Mr. Toolbelt?"

"Nothing worth talking about. I'm trying to be patient. But, like Ellie says, I don't *like* being patient."

"You're right—it's never been your strong point, even though you're much older than our resident five-year-old. But maybe you'll feel better if I give you some *more* good news, besides Ethel's magical reappearance," Paige said.

"Bring it," Harper said.

"Since I got such a good price for my condo, I stopped in the county treasurer's office and paid this year's November property taxes—in full," her sister said.

"Paige. I love you. I *really* love you."

"I love you more."

With Ellie asleep, Caleb and Mariah sat together on the porch swing, but it wasn't like old times. In the early days of their relationship, he would've had his arm around her, and she'd have been leaning into him and probably smiling in blissful innocence. Since then, their lives had done a one-eighty. "So, about the house. I want you to have it. I don't want Ellie's life disrupted more than it already has been. I understand the reasons for that, but still—our daughter belongs *here*."

"You can't just *give* it to me, Caleb. We're divorced, now, and you already had the house when you asked me to marry you." Taking a deep breath, she said, "I appreciate everything you've done. But I need to have faith in myself again, and I can only do that if I learn to stand on my own two feet."

"What does that mean?" Caleb asked.

"It means that I've got a lot of work to do on myself and in my relationships. And eventually, I'd like to buy the house from you—that

is, if you're willing to sell it. It might have to be slowly, but it's important to me."

Caleb nodded. *It was the right thing to do, and, anyway, his plans
were leaning firmly in another direction.* "I'm fine with that. And if it's
alright with you, I'd like to keep my tools and workshop in the garage,
for now. I think a gradual transition is best for Ellie, and this way, I can
spend some time here without being in the house."

"How are we going to tell her?" she asked, softly. "She's been
through so much."

"I think Ellie will be fine, as long as *you're* in her life. She needs her
mom. And we'll both still see her every day, at least at first."

"Are you absolutely sure about this, Caleb?" she asked him, not for
the first time.

He nodded his head. "I am. I don't think you're a bad person,
Mariah—far from it. There's just too much water under the bridge.
It's just life, but I don't think we can get past it." *And I don't want to, he
thought.* "I think a fresh start is best for both of us."

Mariah nodded. "I'm going back inside. But before I do, I want to
thank you, Caleb. I should have had more faith in you. In *us.* You've
been…amazing. I'm just sorry that…I couldn't be the wife you needed
me to be."

He gave her a tired smile. "You just take care of yourself and get
better, Mariah. That's all the thanks any of us need."

Caleb waited until Mariah was asleep, then he climbed into
his truck and drove slowly to the ranch. Turning left at the Coops, he
made his way to the last studio in the row. That damn pup Harper had

adopted would bark its fool head off if he tried for the main house, although he wanted nothing more than to slip silently into Harper's bed, mold himself around her warm, supple body, *and never leave.*

He'd left the studio "as is" when he'd returned, briefly, to his own house. Now that he had absolute clarity, he needed distance. And *Ellie* needed to wake up and crawl into bed with her Mama and trust that she would be safe and cared for. Meanwhile, her father would be only a phone call away.

Harper awoke early, her favorite part of the day in the heat of New Mexico's late summer. Puffy white clouds hung just above the horizon, and the sky was a mellow combination of old blue jeans and salmon-pink that made her glad to be alive to see it. She'd had the oddest dream last night, as if Caleb were right there with her. Then, first thing this morning, she'd seen his truck parked up at the Coop Studios. Well, the small, self-sufficient space contained a coffeemaker. *What a brilliant idea that had been.*

She strode slowly through the dew-wet grass, crossed the gravel drive, and followed the sunflower-lined path to his door. Removing her work boots, she slipped silently inside. Her breath caught in her throat when she saw his sleeping form, one muscular leg hanging out of the sheets, one hand thrown haphazardly above his pillow. She stood watching him for half a minute, then slowly unbuttoned her flannel shirt. She slid her shorts to the ground and pulled her t-shirt over her head. Harper lifted up a corner of the quilt and slipped into the bed, pressed her bare chest against Caleb's bare back, and threw an arm around his waist. He smelled exactly, wonderfully, the way she remembered—of his own musk, wood shavings, and a little salty tang from hard work that never seemed to leave him. Caleb put a hand over hers and let out the deepest sigh. She held on tight until his breathing softened and he returned to sleep. *She wasn't going anywhere.*

Hours later, when the afternoon heat began to invade the studio, she and Caleb woke up wrapped in each other's arms. They'd made sweet, quiet love just once, but once was enough to know they were completely right for each other. Harper was so glad to have him back, hopefully to stay.

"So…why are you here?" she asked, smoothing the hair above his forehead with her fingers. "Not that I mind—obviously."

"It's over," he said. "I can't tell you everything—Mariah has a right to her own life, her own privacy. But I needed to be there for her. Now, she's in a good place, and ready to move forward. And…"

"And?"

"She knows I want to be with you—that I'm *going* to be with you."

That night, they made love in her own bed, in the big, comfortable home she'd made with her sister. Each of them had undergone a personal renaissance, and there would be more changes coming down the road, but she wasn't worried. *Together, they could weather anything.*

A long while later, as they lay in bed, she heard Caleb let out a sigh. "I have some news, babe, but it's not good. I wasn't even going to tell you—but if we're going to move forward, I don't feel like there should ever be any secrets between us."

"I'm listening."

"Mariah…when we were apart…she got into an abusive relationship. A cop friend of mine looked the guy up for me, and he's a total creep. He has a record of domestic violence and sexual assault," Caleb said.

She heard the anger in his voice and turned to face him. "Oh, no. Caleb, that's awful! I feel so terrible for her. No wonder she wanted to come back to a place where she felt safe and loved."

He sighed. "Yeah, I get that now, too. But it wasn't *just* that. It's more complicated. Mariah told me everything: he was controlling her and limiting her contact with anyone else, taking all her money. When she stopped getting her period, she thought she might be pregnant, but the guy was such an asshole that she couldn't even go to the drugstore without him looking over her shoulder. Mariah knew she could never bring a child into that situation, and she risked her life to get away from him. First, she turned to her parents, and then she thought, I don't know…maybe, that she might be safer with me. But, more than anything, she missed Ellie and wanted to reconnect with her. For a couple of years, Mariah's had a huge hole in her life—she needed to repair her relationship with our daughter."

"Do you think…she still loves you?" Harper had to ask.

"Yeah, I think she does—as Ellie's father—and as someone who wouldn't hurt her. Mariah *trusts* me, but I don't think that after all this time she's still *in love* with me, and I am definitely not *in love* with her. But I'd kill anyone who tried to hurt her. Or you, or Paige. You can trust me on that."

She believed him. She also knew he'd lay down his life to protect his daughter. Ellie's happiness meant everything to him.

"So, what now?" Harper asked. "Is Mariah getting the help she needs?"

He nodded. "Yes, it's an important part of her treatment program at the Center. The counselors helped her to sort it all out. Her eating disorder was linked, in part, to the lack of control she'd had in an abusive relationship—Mariah said that's when it started. And, if she *had* been pregnant, she was scared of slipping into a deep depression like what she went through after Ellie was born. If *that* had happened, Mariah knew she wouldn't have the strength to get away from the guy. God, what a nightmare! She escaped by the skin of her teeth." Caleb shook his head. "It could have been so much worse. She might never have seen Ellie again, and Ellie might never have seen her mom again, either."

Harper was quiet for a moment. "What a horrible experience for anyone to go through. I'm so sorry. Poor Mariah." She shook her head, trying to get a sense of where things stood in Caleb's ever-changing world. "So, will Mariah continue to stay in the house?" she asked.

"Yeah, that's the plan—it's what's best for Ellie. Mariah says she wants to buy the house from me, eventually, but for now, I want her to concentrate on healing and on rebuilding her relationship with her daughter." Caleb took a breath, holding Harper close, stroking her back with his strong hands. "I'm going to be there for Mariah as much as I can be—but, I made it clear that she has to respect my boundaries, and that I'm ready to move on, with *you*."

"This is all a lot to process, Caleb. Let's get some sleep—we can talk more in the morning. I'm just so glad you're here," Harper said, giving him a kiss on the cheek. He needed peace and support, and that's what she would give him. Nothing mattered more, right now.

She was so grateful to have him in her life and to be closer than they'd ever been.

"Thanks for listening," Caleb said, pulling her tight against him and encircling her with his arms. He kissed the top of her head. "Night, Harper."

CHAPTER THIRTY-ONE

*C*aleb and Mariah sat with Ellie on the front porch of the small bungalow that Caleb had bought for a steal when he'd first started his contracting business. He'd spent years rehabbing a house that, soon, would no longer be his. But that didn't matter. What mattered was finding the right way to tell Ellie what was happening.

"Ellie, you know I love you very much," began Mariah. "And being your mama has made me happier than anything else in the world."

Surprisingly, Ellie shrugged. "Really?" she asked.

"Yes, Ellie, really," Mariah said, pulling her daughter close.

"I thought maybe…you didn't *want* to be my mama, and that's why you left," Ellie said, her voice sounding skeptical and fragile. "Because kids and their mamas are supposed to be together."

Caleb reeled. He'd had no idea of the deep insecurities his daughter had been harboring. But he needed to step back and allow Mariah to handle this part of the conversation.

"Oh, no, baby. I'm so sorry that I left, and I regret it every day. But I wasn't well—I couldn't think straight. The only thing I could think of was to was run away. But running away from you and your daddy wasn't right, and I'm really sorry that I hurt you. Both of you."

"But then you left *again*, and I didn't know if you were coming back," Ellie said in a high, tight voice.

"I know, baby. When I went to the treatment center, it must have been really scary for you. But I'm back now, and I'm not going anywhere." Mariah pulled Ellie onto her lap and held her tight.

Caleb jumped in. "Mama needed the doctors to help her, Ellie. And it took a while for her to get better and come back to us. I promise, it had *nothing* to do with you. Your mommy loves you *very* much and she wants to be with you," Caleb added.

"So, you're all better?" asked Ellie, looking up into her mother's eyes. "Really all better?"

"Well, I'm a *lot* better," Mariah said, which was the truth. "And every day, I will work to *keep* getting better and to stay well. And I'm going to work on being the best mom I can be for you, Ellie. Will you give me a chance?"

"Of course. You're my mama. And you're my daddy," she said, reaching out to touch Caleb's forearm with her fingers. She needed that much contact—he was her home base, her touchstone—and now that touchstone would rock just a little bit.

"Ellie, you and mama are going to live in the house, together. You're not going anywhere, and neither is she. And *I'm* going to go back to living in the Coop Studios at the ranch for a little while, and you can visit whenever you want."

"Just for a while? And then you'll come back and live with us?" she asked, her voice high-pitched and anxious.

"No, baby. Because your mom and I are divorced. We *have* been for a while, now. And, after a lot of talking, we've decided it's going to stay that way. Ellie, your mom and I are *not* getting back together—but we will *always* be your parents, and we'll always be there for you whenever you need us, along with your grandparents, and Harper and Paige, and Maggie, and all of the people who love you."

Ellie started to cry and turned her head into her mother's chest. "But I want us all to live here *together*. I want a baby *sister*. And I don't want any more things to *change!*" she wailed, with her small fists clenched tight.

Caleb rubbed her back and Mariah held a hand over Ellie's head, smoothing her curls and whispering over and over, *everything's going to be alright*. Only once did she look at Caleb, with tears in her eyes.

The situation between them had been developing for years, and it wasn't only Mariah's fault. Caleb had worked long hours building his business, and he wasn't as attentive as he could have been—or as understanding as he should have been when Mariah had suffered from serious postpartum depression. When he looked back at the first few years of Ellie's life, he mostly remembered being exhausted. And then, that exhaustion was compounded by suddenly becoming a single dad. He'd always done the best he could for Ellie, but he drew the line at living a lie—he was in love with Harper Crawley, not the mother of his child.

As for Mariah, she hadn't intended to get mixed up with the guy who had ended up badly hurting her. Like most sociopaths, he'd been charming and generous in the beginning. And then he'd turned the tables on her, taking over control of her life.

Now, Caleb was painfully aware of how much Ellie had suffered from the actions of the adults in her life, and he vowed to do better. And if things turned out the way he hoped they would, someday he *could* give Ellie that little sister she wanted. But this little chat, as hard as it had been, was only 'part one.' Telling Ellie about his relationship with Harper was 'part two,' but it would have to wait until the dust settled a little. *A five-year-old could only take so much.*

Later that evening, Caleb drove his truck back out to the ranch to speak to Harper. He didn't want to talk on the phone. Instead, he needed to see the understanding on her face and the kindness in her eyes. He knew that Harper loved Ellie—he'd watched their bond grow week by week since early spring—and she'd want to do what was best for Ellie, too.

"It's good to see you," Harper said, kissing him on the lips. She led him back to the patio and they sat side-by-side on a wicker loveseat.

"So, how did it go?" she asked.

"About as well as you could expect. Ellie understood what we were saying, but she's resisting the *outcome*. She wants us all to live in the house together, for starters. In her wildest dreams, Mariah and I would get back together as a couple *and* give her a baby sister." Caleb sighed. "I really hated to disappoint her, but we had to be truthful."

"Did you tell her you were moving back to the ranch, and why?" Harper asked.

Caleb waggled his head. "A *version* of the truth. I said I was moving back to the Coop Studios, because she's familiar with them and she'll be able to picture me there. I said that she and her mom would be living in the house from now on, and that her mom and I aren't getting back together. But...I *didn't* tell her about *us*. I just said that she has a lot of people who love her, including you and Paige. I'm sorry, Harper, but I had to do what was best for Ellie in the moment. She needs time to accept the changes we talked about, and I know she will. Then we can move on from there."

Harper nodded. Even though it was frustrating that, yet again, their relationship was being put on the back burner, she understood. "Well, I'm not going ask you when you think that's going to happen, or when Ellie will be ready," she said, lightly. "I agree—you have to do what's right for her. But...I don't want us to stop seeing each other. Do you? We need to stay connected, whatever it takes. I know you'll find the right way to tell Ellie—and the right time."

Caleb wrapped his arms around her and kissed her with emotion. "God, Harper, you've been *so* patient. Sometimes I feel like I don't deserve you."

"No, don't even say that," Harper said, shaking her head adamantly. "I was married to a man who fits that category, and you're *nothing* like him."

Caleb released his arms and looked her in the eye. "I *can* promise you one thing—you won't have to wait forever. When Ellie's ready, I'll tell her. After that, I'm not going to wait a second longer to announce 'us' to the whole world," he said. "I hope that's what you want, too."

"You don't even have to ask, Caleb. I'm right there with you," she said, leaning in to kiss him properly. "Do you have to get back, or..."

"I think Mariah and Ellie can use some alone time tonight. But I'll have to get back before she wakes up in the morning—when I do leave, I want to make it clear that I'm leaving. So, sorry, no sleepover."

She stood and pulled him to his feet. "I think what *you* need is a nice, relaxing bath," she said.

"Why? Do I smell? I showered before I came over," he said, sniffing an armpit. "I even put on aftershave."

"And I was thinking…you might want some *company* in there," she said.

"Oh, absolutely. Who bathes alone these days? It's so last millennium." They walked up the long staircase, their arms snug around each other's waists, and for a little while, everything was alright.

The next morning, Harper and Paige were eating breakfast together, when Paige came up with an excellent idea: "Since you and Caleb are keeping things on the downlow for a while, let's go somewhere. Let's get away for a few days. We don't have any bookings next weekend, but after this, we'll both be busy with our fall weddings."

"Where do you want to go?" Harper asked.

"We've been so busy that I've hardly seen any of New Mexico. I'd be happy taking a few short road trips to Taos, Red River, or Angel Fire…and I want to go to a spa. We're overdue for a pampering, and, frankly, we both deserve one," Paige said. "And I want to hook up, in a nonsexual way, with a caring professional who wants to rub my feet until I fall asleep. So, somewhere not too far away?"

"Well, there's Agua Caliente. Aunt Sabina took me there once. It was gorgeous, but I don't know what it would cost. She insisted on treating me."

"Well, how about this? You could treat me, and I could treat you," Paige said.

"I'm in. Actually, Paige, this sounds like fun, and maybe it'll take my mind off the Caleb situation. Let's see if Agua Caliente has any openings."

"Bite your tongue—there's no 'situation.' He wants to be with *you*," Paige said. She knew this for a fact. She'd lay money on it—but she was almost certain that somebody already had.

CHAPTER THIRTY-TWO

*I*t was September, the spectacular month when every roadside in New Mexico was lined with annual sunflowers, and the aspens in the higher elevations were beginning their slow turn to gold. Harper drove while Paige read the blurb on her cell phone: Agua Caliente had thermal soaking pools, an award-winning spa, delectable dining, and luxurious rooms. *We'll see about that*, Harper thought, not that the Inn at Verde Springs was trying to compete. Besides, the ranch did not have a hot-springs of any kind.

Since they'd be passing through Taos, Paige wanted to spend the morning shopping, then have lunch at any place where Mexican food was not even on the menu. When her sister had been dined and wined, they'd proceed to the hot springs resort, find their rooms, and schedule their spa appointments.

A spa getaway was Paige's idea, but Harper was uncharacteristically agreeable. She'd be unlikely to run into a certain family of three at Maggie's, and it would give Caleb some quality time at the Coop Studio with Ellie. This weekend, he was building bunk beds, because Ellie wanted them, and Harper had agreed they'd be a nice feature in one of the Coops. Caleb and Ellie were watching Sunny and Birdy for a few days, and the pups would be endlessly entertaining for the little girl. Harper smiled, creating a vivid picture in her head. *Would she ever get to be in the picture with them?*

In Taos, Paige spent some of her real estate windfall buying cow-girl-chic clothing, which Harper had to admit looked really cute on her petite sister. Then they browsed art galleries before agreeing on a lunch spot. It was still warm enough to eat outside, which wasn't always the case in late September in Taos. They feasted on Middle Eastern tapas and good wine, feeling almost as if they were on vacation. They needed to get out more—but that was only likely to happen during their off-season in the winter months. Hence their mutual agreement to fly south of the border to one of Mexico's sunny coastal resorts. *Sayulita was calling…* after the Inn began to show a profit, which hopefully would be soon.

Caleb held his hand out for the last washer and nut and Ellie dropped them in. He used a wrench to tighten the bolt, then asked Ellie to sit out of harm's way on the futon couch, while he carefully tipped the bunk beds upright. The beds were made of sturdy pine boards that he'd stained outside, first, before putting the beds together. Mariah had helped him pick out matching sheets and twin comforters that Ellie was going to love, and now it was all coming together.

"What do you think, Ellie?"

"I think they're awesome! Can I sleep in the bunk bed tonight?" she asked.

"I don't see why not. But let's check in with your mama, first," he said.

"Check in with me about what?" Mariah's voice asked, from the doorway. "I brought some takeout from Maggie's. I thought the three of us could have dinner together," she said.

"That was nice of you," said Caleb, treading carefully. "Let me wash up. You, too, Ell." They ate together on an old Mexican blanket on the grass in the shade of the New Mexico locusts, their leaflets now turning golden. Enchiladas for the grownups, grilled cheese and fries for Ellie. Mariah had brought fruit spritzers, too.

"Well, *that* hit the spot. After we clean up here, you can help me make the bunk beds," Caleb said, thirty minutes later. "That is, if you want to."

"Sure. Ellie can help too. Which bunk are you going to choose to be yours, Ell?" she asked.

"I think the bottom bunk. Maybe when I'm older, the top bunk," Ellie said, reasonably. "Daddy, can I have a friend over sometime?"

"Sure, Ellie. We can talk about it." He didn't want to leave her with the impression that he'd be living here, alone, forever. His daughter had been through so much, and he wanted to get this last part *exactly right*, so he could build the kind of future he already envisioned.

"Thanks, again, Mariah." He handed her two twenties and gently pushed her hand away when she protested that it was too much.

Mariah nodded. "Thanks, Caleb. Well, I came over partly to share some good news: Maggie offered me a job starting next Monday, through the end of fall. She warned me that she might have to let me go in the off-season if business is slow. I guess that'll depend on the weather this winter."

"That's great, Mariah, but are you sure you're ready?" he asked. "There's really no hurry—I can handle things for a while."

"I'm ready. Ellie's started kindergarten, and I need to start moving on with my life, too. I'll be alright at Maggie's. It's familiar, and it's only part-time. But if I do a good job, she might take me on full-time in the spring."

Mariah's hazel eyes caught the evening's golden light, and for the first time since she'd come back to them, Caleb had a feeling that she was finally going to be alright. After all that she'd been through, she was due for some sunshine.

He nodded. "I'm proud of you, Mariah. None of this has been easy. But I have faith that you can do whatever you want. You've always been creative and a hard worker."

"And, I've not made the best decisions," Mariah said. "I know I've messed up, big time. But one thing I got right was having *this* little girl," she said, resting her hand on Ellie's head. Ellie, in turn, wrapped her arms around Mariah's legs and leaned in for a snuggle.

"Yeah, she's alright," said Caleb, with a grin. "I think we'll keep her around. Okay, let's go make up the bunks, kiddo."

During the drive to Agua Caliente, which was forty-five minutes or so past the edge of Taos, Paige answered her phone. "I'm really glad. Yeah, let me know how it goes. I hope so, too. Of course, you can call me. Anytime. Keep me in the loop, okay?"

"Who was that?" Harper asked. "A client?"

"Mm, hmm," said Paige, turning to stare out the side window.

"What did they want?"

"Nothing to worry your little head about, Harper. I'm a big girl. I can take care of things."

"Was it Ed? I kind of like the big guy. He's almost a dead ringer for that Ben dude, on *Home Town*. Are you secretly seeing each other and not telling me?" she asked her sister.

"No, we are *not*—and that is one hundred percent my business. For the record, I have not made any decision about Ed, because I've been focused on other things, like, making money. It doesn't always have to be about the guys, you know. Anway, this weekend is supposed to be relaxing," Paige said. "When it comes to relationships with men, I rarely find them to be relaxing."

"Caleb and I can get plenty relaxed, if we work hard enough at it. But, have it your way," Harper said, shaking her head.

"I plan to have it *exactly* my way. That's why we're going to go to a spa," Paige said, matter-of-factly.

CHAPTER THIRTY-THREE

*W*hen Caleb and Ellie took the dogs for a long walk the next morning, the cool air held a hint of autumn's chill. Since the studio didn't have a full kitchen, Caleb had made toaster waffles and microwave bacon for breakfast, and Ellie was in a chipper mood after having spent her first night in a bunk bed.

"So, who do you want to invite to stay over with you, Ellie? Is it a friend from school?" Caleb asked.

"Yes, my friend Jacob. He started new at our school last year. He used to live in Colorado."

"Oh, and what do you like about Jacob?" he asked.

"Um, he talks to me. He isn't hardly ever a brat like some of the other boys, and he brings in the best stuff for show and share."

"Like what?"

"Well, once, he brought a horned lizard that he caught on a hike with his dad. And on the last day of school this year, he brought a rat."

"A live rat or..."

"Of *course,* a live rat, Daddy! And he took her out and we got to play with her—and her fur was as soft as a kitten's. Her name was Guinevere," she said, with reverence.

"Did you get a chance to hold Guinevere?" he asked.

Ellie nodded her head, vigorously. "Some of the other girls were scared, but not me. Jacob put Guinevere on my hand, and she climbed all the way up to my shoulder. And then she just sat there!"

"So, you like this Jacob kid?" he asked, his ears perking up.

"Yeah. Better than any other boy in my class. He's nice, Daddy. We're friends, and maybe when I grow up, he'll be my boyfriend."

Caleb sensed a possible opening, and decided to put some feelers out. "I think I feel that way about someone, too, Ellie. Like, we're good friends, now, and I think she *could* be my girlfriend."

"Who, Daddy? But, wait, are you *allowed* to have a girlfriend?" she asked.

He smiled at the question. "Well, since your mom and I have been divorced for over two years, yes, I think I'm 'allowed' to have a girl-friend. And I haven't had one in a long time because I've been focused on taking care of *you*—and I have loved every minute of it."

"But if you have a girlfriend, will you still take care of me?" she asked.

"Yes, of course, Ellie. I will *always* take care of you. Now your mama is here and she wants to take care of you. And your grandpar-ents in Santa Fe, love you, too."

"Have I met your friend, Daddy? Would I like her?" Ellie asked, looking up at him.

"Yes, Ellie. You *have* met my friend. You've seen her almost every day this summer, and we're walking her dogs, right now! And the best part is, I already know you like her, and she likes you!"

"Is it Harper? Remember, I told you, Daddy? I said, 'this lady is nice,'" Ellie said, the light shining in her eyes. Her smile was entirely genuine and a source of profound relief after a very long journey.

"Well, you were right, Ell, and that makes me really, really happy."

"Yeah, I think that'll work, and I'll let you know if anything changes. Okay, gotta go. Later," Harper heard her sister say, her voice low enough that she strained to hear the words from the doorway of their adjoining rooms—all very Taos-style, with warm colors, woven fabrics, and minimal furnishings. She was trying to enjoy it all, and not particularly succeeding.

"Ah, the mystery client again—the person whose name *isn't* Ed Barrett," Harper said, poking her head around the doorway.

"Mind your beeswax, Harper. When I want your two cents, I'll ask for it."

"Come on, one more lame cliche. You could totally go for a hat trick, Paige."

"Okay, smartass—there's no need to stick your oar in," she said.

"And it's three for the win!" Harper said, giving her sister a fist-pump. "You really should turn your phone off, anyway, Paige. This is supposed to be a health spa, and you're probably interfering with the other clients "spa Zen" with your 5G, or something."

Paige sighed with exasperation. "That's a ridiculous fear-mongering rumor, Ms. Conspiracy Theorist. Anyway, my cellular carrier says it's only 4G. But, alright," she said, setting her phone aside. "Since you insist on being nosy, it's a good thing that I insisted on a private room. And you might want to respect that," Paige said, pointedly.

The adjoining rooms were a compromise—Harper had wanted to double up to save money. But sharing a room with her sister was not the spa experience Paige had in mind.

Alone in her private room with the connecting door now closed, Paige lay on the comfortable bed admiring her fresh pedicure, the first she'd had in months. "Yeah, it's been fun, despite having to put up with Grumpy, here. I know, I can't wait! But I have to hang up now because I'm going to start crying."

CHAPTER THIRTY-FOUR

"*W*hat are you smiling about? The effects of a pedicure and a facial never last *this* long," Harper grouched. She'd tried to be a good sport, but rather than taking her mind off the Caleb situation, her two-day spa stay had only made her miss him more. And at a time when their financial picture was still less than perfectly rosy, it had cost a lot more than she'd been comfortable spending.

"Aren't I allowed to be happy? I'm the beautiful, independent, semi-successful entrepreneur of a former chicken ranch," Paige replied. "And I've just had two whole days off during which I didn't have to take care of anybody else." She leaned back in her seat and sighed. "I want you to promise me that we can do this more often."

"Yeah, yeah. Whatever. It was nice, I guess. I liked the hot stone massage. If Caleb doesn't follow through, I might ask that big masseuse to marry me—you know, the one that's built like a brick house. Hey, do you want to stop in Taos for dinner? It'll probably mean getting home in the dark."

"No, let's skip it. I brought lots of road snacks, and I'll share if you get hungry. Let's try to make it back tonight," Paige said. "For some reason, I've been really craving carbs, lately," she said, diving into a biggie bag of sour cream potato chips.

Harper drove on, deep in thought, while Paige tilted her seat back and closed her eyes. Glancing at Sleeping Beauty, she thought a summer in New Mexico looked damn good on her sister—and it was pretty fun having her around.

Harper tried to avoid looking for Caleb's truck, but there it was, parked right in front of the Coops. So, he was home. *Should she go up and see him? What if Ellie was there? Should she should wait for him to make the first move?* Her brain buzzed with questions, as her limited amount of 'spa Zen' evaporated into thin air.

It was an unusually gorgeous day, with a hint of fall in the air as the sun began to head toward the horizon. Beyond the sunflowers, her eyes caught the periwinkle blue of asters in full bloom, along with little flickers of yellow and red poking up in her flourishing gardens. She couldn't wait to watch her handsome ring of aspens turn gold for the first time, and she made a mental note to take lots of photographs so Paige could have her pick for the Inn's website. With any luck, they were actually going to pull this off and become successful entrepreneurs. *Who knew?*

Harper had just finished bringing all of her things in from the car when the front door opened, filling the spacious central hall with bright light.

"Oh, good, you're home. Long drive? Feel like taking a little walk with me?" Caleb asked.

Well, that sounded promising. Harper abruptly dropped her bags at the foot of the staircase. "Sure, happy to. Let me freshen up and change my shoes," she said, before running up the stairs like it was an Olympic event. She cupped her hands over her mouth to check her breath, then splashed cold water on her face. She brushed her teeth for good measure and changed from her spa shoes to her comfy Keene's, which could take her anywhere she wanted to go.

Caleb heard the water running in the sink, just before Paige poked her head out of the downstairs bathroom.

"Are we ready for launch?" she asked.

"As ready as we can be. I'll walk Harper the long way around, but you won't have a lot of time, Paige."

"That's okay. I'm pretty fast. Where did you stash the goods?"

"Up at the Coop. Maggie did a fantastic job. Be sure to check the fridge—there's some cold stuff in there. Everything else is in the wicker basket sitting on my bed. You might need to drive—so if Harper hears your car engine, where do I say you're going?"

"Um…tell her I went to get the mail, and then to recheck the measurements on the Coop Studios, because a client called with a question about work space. That seems possible."

"Paige. Thank you. I promise, you won't regret it," Caleb said, giving her a quick hug.

"Should we bring the dogs?" Harper asked, as she came down the last two stairs.

"Ellie and I already took them on a long walk this morning," he said. "And anyway, I want you all to myself."

Hmm, even more promising, she thought.

They walked a circuitous route because Caleb said he wanted to show her some unusual wildflowers that he couldn't identify. *Lame.* And then, he couldn't even manage to find the stupid things. It was a flipping wild goose chase, on top of the long drive home from Agua Caliente.

"If we're all done here, I might go make us a cup of tea and we can sit on the patio and chat," Harper said. *Was she born in the Victorian era?* She was seriously off her game, tonight.

"Oh, *now* I remember," Caleb said, a little dramatically, she thought. "Actually, I think I saw it up closer to your perennial border—the one you planted around the aspen grove. Come on, I really want you to see it before it gets too dark. What if it's an endangered plant and someone accidentally yanks it out?"

She wasn't going to budge. "No, Caleb! I'm exhausted. If you want me to walk another foot, you're going to have to do better than this. I want a kiss. *Several* kisses, in fact. I haven't seen you in days—and I haven't seen *all* of you in many, many days."

"Will this do?" he said, tilting her head back and giving her the softest of kisses.

"Maybe as an appetizer. Lead on," she grumbled. *What was the knucklehead up to?*

They kissed their way up the path, stopping once to sit on a conveniently placed boulder so she could meld herself around his deliciously strong body. *Mmm...good kisses.* She lifted up his shirt and pressed a few kisses on his washboard abs—but he pulled her up by her hands, and gently moved her onward toward the aspens, shining in the evening's last light.

Finally, when they'd nearly reached the grove, he kissed her for a full minute until she was weak in the knees, as she thought she heard the sound of a car engine fade into the distance.

He led her into the grove to a huge quilt piled with heaps of pillows, a down comforter, and a picnic basket containing Maggie's best aphrodisiacs. *And a small, blue velvet box, tucked under a wheel of Brie.*

Caleb reached down and pulled out the remote, clicked the button, and the grove was filled with magical light, creating the perfect ambience for his intended purpose.

When they were both sitting in a delicious tangle, snuggled in the down comforter, and some more kissing had completely transformed Harper's salty mood, Caleb reached into the picnic basket and pulled out two narrow crystal flutes, a bottle of Gruet Champagne, and a small velvet box.

Harper's luminous, blue eyes filled with emotion, and he knew this was the right moment.

"I know you've had to wait a long time, and you've been incredibly patient, but it's finally over. *Harper Elizabeth Crawley*, you've had my heart almost since the second I laid eyes on you. Ellie loves you, too, and she's okay with us being together. No, scratch that—she's *happy*, and that makes me happy, too." He opened the box and showed Harper the ring, which was so entirely *her*—a slim, white-gold band with three lovely diamonds flanked by scrollwork in a fern pattern. "It's the three of us, ready to be a family. Harper, will you marry me?"

"Yes. Yes, of *course*, I will. Oh, my God, Caleb, it's so incredibly perfect! I love you so much, and I love Ellie, too. Are you sure she's really okay with this?" she asked, hope reflected in her eyes.

Caleb nodded. "She's more than okay. I wasn't planning to tell her so soon, but the moment presented itself, and I'm glad I did. The waiting nearly killed me, Harper. I love you more than I thought I could ever love anyone. I hope you didn't doubt it for a minute, and I'm sorry you had to wait so long."

"I'm not sorry about anything, Caleb. Tonight, all of this, it's absolutely perfect! Now, are you going to put this ring on my finger, or what?" she said, holding out her left hand.

"Hey, I don't work for you anymore," he teased. "But I *definitely* want to be your husband."

Since Ellie was at her grandparents and most of the work on the ranch was completed, Caleb spent most of the weekend in bed with Harper. For the second evening in a row, Maggie's picnic basket came in exceedingly handy. They set it on the antique trunk at the foot of Harper's queen-size bed and chowed down when they needed sustenance, because they were burning a *lot* of calories.

Paige yelled a few things through the bedroom door and Harper answered, but for the most part the elder Crawley sister left them blissfully alone. He and Harper had sex in every conceivable position, including twice in the shower when they got hot and sticky, and Harper kept wanting him, more than any other woman had. He'd made her happy quite a few times, and gradually, he sensed a different Harper emerging from the ashes of her difficult marriage and recent divorce. Maybe *he* was different, too. He'd never had the kind of love and support, loyalty and strength that he'd found in Harper, as a friend and now as his partner and lover. *It had been a long time coming, but that only made it sweeter.*

This is what he wanted. Although he might have wobbled out of good intentions when Mariah first reappeared, he knew exactly where his heart belonged—and he knew it would be safe in the hands of this amazing, strong, beautiful, good-hearted woman.

"Caleb, I need to get vertical," Harper whispered, when morning came. "This has been the most awesome, sensational, and fantastic experience of my life. But I may be suffering from dehydration. I need another shower and a real meal, and then, maybe we can go for a walk and do some more kissing."

"Where do I sign up?" he asked, going in for a taste of what was to come.

"Follow me, honey, and I'll make all your dreams come true," she said, laughing. "But first, there's something I need to do."

"And I should check with Ellie and see how she's doing," Caleb said, agreeably.

"I will see *you*, later," Harper said, punctuated by three enthusiastic kisses.

Harper dug through her closet until she found her beat-up day-pack. Slinging it over her shoulder, she went downstairs to their beautiful living room and took a deep breath. *Time to do this.* Standing on her tiptoes, she carefully removed her aunt's urn from the fireplace mantel, then, making sure the lid was tightly secured, lowered it into her daypack. Whistling up the dogs, she headed outside into the cool morning air, but she didn't go far. In the six months since Sabina had died, everything in her life had changed, and she had a lot of thanking to do…

She started with the patio. It was lit up by the morning sun, the only time of the day the space wasn't a cool, peaceful haven. "We love this space, and sometimes, I can imagine you here with us. But…since you're not, I wanted you to see it, and to know how much Paige and I appreciate hanging out here together at the end of our busy days on the ranch. It's the perfect place to unwind, and it's excellent for other things, too."

"Next, I really want to show you the gardens, and the magical place that the three of us made for people to marry each other. I might even want to get married here, myself," she said. "Speaking of, thank you, for giving me Caleb. Not long after Paige and I found out about the ranch, I hired a local single dad to help me fix this place up. He has a darling little girl who I've fallen in love with, and we're going to be a family, Sabina."

She wandered slowly down the path to the aspen grove and spoke about her design for the gardens, and about how she hoped they'd fill in over the years to come. Crossing the ranch drive, she followed the line of sunflowers to Caleb's Coop Studio and opened the door. She hoped he'd at least made the bed before he left it to join her in the main house. "These old chicken coops turned out to be the *biggest* surprise. At first, we didn't know what to do with them, but I think they've turned out pretty well. And I want you to know that *this* one gave the man I love a place to land when he really needed one. So, I'm very grateful for that, and I know he is, too."

Harper snagged a bottle of water from the well-stocked mini-fridge and headed outside into the New Mexico sunshine, the cure for what had ailed her, apparently. "So, this is it, Sabina," she said, doing a little one-eighty and taking it all in, from the backdrop of blue-shadowed mountains to the drifts of goldenrod and asters, late roses in bloom, fragrant purple lavender, and cheerful yellow sunflowers that towered over her head. In the distance, the morning sun lit the warm adobe walls of the ranch house and glinted from its shiny windows. Two tired dogs lay flopped out on the sandy ground, their tongues lolling out to the side after chasing whiptail lizards. And she'd never been happier than she was at this moment. "Anyway, I hope you like what we've done with the place. I just wanted you to see it—and to say thank you from the bottom of my heart, before I put you back right where you belong."

"Okay pups," she called out. "Let's go home."

THE INN AT VERDE SPRINGS TRILOGY:

Book 1 – The Renaissance Sisters

Book 2 – Love Child

Book 3 – Gifts and Revelations

ABOUT THE AUTHOR

Wendy Cohan writes character-driven women's fiction, short stories, and narrative essays. Her work has appeared in *Pittsburgh Magazine*, *Verge Magazine*, *Cricket*, *The Manifest-Station*, and *Be Their Voice: An Anthology for Rescue*. Her debut novel is *The Renaissance Sisters*, Book 1 of *The Inn at Verde Springs Trilogy*. Wendy lives and writes in Albuquerque, New Mexico, where much of her fiction is set. When not writing, she enjoys spending time with her two adult sons and their partners and hiking in the nearby mountains with her rescue dogs, Birdie and Lola. Prior to writing full time, Ms. Cohan was a registered nurse for two decades and is the author of *The Better Bladder Book*, (2010, Hunter House Publishing). She also holds an undergraduate degree in Environmental Conservation from the University of Colorado where she was a botanical field assistant at the University's Mountain Research Station. She's a big fan of wildflowers and bear-grass. Wendy caught the writing bug while living for several years in Missoula, Montana, where she studied creative writing with the Beargrass Writer's Workshop.

ACKNOWLEDGEMENTS

The Renaissance Sisters, Harper and Paige Crawley, and "The Inn at Verde Springs" trilogy came to me after more than a year of writing fiction full-time. My quiet house in Northwest Albuquerque, and the roadrunners, quail, and whip-tailed lizards that visited me often, kept me focused and made the writing possible. But I couldn't have done it alone.

I would like to express my heartfelt thanks to Echo Garret and the team at Lucid House Publishing for seeing something unique in *The Renaissance Sisters* and the Inn at Verde Springs series. I would like to add a special thanks to designer Jan Sharrow for the book's cover, which helps to tell the story.

I owe a huge debt of gratitude to my dedicated readers, who have encouraged me, helped me course-correct, and celebrated my successes. To *Carin Willis*, *Jennifer Stout*, *Peggy Delaney*, *Julie Rall*, and most of all, my sister and chief supporter, *Kim Kenley*, thank you. Without your support, I wouldn't have had the courage to pursue the series through to its conclusion. Thank you to Bridger, Bryce, and Emma for believing in me. It means so much.

Thank you to all of the quirky characters who ask me to tell their stories, and to the many twists and turns in my life that brought me, finally, to my home in New Mexico, truly, *The Land of Enchantment*.

Finally, I will be forever grateful for the love and companionship of the world's best dog, who never left my side, from 2010-2022. He was here at the beginning of "The Inn at Verde Springs" series, but gone by the end. I like to picture him, still, running through the high desert chasing rabbits, and most of all, walking by my side. And I can't leave out my new pups, Birdie and Lola, who show up in *The Renaissance Sisters*, and in my real life, every day."